Dirty Pictures

Patricia Ketola

Betimes Books

First published in the English language worldwide in 2016
by Betimes Books

ISBN 978-0-9934331-3-9

Cover image © Ruslan Olinchuk

Cover design by JT Lindroos

To Clarice Helen Doar

TABLE OF CONTENTS

PART ONE

I'm in a white room laid out on a single bed. My head is propped up on a pillow and I've got a glass in my hand that contains two inches of tequila. There's a night stand next to the bed and that's where I keep my bottle. Sadly, it's the last of the Patron. Scattered next to the bottle are some of mother's leftover pain pills. Taken with the tequila a couple of Percocet should do wonders for my mental health.

My ritual of semi-annihilation was interrupted by the rude sounds of the phone. I was reluctant to answer, but knew I had to pick up because I was expecting a call from the crematorium. I struggled to find the phone, it was buried somewhere under the duvet, and when I finally located it and put it to my ear I heard the voice of my lifelong friend, Terry Volkov. He was talking fast and loud, and I wondered what bizarre combination of meds he was on to give his voice such a sharp and staccato delivery.

He wanted me to come to an immediate meeting at his house. Terry has a serious physical disability and I am usually at his beck and call, but not this time, I was too wasted to drive. He finally shut up long enough for me to explain that I was conducting a private funeral ceremony for my mother. He said he understood my grief and we agreed to meet the following day. I rang off and stuffed the phone back down under the covers. My glass was empty and I added another inch of tequila and popped two Percocet.

After finishing the tequila I put my head on the pillow and closed my eyes. I was trying to think of something pleasant so I could pass out in peace, but all that came up was a mental video of me and Hendrik Van der Saar indulging in long, languid, and slightly kinky lovemaking. We had been lovers twenty years ago. I must have fucked a lot of people since then, but whenever I tried to evoke sexual activity Hendrik was the one who appeared. His hand reached out of the video and I felt his caress and let him soothe me into sleep.

Since Terry fell off his motorcycle and became partially paralyzed he's been living in an environment of dust and gloom that testifies to the enormity of his physical and emotional problems. When I entered his room I was surprised to see that a change had taken place. Previously the frowzy reek of stale cigarette smoke had hung in clouds near the ceiling and the drapes had been tightly drawn. Now, the sun shone through sparkling panes of newly washed glass and the room was bathed in brilliant, natural light. There was even a vase of fresh peonies, whose lush, pale blooms gave off a faint, but sweet perfume.

'What the fucks going on here, Volkov? Did you get a new lease on life?'

'Hardly,' he snapped. 'My assistant cleaned the place up. He said the environment was bad for my mental health.'

Terry pulled a bag of *yayo* and a straw out of his pocket and started to lay out some lines on his desk. 'Why don't you give us some vodka?' he asked, gesturing toward an ice bucket sitting next to the vase of peonies.

There were two small glasses stuck in the ice next to the vodka. I picked them out and started to pour. The vodka had been chilled to perfection and it glided out of the bottle in a viscous stream of pure crystal syrup.

'Sorry to hear about your mother,' Terry said, raising his glass in a toast: 'Here's to Clara, she was an amazing woman. I remember when she used to take us to the public library and feed us milk and cookies afterwards.'

'Her name was Carlene and she never took us to the library. We went on our own.'

'Well, she did give us milk and cookies.'

'Just store bought cookies. She never baked anything in her life.'

'Have it your way, Martel. You always were a killjoy.'

He held his glass out for more vodka. I poured, and then he put the glass down on the desk and clutched at his stomach in the vicinity of his shit bag.

'Do you need to empty that?' I asked.

'No, it's just gas. My wife hated my bag, that's why she ran off with the lesbian.'

'Oh, don't get started on that.' Terry could be a bore when he ranted about his wife's desertion. I helped myself to another line of coke. It really did wonders for a hangover.

'So what's this big plan you've got in mind?' I asked. 'Don't expect too much from me, I'm in mourning for Carlene.'

'Are you still an expert on old master paintings?'

'Of course I'm an expert, I just choose not to work in the field. My area is Flemish and Dutch painting, but I can do the Quattrocento. What do you need, a false provenance, or a phony attribution?'

'No, no, nothing like that,' he said, taking his hands off his shit bag and rubbing them together. 'I went to an opening at the Art Institute last week.'

In spite of his disability Terry was on the local A list and got a lot of invitations to pretentious events. He was popular among the elite because he'd made a fortune in one of the first dot com scams and was widely respected for his financial savvy.

'Was it a group show?' I asked, wondering when he was going to get to the point.

'No, it was a Leon Kossoff retrospective. I'm no connoisseur, but I could see it was important work. The man put some heavy magic down on canvas. Looking at his paintings was as close to rapture as I care to get.'

I was stunned. Leon Kossoff was one of my heroes and I'd missed his opening. Kossoff was the last great representational painter, he lived in London and his work was never shown in the States. He had labored in semi-obscurity for most of his life, and now that he was closing in on ninety the art world was finally taking notice and dealers and private parties were fighting over his work. This late recognition was not surprising, because when Leon died his pictures would be auctioned off for millions of pounds.

'Terry, what you saw was a rare event. For god's sake, why didn't you invite me?'

'Because your mother was dying and you were glued to her bedside.'

Terry was right. I wouldn't have gone if he'd asked me.

'Hey, don't look so glum Martel. The show will be here for two months. You can go on your own some weekday morning and study the whole exhibit in peace.'

He moved his empty vodka glass across the desk but didn't ask for a refill: 'I met up with Preston Greylander at the opening. We got to talking about paintings and he confided he has a Rembrandt that needs to be cleaned. It seems he has a lot of anxiety around this particular work of art. He may be the biggest player in agri-business but he doesn't know dick about the care and handling of paintings. I happened to mention I have a friend who might be able to advise him on restoration and such matters. He'd like to take a meeting with you.'

'I'd rather have a rattlesnake up my ass than meet with Preston Greylander. People like him are the reason I got out of the art racket.'

'You must need money. You haven't worked in years and I doubt Clara left anything after the health care system got through with her.'

'Carlene, her name was Carlene!' He couldn't remember my mother's name, but he was right about the money.

'Sorry, I didn't mean to offend, but I'll always think of that sweet old gal as Clara.'

He moved his wheelchair to have better access to the *yayo*.

'My mother wasn't sweet. She was a hard-nosed anarcho-syndicalist.'

'Whatever,' he shrugged. 'I'll pay you ten grand in front to help Greylander get his Rembrandt cleaned.'

Although I was desperate for money I wasn't eager to accept the mission. Greylander was a vicious oligarch whose life's work was to rape the land and destroy the topsoil. Dealing with him could be dangerous; he'd already killed off half of Africa and parts of the Balkans. Still, my art history training got the better of me. I was curious about the picture: 'Do you really think he owns a Rembrandt?'

'He said his grandfather brought it back from Amsterdam in 1910 and it's been in the family ever since.'

'That was the golden age of the European forger. They were cranking out Old Masters to sell to the rich American's. It's probably a fake.'

'It doesn't matter what the fuck it is. I'm not interested in the painting. It's Greylander I want.' He reached in the desk drawer and pulled out a check book.

'OK, I'll do it.' I said. That ten grand looked mighty attractive, particularly since I only had sixty five dollars in my checking account. Still, I had misgivings: 'You're being awfully vague about this, Terry. Can't you give me an idea of what you're up to?'

'I'll tell you after you meet with Preston.' He wrote out the check and handed it to me: 'He wants to see you on Thursday at 7 P.M. at his place. He'll show you the painting and you can take it from there. Try and manage to look attractive, do something with your hair.'

'What's wrong with my hair?' It was pulled back in a messy ponytail like I always wore it.

'Well, for starters it's dirty. Listen to me, Martel, this may be your last chance to make some serious cash. Don't fuck it up. Preston will pay a lot more than this piddling 10K if he's convinced of your professionalism.'

On the way home I stopped at the bank and deposited the check. Flush with new money I went to Trader Joe's and bought some frozen Korean and a bottle of soju. My mind was working overtime from the cocaine, and at the moment it was split in two parts. Part number one was worried about what Terry was getting me into with Preston Greylander, and part number two wondered when the crematorium would finish burning my mother's corpse and give me her ashes.

Preston Greylander was an old school wasp dressed in a conservative, but well cut, suit and a Hermès tie. We had our meeting in a panelled library that was decorated in a correct and mannered style that emulated a proper gentleman's retreat in Edwardian England. The light was dim and indirect and it was difficult to see the paintings on the walls. I was able to make out several landscapes done in the Hudson River style and what looked like a Rembrandt portrait of a Dutch burger and his wife. All the paintings were covered in ancient brown varnish and badly in need of cleaning.

Looking immaculate with my hair done up in a French twist and wearing my last piece of expensive clothing, a slick black suit from Yohji Yamamoto, I settled into a worn leather armchair and watched as Preston made drinks. I wasn't surprised when I was served an off brand of blended scotch. Previous experience had led me to believe that certain elite assholes pinched their pennies by serving cheap drinks. It was even probable that the water in the Evian bottle he used to top off our scotch was from the tap.

Just after Preston handed me my drink a man in a dark suit came in carrying a silver tray. The man set the tray on the bar and left without a word. Preston, acting the host, put the tray on a mahogany cocktail table, and smiled with delight as he grabbed a potato chip and smeared it with an odious smelling concoction: 'My cook, Lena, makes the best onion soup dip in the world,' he said.

The dip was not for me, I'd had it once at a high school drinking party and it had made me vomit: 'It looks delicious, Mr. Greylander, but I can't eat it. I'm allergic to onions,' I lied.

'That's a pity,' he said, greedily loading up another chip. 'And don't be so formal, my dear, I think we should be on a first name basis.'

'You're right, Preston,' I grabbed a handful of chips in an effort to appear convivial, 'but please call me Martel. My friends call me by my last name. It's been that way since childhood.'

'Martel,' he said savouring my name on his thin lips, 'I imagine you're dying to take a close look at the Greylander Rembrandt.'

'Yes, it would be a rare treat. You don't see many Rembrandt's in private collections these days. Would you mind telling me how long it has been in your family?'

'Oh, years, and years, my grandfather brought it back from Europe in 1910.' Preston gave me an encouraging smile: 'Go ahead, don't be shy.'

I pulled myself out of the leather armchair and walked over to the painting. I searched for a signature, but none was visible in the murk. I was finally able to make out a gold brooch pinned to the man's hat. This was a hopeful sign, and could be interpreted as being typical of the master because Rembrandt never hesitated to add a bit of glitter and glitz to his work. 'It does need to be cleaned,' I said, stating the obvious.

'Thanks for your opinion, Martel. I've been uncertain whether to have it cleaned or leave it in its present state. Other experts have told me the darkness is part of Rembrandt's style.' Preston looked uncomfortable, old master paintings were obviously not his area of expertise.

'Yes, that's true to a certain extent, but I'm afraid this painting is desperately in need of restoration. You can see for yourself that the figures are barely visible. If you like I can contact the conservators at Van der Saar Fine Arts in Amsterdam.' I wrote the Van der Saar name on my business card and handed it to him: 'Have your staff check them out, they're top in the field.'

Preston was all business now: 'I'll do that and get back to you within the week.'

'I'll wait for your call,' I smiled, and stood up. I didn't believe for one fucking minute that the dirty old canvas on the wall was a Rembrandt, but my eye told me it might be of the period and not a late nineteenth century forgery. A lot of people painted in that style back in the day.

Preston took me to the door and actually walked me through the security system and to the front gate where I was parked. We shook hands while an armed guard opened the gate and let me escape from the Greylander mansion.

Two days later a person named Margaret called and told me the deal was on and that I should meet Preston for lunch at an Italian restaurant close to the Greylander headquarters in suburban Lake Washichu to firm up the details. I celebrated by calling Terry and telling him that I'd bagged the job. He told me to come over right away.

The sitting room was still clean and bright. The only difference since the last time I'd visited was that the peonies had been replaced by a vase of yellow roses. Terry was seated at a highly polished table cleaning a handgun. He was smoking a joint and seemed to be deeply engrossed in his task. He glanced up when I entered and smiled. I sat on the sofa and told him about my meeting with Greylander. The handgun was in pieces on the table and as he listened he began to reassemble it with quick, sure movements. It was obvious that he was no stranger to the world of guns and I watched him with grim fascination.

'What kind of gun is that?' I asked.

'It's a Sig Sauer P226. Do you know anything about guns?'

'Not a thing.'

He got it all together and put it down on the table. The Sig Sauer was black and menacing. It was slightly chunky and had some heft to it. I wanted to pick it up and hold it, but I didn't dare.

'This is a semi-automatic,' Terry explained. 'That means it fires one cartridge every time you pull the trigger. It's a reliable piece of equipment and doesn't jam when you're trying to fire it. It was manufactured by a German-Swiss outfit, they're sticklers for precision.' He turned the gun over in his hand admiring the Teutonic design: 'You want to hold it, don't you?' he asked. Among his other skills Terry was something of a mind reader.

'I guess so,' I said warily.

'Go ahead, pick it up. There's no danger, it's not loaded.'

The gun weighed about two pounds and was heavy in my hand. I can't explain it, but there was something solid and comforting about that gun. I liked the feel of it and the heft of it, and I began to understand why people could make love objects of these death dealing weapons.

Terry gave me a sharp look: 'It's too bad I don't have time to teach you to shoot. I have a feeling you'd be a natural.'

'A natural born killer?'

'I don't know about that, but you'd probably be good at target shooting.'

'Come on, Terry, get to the point. You said you'd tell me what's going on after I got the deal together.'

He took the Sig Sauer out of my hand and said: 'You know the score on Greylander International, don't you?'

'As a matter of fact, I do.'

The Greylander outfit was one of my mother's pet bugaboos, she'd been ranting against them since I was a child: 'My mother always claimed they were trying to control the world's food supply.'

Terry nodded: 'She was right about that, in the process the Greylander's have enslaved whole countries and raped several continents.'

'When did you start to care? I thought you sided with the one percent after you got rich in that software swindle.'

'You know that's not true,' Terry was hurt and offended. 'What was I supposed to do, throw the money away?'

'That's between you and your conscience,' I sneered. 'Now what the fuck's going on with you and Preston?'

'I want to take him out.'

The light bulb finally went on over my head: 'So what do you need me for? Can't you handle that on your own?'

Terry clutched his shit bag and glanced pointedly down at his useless legs: 'I'm not the man I once was, surely you can see that.'

'No, but you've got a big gun.'

'I have to get him in range. That's where you come in.'

'Just hire a professional and leave me out of this.'

'What's the matter with you, Martel? Don't you want to get a little revenge on the people who are destroying the earth? I'm giving you a chance to act on your beliefs. You ought to be grateful.'

I took his point. Since I was a kid I'd been yapping about the scumbags who were poisoning the earth and the people on it. Maybe it was time to put my money where my mouth was: 'What do I have to do?'

'Not much. Now that you're working for him you have his ear and possibly his trust. Just invite him to a cocktail party at my place on November tenth. My sources tell me he's going to be in town that day.'

'Why can't you invite him?'

'I hardly know the man. I've only met him at bullshit gatherings of the local one percent. I don't know if he'd come. I'm thinking if you sweet talk him he'll show up.'

'So, I invite him and he shows up, then what?'

'You'll have to be here and let him in and escort him to the sitting room. You walk out and I kill him and then I kill myself.'

'Oh, Terry,' I sighed, glancing at his useless legs. I agreed that he didn't have much left to live for. He was crippled and in constant pain. His wife had left him and was living it up with a pretty woman in London. And, his only child, a girl of nineteen, had been killed in one of the wars.

'I'm through with this life.' he said. 'I have a need to get it over with, and while I'm doing it I might as well take that rotten bastard with me.'

'Killing Preston won't stop Greylander International from destroying what's left of the grasslands and the rain forests. They're a huge mechanism that's running out of control. Nothing can stop them.'

'I know that, but at least I'll have made the effort.'

I thought about what it would be like with Terry gone: 'You're going to leave me alone in the world. You're the last friend I've got left.'

He smiled: 'I can take you along if you want.'

'No, no, that's OK. I've still got a few things to do.'

'Like what? Do you want to find true love and live happily ever after?'

When he mentioned true love I had a fleeting glimpse of Hendrik Van der Saar, but I quickly let that go.

'No, like visiting the Kossoff exhibit.'

'Martel, you're a real freak, nobody gives a shit about art any more except as a tax dodge.' He held out his hand and I took it. We sat in deep contemplation for a few minutes and then Terry asked: 'How come we were never lovers?'

'We used to play doctor together when we were kids. Does that count?'

"I don't think so.' He let go of my hand: 'Want to smoke some *yayo*?'

'No, I have to pick up my mother's ashes at the crematorium.''

'Are you going to keep them and make a shrine to her memory, or are you going to scatter them?'

'Scatter,' I said. 'It's cleaner that way.

My mother was presented to me in a cardboard carton. Inside the box was a heavy plastic bag containing her ashes. When I got to my car I opened the bag and ran my fingers through the ash. I was looking for relics, pieces of bone and teeth that had survived the cremation fire. My understanding was that certain Buddhist sects kept the relics and considered them holy.

I hoped my mother had left some bits and pieces for me because I was going to put them in a red plastic pill box. I'd found the box in the back of a dresser drawer in my childhood room and it too was a relic of sorts. I used to carry little candy hearts in the box when I was a kid, now I was going to put Carlene, or what was left of her, in it.

For a small woman Carlene had certainly left a lot of ashes. They were heavy and thick and I could easily imagine turning them into a paste and making a fetish statue out of them. Those statues were heavy voodoo, serious black magic, and maybe Terry and I could use some protection if we were going to kill Preston Greylander. Still, I could never do that to my mother, I'd have to settle for the benign and sentimental act of putting a part of her in a pill box.

I found a few slices of bone and what looked like part of a tooth, they were mostly grey-blue in colour, but one piece was a curious light russet shade. I stashed the relics in the box and drove on to Cedar Lake. Before she became ill and lost the use of her legs, the path around the lake had been one of Carlene's favourite walking areas.

Like so many necessary acts, the disposal of human remains in a public area was illegal. Fortunately, it was dark autumn, and getting on towards dinnertime, so no one was around to see me break the law and call the park police. I walked down through a forested point and on towards the water chanting *Nam Myoho Renge Khyo* all the way. My Buddhism is eclectic and personal, I'd cobbled it together from readings, teachings, and observations I'd made throughout my life. I'd never had a guru, but I'd learned to chant with a faction of the Nichiren sect. I continued with the chant as I tossed handfuls of ash into the water and watched them float away. When I was finished, I wasted no time on tears but hurried to my car and drove back to mother's house.

The final part of the funeral ceremony was the drinking of champagne. Carlene, despite her populist stance and radical political beliefs, had been a constant consumer of the elite beverage. No matter what her financial status she always managed to have a few bottles of California bubbly on hand. For this special occasion I pulled the cork on a bottle of Roederer Brut and poured two glasses into Carlene's best crystal flutes.

Before I drank, I made a little speech in honor of my mother and talked to her about the plan to murder Preston Greylander. She would have been delighted to learn Terry and I were involved in such a plot. Carlene had a personal grievance against the Greylander's; back in the old days the grain merchants had pulled a land grab in the Dakota's stealing precious acreage from the wheat farmers and sending them into penury. My ancestors had been among the dispossessed. After being thrown off their land they went to Colorado and worked in the mines. At some point they joined the IWW and became Wobblies. That was my heritage, and just because I'd studied art history I didn't forget it. Actually, Carlene never let me forget. She'd schooled me well on all the rotten, despicable acts of the hated Greylander's and that was why I had no problem helping Terry assassinate Preston Greylander.

After I made my speech and confessed all to my mother, I drank both glasses of champagne and when they were empty I took one of the flutes and smashed it in the fireplace and that was the end of Carlene.

After getting lost on a winding suburban road that ended up in a dead end with a beautiful view of Lake Washichu, I finally found the restaurant where I was due to meet Preston for lunch. The building was faux Mediterranean in style and looked like it belonged in a strip mall. I parked my car and went inside. I found myself in a dimly lit vestibule and asked the host, who was fully outfitted in black tie, if Preston had arrived. The man looked blank, as though he didn't recognize the Greylander name, either he was new to Lake Washichu, or Preston was booked in under an alias.

'Do you mind if I take a look?' I asked.

'Certainly not, Madame, please follow me.'

He led me into a larger, equally dim, dining room that was dominated by a boldly painted ceramic pizza oven. The walls were brick and board and sported colored tiles assembled in mini murals of peasants stomping on grapes. I spotted Preston lunching alone in a secluded corner and told the host his assistance would no longer be required.

As I approached the table Preston raised his glass of red and took a big gulp. Seeing me, he didn't bother to stand up, but merely gestured to the chair across from him. I sat down: 'So, Preston, are you going incognito these days?'

His thin lips parted and made a slash in his face that was supposed to be a smile: 'Didn't Margaret give you my alias? When I'm at the Lake Washichu headquarters I generally book in under a false name, I don't like these preening twits fawning over me.'

'I can understand that,' I said.

Preston picked up the bottle of Tuscan red and poured me a glass. There was a plate of olives, and what looked like a plate of French fries on the table. He pushed the French fries towards me: 'I hope you don't mind that I started without you, my time is limited, and, frankly, I was hungry.'

'No, no, that's fine.' I picked up one of the fries. It didn't look like it was made out of potato. When I bit into it I found out it was polenta. 'This is good,' I said.

'Yes, isn't it? I believe polenta fries are a house specialty,' Preston smiled again, this time his mouth didn't look so much like a slash. 'This is going to be a light lunch for me, but please order whatever you like.' He gestured to a waiter who had been lurking behind a brick pillar.

'I'll just have some greens in vinaigrette and maybe we can split an order of bruschetta.'

'Yes, and we'll share another order of polenta fries.'

Preston was really hot on the fries. They were certainly an improvement over the onion dip he'd favored at our first meeting.

I sampled the wine and it was fantastic, a supple Tuscan that was too complex for such simple fare, but we drank it anyway. It seemed that Preston didn't stint on the wine when he was eating out. I didn't have long to wait for him to get down to business, he started off on the painting right away.

'Martel, I'd like to have my Rembrandt cleaned. Are you available to take it to the restorers in Amsterdam?'

'Certainly, Preston, I'll be happy to help.'

'That's wonderful. I feel like I'm in capable hands now that you're in charge of this whole business. By the way, I was impressed by the information on the conservators; apparently the family has been in the business since the eighteenth century.'

'Yes, they're legendary in the field. I apprenticed at Van der Saar Fine Arts years ago. That's where I learned the trade.'

I was proud of my stint at the august firm even though things hadn't turned out exactly as planned because that son of a bitch Hendrik Van der Saar broke my heart and sent me back to New York before I could finish my training.

Preston slid a business card across the table. 'Please call Margaret in the morning and make the arrangements. She will handle your salary and travel expenses.'

'The painting requires special packing and I'm going to need armed guards.'

'That's fine, dear, work out the details with Margaret.' He glanced at his watch and stood up to leave. 'Sorry, but I'm going to have to cut this short.'

'Before you go, I'd like to invite you for cocktails at Terry Volkov's on the tenth of November. The poor man is in a serious depression, and I'm doing my bit to get him out of his slump. I thought a small party might cheer him up.'

'I'll be happy to attend, Martel. As it happens I'll be in town on that weekend and I don't believe I have anything booked. Give Margaret the address and time when you speak to her.'

He fell right into the trap. Luring him in was easier than I expected: 'Thanks, Preston, I know Terry will be delighted to see you.'

I breathed a sigh of relief; the plan was now officially in progress.

Preston affirmed the engagement and rushed off. In his haste I hoped he wasn't stiffing the restaurant and leaving me with the bill, but when I looked out front I saw him in conversation with the host. I stayed on at the table for five minutes and finished up what was left in the bottle of wine.

On the drive back into the city I started thinking about Hendrik Van der Saar. I'd have to call him and get things fixed up fast. The Van der Saar's were always booked solid and they had a long waiting list, but I had a feeling he'd make an exception for me.

That night I had a dream that showed a scene that seemed straight from biblical times but my mind knew it was set in the twenty first century. In the dream I was traveling through a wasteland. The heat was strong and the sun beat down with relentless intensity while vultures circled overhead in the cloudless sky. I was not alone, but traveling as part of a tribal group of dispossessed women and children. There were no men to accompany us, and I knew they were either dead or off at the wars. Together we trudged through the hot sands, past land that had turned to dust, past the rotting carcasses of dead cattle. This had once been grazing land, but it had been despoiled.

The tribe was searching for water and hoping to reach the next refugee camp. The women, some visibly pregnant, carried desiccated babies hanging between their breasts. The babies, looking like tiny mummies looted from an Egyptian tomb, were wrapped in festively colored shawls of purple, azure, turquoise, hot pink and gold. Some of the infants were dead, but the women refused to put them down, they refused to let the dead bodies of their children become carrion for the vultures.

Even though the soles of their feet were scorched and burned, the women walked with the stately gait of royal concubines from an ancient Nubian Empire. They were gaily dressed in robes and gowns of shimmering color, but they moved with the unbearable precision of the starving. They were a human herd whose only need was to find drink and feed, and to escape the death that lay on their lands. I walked among then and suffered with them, and I carried an unknown child that seemed to belong to me. As we crossed a bridge over a dried up river I felt a breeze come up beside me and with the breeze came the heady scent of a Northern forest. The other women must have felt it too because they began to smile through their cracked and broken lips, their gowns fluttered in the breeze, and suddenly the pace began to quicken. We were moving on with fresh resolve and perhaps, we would soon find water, or the next refugee camp.

I woke in the morning and remembered the dream. It had surely been brought on by the famine in the Horn of Africa. It seemed that, as usual, I was identifying with the dispossessed of the world. That fucking famine could have been avoided if it weren't for the gung ho idiots making their endless wars and land grabs. You could call it genocide if you cared to look at the facts. It was a horror and a shame, and many would die while Greylander International picked up some spare change selling grain and food to the US government and the NGO's.

I brushed my anger aside, there was no time to ruminate on the famine, I had to get on with the job. I was going to Amsterdam to deliver the painting and coming right back so I would be ready for the party on the tenth.

I called Margaret at Greylander headquarters and within a day I had the painting packed and crated for transit. Once the crating was done it was off and away. Two armed guards escorted us (me and the painting), from the Greylander compound to a corporate jet at a private terminal. I was being paid handsomely for my efforts, a check for 25K was safe in my checking account and I had a brand new American Express card to cover expenses.We got on the plane before the rest of the passengers and I supervised while the armed guards carefully secured the painting in the bulkhead. When I was satisfied that the painting could neither slip, nor fall, or otherwise do damage to itself, I dismissed the guards. They were no longer needed because the Van der Saar's were supplying security at Schiphol.

An old style, curvy hostess dressed in a snappy navy blue uniform handed me a flute of sparkling wine and I sat back in my extra wide and well-padded seat to comfortably watch the Suits embark. About ten mid-level slaves, two of whom were women, got on board and were led to their seats. They were burdened with digital gear and miscellaneous carry-on luggage. They stowed the carry-on in the bins above their seats, but they kept the digital close to their bodies. Thankfully, the seat next to mine remained empty, and I was able to settle down with a paperback titled *The Rich Are Ruining the Earth.*

When the plane was safely in flight the food began to arrive. As it was a mid-level flight the food was bland and mediocre, about the same quality as was served in business class on commercial flights. First came a bit of dried out smoked salmon on wilted cucumber. I pushed it to the side of my tray and drank the rest of my wine. After the stewardess (I use the antiquated term in full knowledge), got rid of the first course each passenger was served with a small bottle of

California red and a plate of sliced roast beef, stinky broccoli, and a microwaved potato smothered in sour cream substitute. The food was not successful, and the stench from the well stewed broccoli fouled the air of the cabin with the smell of a thousand farts. It was a long flight and I needed sustenance, so I held my nose and managed to eat some of the potato and a bit of the beef. The smell of the broccoli was so noxious that the stewardess finally took notice and used a spray can to refresh the air in the cabin. For dessert there were slices of Tarte Tatin. It was delicious; although I couldn't help but notice that it looked and tasted suspiciously like the tart I sometimes picked up in the frozen food section at Trader Joe's. I waved away the coffee and kept on with the red until I was mildly buzzed and ready to sleep.

We had barely landed at Schiphol when Hendrik Van der Saar, accompanied by two ex-military types, boarded the plane. Hendrik, an up-scale gent with a suave, slightly Spanish look, greeted me with a kiss on both cheeks while his aides took possession of the painting. Hendrik looked terribly posh in Italian tailoring, but one glance at his hands gave him away. He had the gnarly hands of a manual worker, and although he was now the front man and did not participate in the restoration process his short fingernails were still stained from years of contact with solvents and pigments.

While we deplaned the Greylander clones were still taking their bags from the bins. Hendrik got us through customs in record time and we were soon on our way to Amsterdam in a Mercedes SUV. Hendrik sat beside me in the back, we didn't talk much, and I looked out the window to avoid his gaze. There was a light mist in the air, and the flat, reclaimed land seemed to stretch out to meet the grey and eternal sea. Occasionally, a large canal ran through the fields like a thick, silver thread. Some visitors found the landscape dull and not worth a glance. I found it unique and inspiring. I loved the Netherlands and the Dutch people; they were civilized with a capital C, and had successfully managed to blend commerce and fine art since medieval times. The Van der Saar family had been in the business of sales and restoration of art works since the eighteenth century. Hendrik and his brother Willem had inherited a tradition that was rich in craft, artistry, and knowledge. They had also inherited plenty of street smarts and an uncanny ability to cater to the needs of the ultra-rich without debasing themselves or their work.

We arrived at the Van der Saar shop in the Museum Quarter and the painting was quickly hustled inside. It seemed that events were unfolding at a very fast clip and I assumed that Hendrik and Willem, the chief of restoration, were eager to have a look at the Greylander Rembrandt. I paused for a brief moment to admire the high style of the sales room. Surprisingly for an establishment dedicated to the art of painting, there were no pictures on the walls. The only object of decoration was a gigantic arrangement of blowzy red and white striped tulips, pale pink roses, white peonies, and purple iris in an enormous crystal vase. The flowers looked particularly fine because they were set off against walls which were painted in an acidic shade of Van Gogh yellow. You had to hand it to the Van der Saar's, they knew how to put a still life together.

Willem was waiting in the coldly utilitarian studio. He gave us a bright smile and pulled me into his arms with such rugged enthusiasm that I almost felt my ribs snap. He was a big guy with long, blonde hair done up Viking style in braids that hung down on each side of his face. In contrast to his ultra-chic brother he was dressed like a *clochard* in baggy cords and a moth eaten sweater.

The big joke in the Van der Saar family was that Willem had to be kept hidden from the clients because, if he were to be seen in all his disheveled glory, the big money collectors would recoil in disgust and take their business elsewhere. The truth was that Willem was a druggie and smoked a lot of weed to enhance his concentration and enrich his detail work. He was often too stoned to speak coherently to customers and that was why he kept to the studio.

'So, Martel, you bring us a mysterious Rembrandt with no provenance,' Willem said, as he loosened his hold on me.

'Yes, it was sold to one of the American millionaires in 1910.'

Both Willem and Hendrik frowned; it was well known that the European fakers and forgers hit the jackpot when the naïve American *nouveaux* began to try to embellish their social superiority by purchasing old masters.

'Let's have a look,' Hendrik said.

Willem expertly broke open the crate and began to remove the layers of packing that covered the painting. Hendrik watched with an eagle eye: 'This is well done, Martel. May I ask who made the crate?'

'I did,' I said.

'Of course,' Hendrik nodded, and absently patted me on the back: 'Very well done, my dear. You are a credit to your teacher.'

'As I recall you were the one who taught me how to make crates.'

'Yes, yes, so I was,' Hendrik said, still keeping his eye firmly on his brother and the business at hand. I wondered if he remembered that while teaching me the finer points of packing and crating we had engaged in hot sex. In fact, we had fucked in this very room. When the work was finished Hendrik had shoved me up against the wall and we had indulged our animal natures to the fullest. For such a suave looking character he often behaved like a boar in rut.

The painting was now free of its wrappings and placed on a long table for inspection: 'The frame is nineteenth century, it should come off easily enough.' Willem said. We all knew this, but it had to be commented upon.

'Is there anything on the back?' he asked.

'Not that I could see, you guys will have to give it a closer look.'

'Let's clean off a bit of the dust.' Willem took a brush and a swab that had been dipped in *sapone* solution and delicately cleaned a tiny square at the top left of the canvas. When he finished, the square was noticeably lighter. It had been covered with filth of an indescribable murk, now it was black.

'It looks to be in good shape,' he said.

'It should be, it hasn't been disturbed since 1910,' I said. 'Mr. Greylander claims there was a provenance, but apparently it's been lost.'

'No doubt,' Hendrik said drily. He'd heard all this kind of bullshit before. 'Do you have an opinion, Martel?'

It was polite of Hendrik to ask my opinion, he and Willem hardly needed it, but the question was part of the professional repertoire.

'I think it's of the period,' I said.

'Yes, I believe you are correct. It is definitely not something that was manufactured for sale to rich tourists.'

'I'll start on the preliminaries today,' Willem said. 'Will you be staying on in Amsterdam?'

'Just for the night, I've got business back in America that can't wait.'

'Call me before you leave. I could have some news for you.' He smiled, showing his well- spaced, but slightly stained, teeth. 'Who knows, maybe we will find a signature when we take the frame off.'

'The client believes it's a Rembrandt. I'm afraid he won't accept another author.'

'We all know that cannot be,' Willem's smile was gone and his face was grave.

'He will accept what we tell him,' Hendrik said, he was used to dealing with the rich, they didn't scare him. He turned to me: 'Where are you staying, Martel? I'll take you to your hotel.'

'I'm at the Bilderberg Jan Luyken.'

Hendrik took my arm and steered me towards the door while Willem stared avidly at the painting. You could see he was anxious to have a go at it. After all his years in the business, he still wanted to see if a miraculous surprise existed under the layers of dirt.

On the way to the hotel Hendrik and I agreed to meet for dinner that evening. It was just a business meeting, but it gave me some hope, because now that we were in close proximity the old feelings were coming back in a mighty rush of manic desire. I longed to throw myself in his arms, attack him with ardent kisses, and make him a prisoner of my body. Whatever he felt, if anything, was not apparent.

We had dinner at a small Indonesian restaurant over by the Rijksmuseum. The only item on the menu was the complete Rijstafel, a feast of Indonesian dishes that are delicately spiced and beautifully presented. As I had eaten nothing since the morning when I'd breakfasted on a stale croissant and American coffee, I was ready to dig in and enjoy the food.

Over dishes with names like *Gado Gado* and *Krupuk* Hendrik updated me on the status of the painting. Willem had examined the back, and I was correct, there were no marks of identification, no signatures, dates, or any other significant data. As predicted, the frame was removed without difficulty or damage, and the medium was identified as oil painted on panel. Currently there was no signature. There was always a possibility that the signature was buried under the dirt of centuries, but neither Hendrik nor Willem held out much hope on that point. The painting would be sent to the lab for age dating, but presently we all agreed that the visual signs indicated it was made in the seventeenth century.

When we finished the meal Hendrik took my arm and escorted me back to the hotel. We didn't speak, but I could feel the heat of his body coming through his elegant suit loud and clear. From the vibes he was sending my way it was apparent that he, too, felt a rekindling of our lost passion.

Upstairs in my hotel room we didn't bother with the niceties of seduction. He was the first to disrobe and I watched avidly as he removed his stylish garments. He was still well toned and nicely muscled, probably because neither he nor Willem trusted their assistants with the lifting and hauling of precious objects. I closed my eyes for a moment and felt my mouth begin to salivate at the thought of making love with him. He took it from there, the next thing I knew I was naked and we were both down on the bed. It was a royal fuck, Hendrik was so eager and so skillful that I just gave it all up and let him ravish me like we were back in some eighteenth century boudoir. When we were done he kept me in his arms and I rested my head on his chest. His skin was smooth and firm and he smelled like hot peppermint.

'You're still a fantastic lover,' I said, 'What do you take for virility?'

'An herbal from Indonesia,' he said. 'It really does the trick, doesn't it?'

'It certainly does,' I murmured. My sex throbbed from the stimulation it had just received and I rubbed it against his thigh.

'What time do you leave in the morning?'

'I have to be at Schiphol at six.'

'If you like, I'll spend the night and take you to the airport in the morning.'

'I'd like that,' I said. I wanted him to stay. We could fuck again and drop into space and forget about all the shit that held us to the earth.

He put his hand on my sex and opened it with his blunt, stained fingers: 'It's still a beautiful flower,' he said.

I had to smile, apparently after all these years Hendrik was still hooked on flowers. He had once made a sensational bouquet of tulips, iris, and roses to brighten up my grungy room in the Jordaan. My mind's eye flipped to the bouquet I'd seen earlier in the day and I wondered if he was responsible for its creation: 'Hendrik, are you still doing flowers? Did you make that bouquet down at the shop?'

'I arranged every damn flower in that vase myself,' he grumbled. 'It took me two bloody hours to get it right. I was thinking about you and I wanted to make something brilliant and wildly beautiful.'

'You are such a bullshitter.' I started to laugh, but I was secretly pleased he was giving me the sweet talk.

He touched my labia with one of his fingers: 'I can't decide whether it's a rose or an iris.'

'It's an iris,' I said.

'I think you're right,' he said, bending his head and getting down and licking my petals.

In the morning, I stared fondly at my lover. He still looked good, even though clumps of his silver streaked hair stood up on end and he badly needed a shave. He gave me a quick grope, stuck his hard dick into me, and with only a few thrusts we both got off. After that I let him use the bathroom but I kicked him out before he could shower. I was in a hurry, and he didn't complain, he made himself useful by brewing coffee in the cute red espresso machine that came with the room.

We made it to the car in record time; Hendrik drove with one hand and clutched a paper cup of coffee in the other. Half way to Schiphol he began to talk about the Greylander's: 'Madame Pookie Greylander is my client. She's a hundred years old but still in the art game.'

'Madame Pookie,' I repeated the name and snickered.

'Yes, she is a collector of old masters and makes a pest of herself by sending us worthless forgeries to clean and refurbish.'

'I'm sure she's not the only one sending you worthless forgeries. It's never bothered you before. As far as I know forgeries are half your business.'

'Less than half, maybe a quarter,' Hendrik said defensively. 'Let me remind you, Martel that we restore and sell paintings. We leave the serious authentication to the professors and the museums. I mention Madame Pookie because I have done research on her clan. There are fourteen Greylander family members living in Switzerland and my sources tell me they each collect one billion dollars a year from the business.'

'Since when have you objected to dealing with the super rich?' Hendrik was showing a side of his personality I'd never seen before.

'I've never liked that aspect of the business,' he said. 'I don't know how you got mixed up with the Greylander's, but the man you're working for is a shit-eating dog. You need to stay away from him. He's trying to eliminate the entire population of Africa.'

'Thanks for warning me, I didn't know you cared.'

'Don't be so flippant, darling. I do care about you and I hate to see you associating with such an evil man.'

Hendrik looked rather shamefaced and sad. I guess it was hard to admit he cared about something or someone. 'Do you want me to speak to Greylander and tell him the painting is not a Rembrandt?' he asked.

'I'll tell him,' I said. 'You can come in later when he doesn't accept what I say.'

With any luck, Greylander would soon be dead and neither Hendrik nor I would have to explain anything to him.

'Very well,' he said, taking a sip of coffee and giving his full attention to the road.

Conversation lagged and we arrived at Schiphol in silence. I was flying back commercial, so I had Hendrik drop me off at KLM. He seemed rather subdued until I moved to give him a goodbye peck on the cheek, then he got hold of me and his lips caught me on the mouth and we kissed with a lot of passion. I broke away, grabbed my bag, and practically flew out the door. This reactivated romance was a shock to me. Christ, we'd been absent from each other for years and now we were carrying on with insane lust.

When I was outside in the street he leaned toward the open window and said: 'Come back soon, Martel. Don't make me come to the States and drag you back.'

This was a rare concession, he hated going to the States and usually sent an associate in his place.

I stuck my head in the window: 'Why do you want me now, you old bastard? You've been pretending I didn't exist for years.'

'We don't have time for that conversation,' he said.

'Don't worry, you won't have to set foot in the USA, I'll be back as soon as I can because I want to hear your explanation.'

He gave me a crooked smile. Fuck, even his lopsided grin was enticing: 'I'll be waiting for the moment,' he said.

I was tempted to jump back in the car, but good sense prevailed and I turned away and hurried into the terminal. By the time I boarded and took my aisle seat in business class, I was fantasizing about my return to Amsterdam and a couple of nights in a locked room with my former and present lover.

I was fantasizing and puzzling about Hendrik until half-way across the Atlantic when I realized exactly what I was going back to. I put my head in my hands and closed my eyes, unfortunately this simple gesture could not blot out the truth: I was going back to the States to be an accessory to murder, and my beloved friend was going to do the killing and then turn the gun on himself. It was a grim scenario, but I had agreed to play my part and I only hoped I would be able to carry it out with award-winning efficiency.

By the time I arrived at my destination I was a frazzled wreck. Unfortunately, there was no Greylander driver waiting with a sign, so I took the train downtown and transferred to a cab for the short ride to my mother's house. When I got to the house I drank a glass of water and reported in to Margaret. She said she'd have Preston call me within the next couple of days. That might be too late because the tenth was coming up in two days' time. Next, I called Terry and he told me all was well. Preston had actually phoned in an acceptance on the cocktail party. We made a date to meet the next day for a dry run-through on the murder scenario and rang off with fond, but brisk good byes.

I started to review my email but found myself preoccupied with thoughts of Hendrik. I kept reliving the moment when his lascivious tongue began licking away at the petals of my iris.

Terry and I had everything clear by Friday. My job was a simple one. I would answer the door to Preston's ring and then escort him to the sitting room. When we were inside, I would tell him that I would be right back with some canapés. I would walk out of the room, shut the door, and hold it so he couldn't escape. Terry would have the gun beside him hidden in the cushions of the wheelchair. He planned on shooting Preston as soon as I closed the door. He would shoot him three times and then he would shoot himself. It was a good plan and the only way it would fail was if Preston brought another person along with him. Terry said that was unlikely because there was no girlfriend on the scene and the wife lived in Switzerland.

On the day of the big event I walked through the hours until seven like I was living in zombie land. I started dressing around five, making sure I wore a disposable polyester dress that wouldn't leave any fibers scattered around the murder site. It was a plain black number purchased at Walmart for fifteen dollars and it didn't look half bad when I got it on. I brushed out my hair and then sprayed it stiff and put it up in a tight French twist. The effect was *très* Catherine Deneuve, and I prayed no incriminating hair would get loose from the tightly coiled hair style. On my feet I wore flat shoes similar to the ones seen on Madame Sarkozy, but mine were not for the purpose of making a tiny politician seem slightly less miniscule; mine were for running away from a crime scene.

I prepared myself well, no perfume, no lipstick, no jewelry. When I looked in the mirror I was pleased with my image, and decided I would conduct myself as though I was in a French movie, a noir thriller starring Catherine Deneuve where she played a snaky bitch out to kill her double-crossing ex.

By the time I got to Terry's I was well into my Deneuve persona, it was just as well; I probably couldn't go on with the murder unless I was pretending to be someone else. The front door was unlocked and I walked down the hall to the sitting room. Terry was at the bar, drinking a shot of vodka. He looked fine and healthy, and when I kissed his cheek he smelled fresh.

'I guess this is it, isn't it, Martel?'

'I guess,' I said, pouring myself a shot.

'What is it the Irish say?'

'I think they say see you on the other side.'

'Yes,' he raised his glass and we clinked, 'see you on the other side, Elizabeth.' He used my first name, it sounded strange, but it also sounded correct in this solemn moment.

Just then the doorbell rang and we both knew it was Preston. I gave Terry another kiss, a final kiss, and ran out of the room to answer the door.

Preston was standing on the step looking calm and assured in his Savile Row suit and regimental tie. I greeted him with a chilly peck on the cheek and led him down the hall. When we got inside, Preston was surprised that he was the only guest, but I assured him he was early and that the others would be arriving soon. I poured him vodka and excused myself to go make canapés.

Murder and suicide, the corpses don't look like they do in the movies; they look much worse, and, of course, in films you never get the stench that hangs in the air and makes people vomit. Terry had done his thing with the Sig Sauer while I stood outside the sitting room, my back pressed against the door, holding it so Preston couldn't escape. The Sig was equipped with a silencer, but I could still hear a muffled *bang, bang, bang*. There was silence that seemed like it lasted ten years, and then I head another bang. I felt my body weaken and involuntarily slide down the door until I sat on the floor. I waited and no sound came from within. I looked at my watch it was only ten after seven. I waited another five minutes, got off the floor, and opened the door.

The first thing I noticed was the ungodly stink, it was worse than the broccoli smell on the Greylander plane. The killing had only happened five or ten minutes ago, but the place smelled like rotten meat and diseased shit. I stepped over Preston to get to Terry; my mind seemed to be working normally and it advised me not to step in the blood and effluvia on the floor. I wanted to puke, but by some incredible act of will I held it down.

Greylander had been shot in the head, gut, and genitals at close range. The mess was indescribable; blood, organs, meat, brains, mucous, bones, you name it, were all spattered merrily about like so many pieces of a particularly noxious dinner. I could see part of his dick, looking like a limp piece of spaghetti, hanging on the arm of a chair. Terry was slumped over dead in his wheelchair. He had put the Sig Sauer in his mouth and blasted away, so that when his brains hit the wall they made an expressionist pattern that reminded me of the thick impasto once used by the great abstract expressionist, Willem De Kooning.

When I was assured both men were dead, I got the hell out because I knew I was either going to vomit or lose my mind. Maybe both.

Just to be on the safe side, I did a hasty swipe of the door knobs with the sleeve of my dress before I ran outside. I moderated my gait to a brisk walk and made it to my car which was parked five blocks away in front of the Unitarian Society. When I made my plan I knew no one would be suspicious of another PT cruiser parked around the meeting hall. It was the car of choice for the entry level Unitarians.

I took the back route home, and it wasn't until I hit Cedar Lake that I had to stop the car and vomit out the window. Fortunately, I hadn't eaten all day, so it was just bile and dry heaves and a lot of tears for Terry. Safely back in my apartment, I went to the bathroom and retched for an hour or so. When I was done, I drank a glass of water and followed it by a glass of Tequila.

The next day I wanted to go to the art institute and look at the Kossoff exhibit, but I knew I was going to have to hang tough around my apartment for a couple of days. I thought about drinking the bottle of tequila and sedating myself with pills, but I had to remain alert in case the cops came by. Every morning I got online and looked for news of Preston's murder. Nothing! I bought hard copy of all the papers and nobody had anything on either Preston or Terry. Apparently, the long arm of Greylander International was keeping the murder-suicide under wraps.

On the third day I got some action; Sammy Volkov called and told me his brother was dead. The story was that Terry had been decimated by the loss of his wife and daughter and was unable to carry on in his diminished state. The cops were claiming that Terry had left a suicide note to that effect, but I knew for a fact the note was a forgery. Terry left nothing but two mangled bodies. I supposed that somebody in the Greylander mob wrote it, but then again, it could have been the cops. Naturally, I acted shocked and commiserated with Sammy. He sounded genuinely bereft, but I questioned his sincerity when he told me that Terry had already been cremated, and that the family had decided that, because of the circumstances, there would be no ceremony. That made it easy, no flowers to buy, no little black dress, no service, there was nothing to do but mourn for Terry privately. It was beginning to look like we had got away with murder.

That afternoon, just as I finally relaxed and decided to pour myself a tequila, the phone rang, and it was Margaret telling me I was off the Rembrandt case and that the Van der Saar brothers were now in charge. She told me I could keep the 25K, but the credit card had already been canceled and would I please send her an accounting of my expenses. She rang off with no mention of Preston.

I was more than a little surprised about the Van der Saars. Maybe Hendrik had been playing me, and all that talk about the evil Greylander's had been a ploy to gain my confidence and get control of the picture. The sex scene in my hotel room could have been designed to get my mind off business and onto his Indonesian-enhanced dick. There was the remote possibility that I was wrong about the painting, maybe it really was a Rembrandt. Now that I thought carefully about the execution of the work, it looked more like a Rembrandt than something done by one of his major students, it certainly wasn't a Dou or a Flinck. Still, the proportions were all wrong. I knew that. I'd stake what was left of my career on that.

I thought about Hendrik. There was no question I was developing a deep romantic attachment to him, and I wanted to confess to him and have him absolve me of my crime, but it seemed that wouldn't be possible because he was double-dealing me over the picture. I finally took down the bottle of tequila and had a good stiff drink.

I woke up the next day with a hangover only to learn that Preston Greylander had died of an undisclosed disease and that the funeral would be private. Ironically, the family stated that contributions to the Horn of Africa Relief Fund would be appreciated.

The obits were short and to the point and not particularly celebratory. The knowledge of Preston's power and influence was once again kept from the masses; there was no need for a memorial splash on the front page of *The Financial Times* or *The Wall Street Journal* because those in the know knew. The rest of us could continue on in ignorance because we were of no importance in the high stakes game of global domination.

I stayed online for an hour, futilely looking for detailed news of Preston's death. Just before I logged off, I went to my e-mail; I hadn't been there for days and the junk had piled up. Surprisingly there was a message from Hendrik. All it said was: 'Thinking of you. There are new developments, please come back.'

PART TWO

I went to Amsterdam in economy class and checked in at the Ibis Central close to the train station. I was going cheap because I was traveling on my own dime. The Ibis is a no frills chain hotel with tiny rooms that are sparsely furnished with playful Ikea-type furniture. Before crawling under the duvet for a quick nap, I called Hendrik at the shop. He laughed when I said I was staying at the Ibis, it was surely a comedown from my previous accommodation, but he said he'd be over in three hours when he finished haggling over a still life by Pieter de Ringh. I told him to bring a bottle of cognac and some mineral water because there was no mini bar in the room.

Almost exactly three hours later Hendrik knocked at the hotel room door. I had been sleeping in the nude and I wrapped myself in the duvet and went to the door. I let him in and moved toward him. It was only a step or two in the restricted space of the tiny room. I was so close I could feel my breath hitting the skin on his face. He put his hands under the duvet and started moving them over my body. His touch was demanding, almost rough. He was in wild boar mode, but I didn't mind. He didn't even bother to take off his suit. I guess he could afford the dry cleaning.

We had a quick and resounding fuck and when we were done Hendrik said: 'I needed that.'

'Me too,' I said. The jet lag and the tension seemed to have melted away with my orgasm.

Hendrik took off his suit and got under the duvet with me: 'What's going on with the picture?' I asked.

'After you left, one of the Greylander lawyers came to me with a contract. It was written in highly veiled language, but the bottom line was they wanted us to put a signature on the painting. The money was large, and I knew this imbecile would never understand why we couldn't forge Rembrandt's signature. I agreed to their terms thinking we could at least collect some of the money before we told them the deal was off.'

'How large was the money?'

'A million Euros.'

'Will you be able to collect now that Preston's dead?'

'Yes, I think so. Margaret called and told me to continue on with the restoration. Now that Preston's gone, Pookie wants to add the painting to her collection.'

'Is she really a hundred years old?' I asked.

'Indeed she is, in fact she's going on a hundred and two. She lies about her age.' Hendrik was smiling, but then his face went serious: 'This morning a messenger delivered a check for half the money. We'll receive the rest when the picture is safely in Pookie's hands.

'I assume I'll get a finder's fee.'

'No need to ask, Martel. You'll get the standard and maybe a little more if you're good to me,' he said, dipping his fingers into my wet.

'You say that now when you're all happy and sated and playing with my cunt, but what happens in the real world?'

'As far as I know, this is the real world.' He moved down and started licking my labia.

'Hendrik, this is no way to do business; we'll never get anything accomplished if you go on like this.'

He didn't bother to answer because he was too busy licking away. He had me where he wanted me, and the sensation was so intense that I clutched at his hair and yelped like a dog. I felt like my whole conscious and subconscious mind was falling out of my head and into his mouth and I began to sob while my body went off in a frenzied convulsion.

Hendrik had surely fucked some crazy chicks in his day, but this time the woman he was with had gone totally berserk. He got out of my grip and stood up: 'Didn't you like it, darling?' He poured us both a shot of cognac and held the glass to my lips.

'It was great. I loved it. Sorry I started to cry, maybe it's the jet lag.'

He smiled: 'Don't apologize. I got off on all that yapping and sobbing. You really know how to get the most out of an orgasm.'

Hendrik seemed to have genuinely enjoyed my reaction to his tongue job. He was a supreme practitioner of cunnilingus and always had been. Still, my reaction to his passionate expertise had been way out of control. I gathered up my clothes and started to get dressed: 'Can we get out of here and go someplace non-sexual? I need to talk to you.'

'We can go over to 'No Exit' and smoke some weed.'

'Pot always gives me a mushy mind, and I need to keep my wits about me. Is there a Brown Café around here? I could go for a beer and a shot of jenever.'

'We'll have to walk a bit, but I know of a place that hasn't been redecorated since 1850. I think people are still smoking tobacco in there.'

The deal about Brown Cafés is that their walls are supposedly stained from centuries of nicotine. There are, of course, contemporary Brown Cafés that cater to the tourist trade. Their walls are stained brown with varnish and they are decorated with plastic antiques. Smoking is strictly forbidden. You cannot smoke tobacco in an Amsterdam bar or cafe, but you can still smoke pot in a coffee shop.

Hendrik and I trekked out through the streets and canals of the city center until we turned into a tiny street that led us back into a maze of alleys. It seemed as though we were on a journey to a secret destination, and we finally arrived at an old, ramshackle house, hidden behind a brick wall.

Inside, the place was a fucking marvel: the cafe was paneled in dark wood and the upper walls and ceiling which had once been white were appropriately stained with what looked to be genuine smoke and nicotine. Surprisingly, the room emanated a golden glow from artfully placed chandeliers shining on glass, brass, and wood. The smell was incredible, it was a scent that was forbidden, but I recognized it. The room smelled like the inside of my grandfather's cigar box, rich, spicy, and flavorful, not at all like the noxious reek of the death dealing cigarettes we were encouraged to despise and fear.

When I looked around, I saw patrons, Amsterdam locals, enjoying beer and blithely puffing away on forbidden tobacco. It was an unusual sight: the smoking bans had been on for twenty or thirty years; if you wanted to smoke in public, you had to travel to Russia, Japan, or one of the South American Free States.

There was no table service in the café, so Hendrik went to the bar. He had to make two trips to carry the beer and the shots of jenever back to the table. I watched him intently as he moved back and forth. There was something in the way he walked that gave me a weird thrill. His movements were raw and masculine and he had a bit of a swagger. This hint of insolence and defiance was unusual in a man of his status. The fucking dude had attitude, and no matter how he toned it down, you could see it in his walk.

After Hendrik sat down he pulled a box of Gitanes out of his pocket and offered me one.

'Where did you get those?' I asked, taking one. I seldom smoked; it wasn't worth the hassle. Most places in America were smoke-free, and that included your automobile and your apartment.

'I picked them up in Moscow last week. We do a lot of business there.'

He lit my cigarette with a disposable lighter, and when I took a puff I almost choked. 'These are really strong, they taste lousy, but the box is pretty.'

'Yes, the box is a classic example of Art Moderne.'

I didn't feel like discussing the Art Moderne on the Gitanes box, I had an anxious need to get down to personal business: 'So, what are we doing together, Van der Saar? Did you finally decide you wanted me?'

'I've wanted you since the first day I saw you. That's never changed.'

'That's news to me. As I recall you were the one who asked me to leave town. You even paid for my plane ticket.'

'Yes, and I gave you severance pay and saw to it you got a job at Wildman and Son in New York.'

He sounded defensive and looked uncomfortable as he tried to explain: 'Our relationship was too intense. I wasn't ready for that kind of emotional experience. Aside from that you were childlike and naive. I couldn't subject you to the shit that was going on in my life.'

'I was twenty one, that's not a child,' I was insulted. 'You weren't much older. What were you, twenty five?'

'I was twenty six, and I'd just got out of prison for bank robbery.'

I started to laugh. What new kind of bullshit was this? The Van der Saar's committed crimes of a more genteel nature, surely, bank robbery was not in their repertoire.

'I'm serious, Martel.'

'Sorry, Hendrik, I can't picture it.'

'I was robbing banks with the Stelnik-Berghoff gang. I was their weapons expert.'

'Whoa, wait a minute! Didn't your wife run off with one of the Stelnik-Berghoff gang?'

I had been told that Hendrik's ex-wife was a radical with a price on her head. I thought she'd taken to revolution after they split up, but now it seemed that Hendrik was one of her cohorts in the infamous gang.

'Yes, she went to South America with Dieter Stelnik. They went while I was in prison. Greta dropped the baby off with Willem on her way out of the country. It was too dangerous to take the kid.'

'I'm beginning to see why you didn't want me around. With my big mouth I could have been a serious liability.' Hendrik polished off his shot of jenever and reached for mine: 'You can't have that,' I said, slapping his hand away, 'I'm going to need it after you tell me the whole story.'

'You're going to need more than a shot of jenever after I get done talking.' He stood up and went back to the bar. He still had the swagger, but now I knew where it came from, he'd acquired it robbing banks and perfected it in prison.

Hendrik came back holding a bottle of jenever. He sat down and lit up another Gitane. When he started to talk he looked like a desperado in an old French movie. I thought of Alain Delon in one of his more existential roles.

'Martel, I'm sure you understand that Willem and I were groomed since childhood to take our place in the family business and we had no quarrel with that. Aside from our studies in art history, languages, conservation, and restoration, we trained in weaponry. We needed to be able to defend the valuable art works that would soon be in our possession.

'When we were in adolescence, an investigative reporter broke a story that became a huge scandal in Northern Europe and Scandinavia. The events were too far in the past to affect our business, but it was a great shock to us kids. It seemed that our grandfather Gerard and his brother Laurens were criminal accomplices to the Nazi regime. They started out buying low from the Jews and selling high to the Nazis. Our ancestors prospered under the Germans and eventually started to work with the leaders of the Reich, they advised on, and procured, art works for the personal collections of Goering and Hitler.

'When the war ended, grandfather shot himself and Uncle Laurens overdosed on heroin. They were due to be tried as war criminals and, wishing to avoid scandal and imprisonment, they took the sensible way out. Our father, Dries, was born shortly after grandfather died and was not blamed for the crimes of his elders. As Dries reached adulthood his one dream was to restore Van der Saar Fine Arts to its preeminent place in the art world. Papa was something of a genius in public relations and financial dealings,and by the time we were born the business was flourishing.

'Serafina, our mother was a Communist. Her family fled Spain when Franco took over and they settled in Amsterdam. She brought us up as leftists, so you can imagine our shock when we learned of the Nazi collaboration of our elders. We all went off the deep end; Willem became a heavy drug user, our sister, Jasmyn, ran off with a bankrupt Sicilian prince, and me, I joined up with the Stelnik-Berghoff's. At the time they were desperately in need of someone to teach them how to use the weapons they'd liberated from a NATO storehouse in Brussels.' Hendrik grinned and poured himself another shot of jenever: 'The gang members were all typical bourgeois Europeans who'd never handled a gun in their lives. I was of great use to them.'

'So, if you were running around robbing banks and teaching people how to shoot guns why did you get married? I didn't think radicals believed in marriage.'

'We didn't, but at the time you had to produce a marriage license to get conjugal visits in prison. Greta was a good comrade who agreed to a prison marriage so I could get laid twice a month.'

'Jesus, couldn't you have tried celibacy for a while?'

'I was young, celibacy never occurred to me.'

'How long were you in?'

'A year and a half, and it wasn't pleasant. I was in prison in Belgium, and some of the guards had worked in the Congo. They used to beat us for the slightest infraction.'

'Did you have a special boyfriend when you were in jail?'

'Jesus, I knew you'd ask that.' He seemed exasperated. 'In case you haven't noticed, Martel, I'm a dominant male. In prison, the dominants are looking for submissives. I wasn't that desperate. Greta was coming in regularly, and I knew how to jerk off. Still, I had to prove my dominance in the prison world, which means I had to fight a couple of tough cons.'

'So how did you get out of prison?'

'I'm a living example of one law for the rich and one law for the poor. My father spent big money getting me out on a reduced sentence. I had to promise him I'd give up my wild ways and go back to working at Van der Saar Fine Arts. It was an easy decision; by that time I'd become disillusioned with the revolutionary vanguard and figured I could live with my family's tainted past. Besides, I had a child to take care of.'

He looked thoughtfully into his beer glass before he drained it: 'Although I'm legally Venessa's father, I don't know if she is my biological child.'

'That's what they all say,' I said.

'Honest, Martel, it's true. It was a sexual free-for-all back then. We were trying to break all the sexual taboos and, during the crucial period when Greta was impregnated, she was intimate with Nikki and Dieter and me.'

'Who's Nikki?' I asked.

'One of my oldest friends. He was a dedicated revolutionary, but now he's a cop on the Amsterdam Art Squad.'

'So what about Greta? How come she had the kid if it had so many fathers?'

'Everyone in the group wanted her to abort, but Greta had been brought up hard core Catholic and she couldn't break her early conditioning. She wouldn't listen to reason and insisted on carrying the child to term. As I was her lawful husband, Venessa became my child.'

'Does Venessa know about this?'

'Unfortunately something came up a couple of years ago and I had to tell her.'

Hendrik looked so sad and forlorn that I decided not to press the issue: 'Is she OK with it?'

'It's complicated, but basically she's OK. I'm her father and she's still a Van der Saar, that will never change.'

I reached for another Gitane. My hand was trembling and I didn't know if I could take any more of his painful revelations. Just then the music kicked in and he stopped talking. Throughout our time in the bar a tape had been playing softly in the background, it was all low key, melancholy music going from French *chanson* to Leonard Cohen. I hadn't paid much attention, the musical selection was great, but Hendrik's confession had been riveting. Now, the music was no longer in the background, the volume had increased, and the lights seemed to brighten and the chandeliers began to sway ever so slightly in the smoky air. Somebody on guitar started out with a monster riff. It was jazz guitar played at a rapid pace with extraordinary skill and dexterity. The notes cascaded into the room like brilliant strands of sparkling gems. Even though the guitarist was playing insanely fast the tone he got out of the guitar was so rich and so deep you could hear emotion coming through loud and clear. It was a superb performance by a virtuoso musician who presented a vibrant and unearthly sound. The music stopped as suddenly as it had begun and the lights went back to normal: 'Do you know who was playing? That guitarist was amazing.'

Hendrik's mouth twisted into a wry grin: 'That was one of our local heroes, a kid named Bobby Janacek. He's quite well known in the jazz world.'

'Does he always play that well?'

'As far as I know. The critics say he's the best.'

'Did you notice how the lights got brighter when the guitar started to play? I swear to god the chandeliers were swinging.'

'It was probably something to do with the power. This café is pretty far off the grid. As for the chandeliers, I didn't see them move, I was concentrating on the music.'

'I think this place is magic. I feel like I'm in a hallucination. Are you sure this café is real?'

'It's real, alright. It's so fucking real the authorities are trying to tear it down.'

'They have to break everything that's beautiful.'

'Yes, they do, *schatje,* and it's our job to oppose them and see that the beautiful is preserved.'

He pulled another Gitane out of the box. I took one too. I was getting used to the rough tobacco. I knew we were going to smoke the whole pack and drink the whole bottle of jenever.

I was still at the Ibis. Hendrik had gone off to Switzerland to confer with Madame Pookie about her collection, but he'd only be gone for one day and when he returned I'd have to give him an answer. He wanted me to come live with him at the family house on the Herengracht canal. He was alone in that old mausoleum because Venessa had asserted her independence and moved to an apartment in the De Pijp neighborhood. I wondered if her departure had anything to do with the revelation that Hendrik might not be her biological father. There was so much that Hendrik and I didn't know about each other and even though he'd told me a lot about himself that night in the Brown café I had a feeling there was more to learn.

We'd spent the weekend in bed at the Ibis, leaving only for brief walks and long meals. Somewhere between erotic episodes I told him about my mother's long, drawn-out departure from life. There were certain events and images that were stuck in my brain, images of my mother's suffering and pain. I had never told anyone, not even Terry, how emotionally difficult it had been to witness her physical decay, but now, with Hendrik so close, I was able to finally unload. I told him about the bewilderment in Carlene's eyes when she realized her legs were gone, and the terrible intimacy we'd shared when I changed her adult diapers. I'd cared for her alone and with little money, and it had exhausted and defeated me, and now that I was free she still haunted me.

Hendrik held me close and let me cry on his chest. It was strange, I hadn't cried in years, not even when Mother and Terry died, but now that I was with Hendrik I seemed to be crying all the time. Being with him had broken my defenses and opened me up and all the pain I'd stuck up in my head was flowing out of me and onto his body. He stroked my hair and called me sweet names and generally treated me like I was a traumatized child. He'd probably had experience in this area with his daughter. When I finally stopped crying, we got dressed and went outside and walked the streets until Hendrik stopped at a flower stall.

'What was your mother's favorite flower?' he asked.

'She liked orchids,' I said.

I followed him over to a tub of colorful Thai orchids.

'What color do you think she'd like?'

'The electric blue would be perfect for Carlene.'

He selected one stalk of sensational neon blue orchids and a tiny glass vase that would hold the stem and had the clerk wrap them up. We hurried on to a stall that sold incense and hippie items. I chose black opium incense and a tiny ceramic incense holder that just happened to be the same blue as the orchids.

When we got back to the Ibis, Hendrik put the orchids in the vase and set it on the bed table. I put the incense in the holder and lit it. The smoke was sweet and musky and smelled like the orchids looked. Hendrik and I stood in front of the makeshift altar, and I clasped my hands, bowed my head, and chanted *Nam Myoho Renge Khyo* three times. When I finished chanting, Hendrik started talking to my mother, he said: 'Carlene, I'm sorry your passing was so difficult and I hope your next life will be a fortunate one. I'm here with your daughter and I want you to know I love her and I will do everything in my power to comfort and protect her.'

At one time I would have been indignant if someone wanted to comfort and protect me, but now I knew I needed all the help I could get and I was grateful to Hendrik for expressing the sentiment. I still hadn't told him about Preston and I wondered how he'd feel about protecting me once he knew the Greylander combine might be after me.

After Hendrik finished talking to Carlene, he went to the cognac bottle and poured us a couple of shots. We sat on the edge of the bed and looked at the flowers and watched the incense burn.

'Hendrik,' I said, 'I don't want to suffer like my mother. I want to die before I get old.'

'I understand, *schatje*. But remember, you've still got a good thirty or forty years left in you. Why don't you spend them with me, and we can both go out together.'

'Are you serious?'

'Absolutely, I have no desire to sit around like a helpless old fool and watch my body rot.'

That was when he asked me to come live with him in the house on the Herengracht canal. I knew I couldn't make a commitment until I told him about my part in Preston Greylander's murder and at that moment I didn't have the strength to do it. One emotional scene per day was enough.

We were back in the Brown café drinking beer with shots of jenever and smoking a fresh pack of Gitanes. The music was on and Ray LaMontagne was singing *Roses and Cigarettes*. I really liked Ray, but I didn't have time to moon around listening to his incredible voice and poignant lyrics. I had to tell Hendrik about Preston's murder.

'I'm afraid I've got something bad to tell you, Hendrik.'

'You're not leaving again?'

'No, nothing like that, it's something I've done.'

'And what would that be, *schatje*? If you've been robbing banks and committing crimes I think I can forgive you.'

'It's about Preston Greylander.'

Hendrik's eyes iced over and his face turned to stone: 'Don't tell me you were fucking that asshole.'

'I didn't fuck him – I helped kill him.'

'Well, that's a relief.' His face relaxed and he started to smile: 'I didn't see that coming. Why don't you tell me about it? Start from the beginning.'

I told him the whole story in detail, including the guts on the floor and the brains on the wall. When I finished he sat there staring at me with stunned admiration: 'I knew there was a reason I loved you,' he said.

'I'm afraid the Greylander's might find out I was involved and come looking for me.'

'That's possible, but I wouldn't lose any sleep over it. Have you any indications they're on your tail?'

'No, it's just an irrational fear.'

'It's not irrational, you and your friend messed with some of the worst people in the world. They could know about your role in the murder and be looking for revenge. We'll just have to wait and see what happens. For what it's worth I've got your back.'

'I could bring you a lot of trouble. Are you sure you want me around?'

'Of course I want you around! In fact, I'm honored to be in your company. You're a better terrorist than I ever was. We never landed a whale like Greylander, but I was a member of the team that kidnapped and killed Axel DeGroot.'.

'The name doesn't ring a bell. Who was DeGroot?'

'He owned a diamond mine in the Congo and his workers were slaves. They were beaten with bull whips and never got paid for their labor. Most of them died on the job. It was a mode of operation that was popular with the mine owners so we decided to put a scare in them. DeGroot was the most flagrant and vicious of the lot so we made an example of him.

'We took him from a house in Antwerp in the middle of the night and killed him right away. At 4 a.m., when the city was asleep, we dumped him in the gutter in front of the Cartier jewelry store. It was cheap symbolism, but it sent a message.

'We got away with that action, but after we killed DeGroot the war was on. The big money boys wanted our collective ass and sent the cops and the para-militaries after us.' He shrugged, 'As you know we didn't have popular support and we lost. '

'When I first came to work at Van der Saar I knew you were hurting, but I thought it was because your wife had run away and left you with the kid.'

'Maybe that was part of it, but I'd been living off my own adrenaline for years, and when I got out of prison and back to civilian life I crashed. It was worse than kicking heroin. When you turned up at the shop, I started using your body to get away from my demons, but it backfired, the sex was too intense. You and I were involved in a process that seemed to be changing the chemicals in my brain, and I was too fragile to let that happen. I couldn't trust you, or confide in you, so you had to go.'

'You spoiled me for other men. I was always looking for that thing I had with you, but it never happened.'

'I'm sorry, Martel. If it's any consolation I felt that way too.' He took my hand: 'Let's do the next thirty years together,' he said.

'OK,' I said,' just as long as we die at the end.'

Hendrik and I have been together for some months. I adore him; he is like a brilliantly polished mirror in which I sometimes see my reflection. I think he feels the same about me. I have put Preston away in the back of my brain. I don't feel guilt, but sometimes I feel fear. Fear that a Greylander assassin may come at any time, and I remember the old Italian adage that revenge is a dish best served cold. Of course, the Greylanders are Wasps; maybe they are unfamiliar with the concept, and I should stop inspecting dark corners and checking for a bomb under the car.

We live together in a magnificent house on the imposing Herengracht canal. The house has been in Hendrik's family for over two hundred years. The interior walls are painted a pale and indeterminate shade between gray and white and are hung with fine looking pictures which may, or may not, be real. The furniture is arranged in small groups and is of modernist Dutch design. It makes a nice effect in such an old and stately house.

Hendrik and I do not share the same bed as neither of us craves that particular intimacy on a full time basis. I have taken over a suite on the third floor. It's next to Venessa's old room, which has never been cleared out and is still completely furnished in a bright and youthful style. Venessa moved out two years ago to an apartment in the De Pijp. To tell the truth, I find it difficult to live in such splendor and sometimes think I'd like to move to the De Pijp myself.

These old houses need special care, and a professional team comes in to wax and polish and clean. They arrive in a black van that has lettering on the doors that is painted in golden scrolls. Like the Van der Saars, the cleaners are practicing an inherited trade. I make myself scarce when the crew comes round. I wouldn't want to get in their way because they work with a relentless vigor and furious speed that is probably rooted in past centuries when they were likely to get a flogging if they didn't finish the job on time.

Here in Amsterdam on this historic canal we live in a false bubble of culture and harmony where even the grubby hands of the tourists cannot reach us. From my third floor window I watch the world fall apart and try not to weep when I learn of new wars, new famines, and new plagues. Even the honey bees are dying out.

Thankfully, I am far away from the disputes in my home country which has become a failed state led by an insane woman. This misbegotten trollop has become the president of the USA and she wraps herself in the American flag while she prays nightly to an Evangelical Christian god and asks that he guide her in matters of state. America was on the downswing when I left, but now it is the laughingstock of the entire world.

When I first came to live in Amsterdam, I busied myself trying to track down the author of the Greylander Rembrandt. The picture had been handed over to Madame Pookie, but Van der Saar Fine Arts was still in possession of multiple photographic reproductions, so I was able to spend several days at the shop viewing the prints and writing extensive notes. I took a highly detailed copy of the painting and my notes, and went off to the Rijksmuseum to sift through the huge trove of pictures from the Dutch Golden Age in hopes of finding a stylistic clue. All I got for my efforts were sore feet and a headache from looking at pictures that were categorized as 'Circle of Rembrandt', 'Workshop of Rembrandt', and of course, that old standby, 'School of Rembrandt'. I'm surprised they didn't have a "Faker of Rembrandt" classification.

After failing to find any clues at the Rijksmuseum, I scouted The Hague and the provincial museums. When that didn't pan out I went down to Flanders. I had no luck in Antwerp or Bruges, so I went on to Ghent. I checked into an Ibis hotel across the street from the cathedral and called

Hendrik. I told him my search was turning out to be one big bust and that I would be home on Monday. He commiserated with me and said he'd join me in Ghent for the weekend and we could go back to Amsterdam together. When I told him I was staying at the Ibis he chuckled. Hendrik found my penny-pinching highly amusing, particularly since he knew I had just received a bequest of two hundred thousand American from Terry Volkov's estate. In his mind, I should be staying at five star hotels and throwing money around like it was paper. Well, I didn't come from that sort of place, and living on the margins was a difficult habit to break.

We terminated the call and I went downstairs to the café for coffee. I walked inside and was startled to see a vastly enlarged black and white photographic portrait of the jazz legend Chet Baker. Chet, a notorious junkie, had been a real beauty in his heyday, but this photograph had been taken at a later date and he was looking slightly damaged, but not yet totally destroyed. It was an odd choice of decor for a chain hotel, but perhaps it wasn't that weird. Chet had given one of his greatest concerts in Ghent. Maybe he'd even stayed at the Ibis.

After I finally tore my eyes away from the compelling Mr. Baker, I settled at a table and ordered an espresso. The thimbleful of coffee came with two chocolate covered cookies and a tiny glass of Advocaat liqueur. It was a sumptuous mini-feast, and I took my time savoring the delightful mélange.

When I got up to leave I noticed a man seated at a table directly below Chet's photo. He was an innocuous American business type who reminded me of one of the robotic clones on the Greylander corporate jet. His bland, open face was in sharp contrast to Chet's pithy image, and I reflected how odd it was that two such disparate types were manufactured in the same country.

The Greylander clone nodded and smiled as I walked by. I returned his nod but didn't bother to smile. As I hurried out of the café a paranoid thought flashed thought through my mind: Maybe this was the assassin I'd been expecting.

By the time Hendrik arrived, around midnight, I had dismissed my ridiculous fears; after all, this was an inexpensive business hotel and the man was most likely a traveling salesmen from New Jersey trying to peddle a new gadget to the low-tech Belgians. Just to be on the safe side, I asked Hendrik if he'd seen any Americans lurking in the hallway. He said 'no,' but wanted to know why I was concerned. I told him some guy from New Jersey had been bugging me down in the lobby and I was worried he might have my room number.

'Don't lie to me, Martel,' Hendrik scolded. 'If you're in trouble you better let me know.' He sounded like he was talking to his daughter.

'There's no trouble, darling, I'm just being paranoid. I saw a man who looked like he might be one of Greylander's people in the café.'

'That's interesting,' he said. 'Would you be more comfortable if we went back to Amsterdam right now?'

'Of course not, I had an attack of nerves, that's all. The guy was an American and he looked like a robotic clone. It doesn't necessarily mean he's a Greylander, there are a lot of people who look like that where I come from.'

'So I've noticed,' he said drily. He was carrying an overnight bag and a large basket. He handed me the basket and said: 'I thought I'd probably arrive too late for dinner so I brought food and some white wine.'

We had a meal of seafood salad, green beans with walnuts, and French bread, all washed down with a fresh, bright, Austrian white. It was simple but delicious fare, and we ate with gusto. When we crawled into the bed we were replete, but not too replete to make love.

In the morning Hendrik and I went down to the café and stood in the entrance for a moment looking carefully around the room, but there were no robotic clones in sight. Before we sat down he went over to the photo of Chet Baker and eye-balled it. Like most Amsterdam natives he had complex feelings about the trumpeter. They all seem to carry a load of guilt where Chet is concerned. It's not every day that a fabled and adored musician takes a mysterious fall out of a hotel window across the street from Central Station.

Hendrik stopped communing with Chet and sat down beside me. He sipped his espresso and toyed with the chocolate cookie. Finally, he asked: 'Are you really going to give up on the attribution?'

'Yes, I don't have the strength to go on. It's like digging for information in a black hole.'

'Willem and I are starting to believe it's something Rembrandt did while he was drunk. He probably painted it at night, and when he saw it in the morning he threw it in the rubbish.'

'You're a bullshitter,' I said, finishing off my espresso. 'Come on, Hendrik, let's get out of here. We can go to the flea market and walk around and see if I've got a tail.'

'I'm not convinced that the Greylanders are after you, but there's no harm in being careful.'

We left the café and crossed the street to the square where the market was being held. The market was touted as a symbol of ancient Ghent and was said to have been in continuous operation since the sixteenth century. As we circled the picturesque, cobbled square and paused to look at displays of goods it soon became obvious that no one was following.

'There's no need to worry, Martel. It must have been a false alarm.'

'I believe you're right, darling. Let's enjoy the market.'

Hendrik went directly to a junk stall that had huge stacks of old prints and began rummaging through the piles looking for hidden treasure. I left him there in blissful pursuit of the unknown and went next door to a clothing stall. As I examined the clothes on the racks I found the dresses to be surprisingly sophisticated. They were the work of a young designer who had not yet made a name for herself in the Antwerp fashion world. I took a liking to a simple shift of heavy Thai silk. The body of the dress was a vibrant turquoise color and it was trimmed with bands of magenta silk at the hem and sleeves. I purchased the dress for one hundred and fifty Euros and thought I'd made a bargain because it would have cost three times as much in a boutique. The stall keeper wrapped it up in pink tissue paper and put it in a handsome red shopping bag, and I carried it proudly away. I found Hendrik where I'd left him, still going through prints and getting dirty in the process. He had a black spot on his shirt and his hands were filthy.

'Did you find anything?' I asked.

'Not yet,' he said, barely looking at me.

He was so involved in his task I decided this was not the time to show him my dress and went out to explore the market. Some Moroccan guys were selling figs out of a truck and they offered me a sample. The fig that was given to me was the largest, most voluptuous I'd ever seen. It was so succulent it actually oozed juice into my hand. I took a bite out of it. The texture was fleshy and thick. The taste a mixture of honey and spice. It was so rich and juicy that I, like countless others, couldn't help but relate it to the female sexual organ. The fig eating experience was more than vaguely sensual and the Moroccan guys were having a friendly laugh watching me enjoy it. I ordered up a large bag of figs and went on my way, thinking I'd come back later with Hendrik and buy a kilo or two to take back to Amsterdam.

Further down the square I noticed a crowd gathered in front of a stall where three young boys were setting up to play music. The kids were about thirteen years old and their bones had not developed as yet. They were skinny and birdlike and had prominent noses that looked like beaks. All three played guitars, and when they let go with a spirited version of a Gypsy Kings tune, I knew for sure they were Roma. The music excited me, and I ran over to the junk stall where Hendrik was still going through stacks of paper.

'Come on, there's some Roma kids playing across the way and they sound pretty good. Let's go listen. I grabbed his arm and tried to pull him away from his papers, but Hendrik's body stood firm, he was not going to let me drag him away.

'They're probably from the Revata sub-group.' he said. They settled in Flanders hundreds of years ago.' He went back to his work: 'You go ahead. I'm going to finish up here.'

I noticed that his face had grown pale and I thought that he looked sad and fatigued: 'You ought to get out of this musty dump and get some fresh air.'

'I'm fine, Martel. I'll join you in a few minutes, now run along.' He dismissed me like he was swatting away a bothersome fly, and I wondered what was up with him. Surely, if he'd made a spectacular find he'd have shared it with me. Maybe I was imagining things, but Hendrik seemed to be showing signs of stress that had not been there earlier in the morning.

When I got back on the street, the Roma kids were playing their little hearts out and the crowd around them had gotten much larger. It was an enthusiastic audience and they applauded and shouted and threw Euros in the tin. The kids made such brilliant music that even some of the stall holders stopped their activities to listen. Just as they were finishing their set, Hendrik came up beside me and we listened to a wild finale that sounded like *Bamboleo*. I got in line to put some money in the tin. It was full of cash and I threw my five Euros on the top. Hendrik was next to me and I was surprised to see him put twenty Euros down. What the fuck, he hadn't even heard the music, why was he giving so much? I thought it wise not to question him about his generosity because he still looked distressed. He hadn't found anything worthwhile in the junk shop and maybe that was troubling him, but I doubted it. I knew he didn't really expect to discover a Rembrandt etching, or a Rubens drawing – he just enjoyed the process of sorting through the piles.

We stopped for a beer on our way back to the hotel. I fed him figs and showed him my new dress and gradually his pallor vanished and his good spirits returned. When we finished our beer we went back to the flea market to buy more figs. Sadly, the truck had already left for the day, and we were unable to purchase any more of the voluptuous fruits.

Two weeks later, while Hendrik was in London, Willem asked me to a concert. He said he had an extra ticket because his girlfriend was unable to attend due to a kidney infection. When he told me that the performer was Bobby Janacek, the virtuoso guitarist whose music had made such an impression on me at the Brown Café, I eagerly accepted his invitation. Willem explained that Bobby was a Roma who had been brought up in a Revata camp just outside Amsterdam and that he had been playing guitar professionally since he was nine years old. Now he had reached the age of twenty and was regarded as a contemporary master.

When we got to the concert hall I was in for a shock. I'd never seen a picture of Bobby Janacek, and when he took the stage he turned out to be a dead ringer for Hendrik Van der Saar in his younger days. I could feel Willem eyes on me searching for a reaction, but I wouldn't give him the satisfaction. Thank god Bobby hadn't started to play because I stood up and walked out. Willem was hot on my heels and when we got in the lobby I put my fist in his face.'Motherfucker,' I said. 'Do you want to explain this to me or do I have to hit you again?'

Willem winced and held his hand to his jaw: 'I didn't know you were a violent person,' he said ruefully.

'I *am* a violent person, and you deserve it.'

'I guess I was being uncool. Sorry, Martel. I had to take matters into my own hands because it seems Hendrik can't tell you about his son.'

'He told me about his life as a member of a terrorist gang and his time in prison, so why can't he tell me about Bobby Janacek? From the look of the kid, it's hardly a recent indiscretion. What's the big fucking deal?'

'Let's go around the corner and get a beer and I'll lay it all out for you. It's a complicated scenario.'

'Complicated, complicated,' I ranted, 'ever since men first started sticking their dicks into women it's been complicated!'

I don't think I've ever been so angry, my love and trust had just been shattered, and I felt like kicking the shit out of Willem. Fortunately, the café actually was around the corner because I had a real need for liquid sustenance. We ordered beers and shots of jenever while Willem squirmed in his chair looking guilty and scared. Guilty about taking me to see Bobby Janacek in concert, scared that I might hit him again.

'Alright, dude, spit it out.' I ordered.

'Hendrik didn't even know of Bobby's existence until the kid was fourteen years old. Bobby's mother used to be a whore and she came by Hendrik's every couple of weeks. One day she broke an appointment and he never saw her again.'

'I didn't think Roma were whores.'

'She's a Revata. Here in the Netherlands they've assimilated and given up a lot of the old ways.'

Willem smiled when he said the word assimilated, and I wondered if he was trying to be ironic.

'Hendrik never saw Anoushka again until years later, when she came to the house on the Herengracht and presented a photo of Bobby. He had to admit there was a likeness, but he wasn't taking any chances and demanded a DNA test.

'Anoushka's husband, a guy named Zonzo Janacek, was the only person who could keep Bobby in line, and he was doing a long jail term for people smuggling. In Zonzo's absence the kid was running wild and shooting heroin. The boy was a valuable commodity, and neither his mother nor any of the Revata crowd could handle him, and that was why she turned to Hendrik.

'At this point my brother had never heard of Bobby Janacek, although the boy was already famous in certain circles. Even at that early date the jazzers were saying the kid was the greatest player since Django Reinhardt. Others went so far as to say he was the actual reincarnation of Django.'

Willem paused and sipped his beer.

'Go on,' I said, 'this is getting good.' My anger was starting to cool and I was becoming engrossed in the story.

'When the tests came back, they proved that Hendrik was Bobby's father, and to this day he doesn't know how Anoushka got pregnant.'

'I bet I know,' I said sarcastically.

'It was so long ago he doesn't remember what they did. I hate to tell you, Martel, but Hendrik wasn't buying whores for regular intercourse.'

'He told me he didn't go in for butt fucking,' I said.

'I think it was more like bondage.' Willem looked uncomfortable; he was really spilling his brother's secrets tonight. He drank the rest of his beer off in one gulp and went on with the story.

'After paternity was established, Hendrik began investigating Bobby and his environment. He learned that Zonzo, a good, but limited, guitarist, had been in charge of the child's musical education. By the time Bobby was nine years old he had surpassed his putative father in musicality and improvisational skills. The gossips claim that the old man was jealous of the kid and began beating him on a daily basis. They claimed he was practicing psychological torture by taking Bobby's fingers and pretending to break them. There was a sensational story going around that Zonzo burnt Bobby's fingers when he didn't play fast enough. His mother stepped in before the boy's hands were broken and burned for real. She didn't want the child damaged, she wanted him to work. A manager was found and Bobby went on the road and became famous in the countries that care about jazz. By the time Hendrik got involved the damage had been done and it was already too late.'

Willem was starting to tear up and I waved for the waiter to bring us more drinks. Although I was intrigued by his story, it sounded overly dramatic, and I doubted the stepfather was as vindictive and evil as Willem was portraying him.

'Besides being a musical genius, Bobby's been a hard core, no hope, junkie since he was fifteen.' Willem was crying now: 'He's such a great artist and he is so fucked up.'

'So much for the redeeming qualities of art and the power of creativity,' I said scornfully. I had to act like a snotty bitch, otherwise I'd break down in tears myself.

'Bobby's been in rehab three times and he even went to jail for a couple of weeks for getting in a bar fight.'

'He sounds just like Hendrik. It must be in the genes.'

'I don't know why you have to be so hard, Martel. Have a little compassion for the kid, he's a lost soul.'

'I'm not mad at Bobby, he's a helpless victim. You're the one that's pissing me off.'

'I had no idea you'd get so upset. I thought seeing him perform on stage would be a good introduction to the problem.'

'You better go back to school and take a course on human behavior. Trust me, it was the worst thing you could do. Was bringing me to the concert something you and Hendrik cooked up?

'Oh, no, he wouldn't approve. He wants to tell you on his own.'

'Isn't it about time? I've been living with him for three months.'

'You have to understand that this boy is the biggest scar on Hendrik's heart. It's such an emotional subject he can barely speak of it. He loves the kid to distraction and is hated in return. Bobby is killing my brother and I can't take it,' Willem was crying again. 'He looks just like Hendrik did when we were young,' he sobbed.

'I noticed that,' I said. 'Why don't you drink that jenever? It might help.'

'Bobby wants to meet you, Martel. Hendrik saw him recently and told him about you. I think he's curious to see his father's choice in women.'

'Oh god, what next,' I groaned. I supposed it would have to happen, but I was going to cut Hendrik a new asshole before it did.

Willem and I got drunk together and he talked about Bobby and Hendrik all night long. By the time we left I was crying too.

Hendrik got home two days later, so I had plenty of time to think about the relationship between father and son. I empathized with Bobby, in fact felt great compassion for him, but I loved his father with every cell in my body and I could not bear to watch him being dragged down into hell because of an unthinking moment in his past.

I knew that blood disputes often result in tragedy, or at least in death, and I was totally backed up in my opinion by a whole library of Greek classics. Bobby could go through detox a hundred times, but there was nothing that could make his head come out clean. It was the bleakest, saddest, situation I'd ever encountered, and it was made even sadder because Bobby had given up so much of himself to bring joy and transcendence to those who bothered to listen to him play.

There was something else happening to Hendrik. It was my belief that he was burning up past karmas at a rapid pace and the doppelganger effect was evidence of his struggle. His son was an exact physical replica who seemed to have been brought on the scene to make him suffer and grieve.

The nineteenth century literary masters, many of whom were fascinated by duplicates, would have been intrigued by the situation.

Hendrik walked in carrying a briefcase and a garment bag. I took the garment bag and hung it in the hall closet. He put the briefcase on the bottom step of the stairs. The weather was getting on towards winter, and when we embraced I could feel the cold on him; it was seeping out of his skin.

I followed him down the hall and into the kitchen. He went to a cupboard, pulled out a bottle of cognac and poured two stiff drinks. We sat down together at the kitchen table and we each knocked back a slug.

'I've got a question,' I said.

'What's that, *schatje?*'

'Who's the evil twin, you or Bobby?'

He started to laugh, real laughter, you could even see it in his eyes: 'Me, I guess.'

'I can believe that,' I said. 'So why didn't you tell me?'

He was suddenly grave: 'Martel, you bring me the first happiness I've had in years. I must seem like a coward, but I had no idea how you'd react when I told you about my son. I only wanted to have a few months of peace and tranquility with you before bringing him into the equation.'

'I know you're not a coward, but sometimes you're kind of dumb. Did you think I'd be upset because you have a brilliant little bastard running around?'

'Not really, but the kid is a major problem and our relationship isn't the best. I've failed with him, Martel, and maybe I didn't want you to see me as being so weak and ineffectual. Can you forgive me for being such a selfish jerk?'

'Yes, of course I forgive you. Why don't you cut yourself some slack? From what Willem tells me, you came in late and didn't have much chance of influencing his life.' I put my glass to my lips and ran the brandy over my tongue: 'You really love him, don't you?'

'More than my life, I would give up my life to make him whole.'

'Darling, you're going to have to face up to the fact that Bobby is never going to be a whole person. If he makes it to forty, he'll be lucky.'

'How do you know? You've never met him. Willem said you didn't even stick around to listen to him play.' Hendrik sounded aggrieved.

'How could I listen? I was shocked and upset.

I'm sorry it had to be like that. I wish you could have stayed: There's something remarkable about him when he performs before an audience,' he paused and added wistfully, 'He plays with such dignity.'

'I noticed that, I've watched a lot of YouTube since I found out he's your son.'

'He's really great, isn't he?'

'I'm no authority,' I said, 'but he's surely the greatest since Django. And, aside from his playing, he's got a style about him that's almost unique. He makes an extraordinary presentation and his clothes are perfection. Did you teach him how to dress?'

'I'm afraid so. He came to live with Venessa and me when he was fifteen. He only lasted a month because he couldn't adjust to our lifestyle. The rotten brat stole my red paisley scarf and some of my sweaters. I don't think he'd ever felt cashmere before.

'One day I caught him parading around the house in an unlikely getup of my beige sweater, black jeans, and his very own red jacket trimmed with gold spangles. After that, I took him out and bought him clothes and taught him how to wear them. For once he actually paid attention to what I said.'

'His fans say he's a god on earth.'

'Yes, they do,' Hendrik sighed.

I could see he didn't like hearing about that aspect of Bobby's legend.

'You helped him look like a godlet,' I scolded. 'You made him into a mini-me, and he copied you by acting princely and aloof. If he were just a superb jazz player in a red jacket with gold spangles, he wouldn't get half the adulation.'

'How do you know that, Martel?' Hendrik bristled, 'Don't blame me for the stupidity of his fans: They were calling him the reincarnation of Django Reinhardt before I even knew he existed.'

'Yes, and speaking of existence, just how did he come into being?'

'Fuck if I know. He could be the Immaculate Conception as far as I'm concerned. Maybe Anoushka used some of her old time gypsy magic to conjure him up.'

'Maybe she got hold of some of your sperm and put it in a turkey baster.'

'Anything's possible,' he shrugged, and drank more of his cognac. "Do you want to hear the rest?'

'Of course, darling, I'll try not to be too rough on you. I know none of this is really your fault. It seems to me you've reached a place where your karma and the randomness of the universe collide.'

Hendrik gave me a startled look, like he'd never considered such a thing. I could see the thought taking root in his mind. Then I saw him bury it.

'One morning when Bobby was staying with us I walked down the hall on my way to work, and what I did see but my son and his little tan ass high stepping it out of my daughter's room. He stood there naked in front of me, a shit eating grin plastered on his mouth and his dick hanging down in full view. He looked so pleased with himself I wanted to smack him, but instead I said: 'Don't do that again, she's your sister.' He gave me a big smile and said, 'She's only half, so it doesn't count.' 'I told him to go to his room. Then I fled the house and stood on the banks of the canal and vomited into the water. Later that day I pissed blood.'

'Poor, baby, that little shit was really putting the hex on you. How did Venessa take it?'

'She took it just fine. When I confronted her she told me that Bobby was still a child and that he was sleeping with her because he was afraid of the dark. The reason he was naked was because he had no pajamas. She actually had the nerve to tell me I ought to buy him some pajamas, so he wouldn't have to walk around nude. The incestuous little wench insinuated I was a negligent father.'

I giggled, I couldn't help it, I could just picture Venessa lecturing Hendrik on his parental responsibilities: 'She may have been telling the truth,' I said.

'Yes, yes, I know,' Hendrik said impatiently, 'but true or not, Bobby couldn't stay with us anymore. Anoushka's old man was still inside and couldn't harm him, so I sent him back to the Revata. He wasn't at home for long. The next thing I knew Bobby was in Tokyo with a new manager. That was when he signed the million dollar contract. The audience was clamoring for him over there and they were willing to pay top dollar to catch his act. The Japanese were as enchanted by his music as the Europeans, but they didn't call him a god, they called him a Bodhisattva.'

'A million bucks was huge money back then,' I commented.

'The money didn't last long, because Bobby supports the whole clan. After he bought a Lamborghini, his mother took her cut and doled out the rest to the relatives.'

'Those Italian beasts are hard to handle. Could he drive it?'

'No, he didn't even have a license. The car was totaled out within two weeks, and after that he went back on tour, this time to Scandinavia. While Bobby was in Iceland, Zonzo got out of prison and threatened to kill me. Anoushka had waited till he got out of jail to tell him I was Bobby's real father. You can't blame the guy for going berserk when he found out she'd been selling her ass to a rich *gadjo*, but I really took offense when he planted a bomb under the SUV and left messages on my phone saying he was going to torture and kill my family in front of my eyes.'

'Did the bomb go off?'

'Yes, but it didn't do much damage, all it did was blow the exhaust pipe into the street.'

'It sounds like Zonzo was really going for the drama,' I said.

'You could say that,' Hendrik said. 'I wanted to strangle the miserable fuck with my bare hands, but my old pal Nikki Gripsa advised against it. Nikki's a police detective and he knew Zonzo from being on the cops. He arranged a meeting between us. I can't say we became friends, but we didn't kill each other. Zonzo and the rest of the Revata found it extremely difficult to accept me as Bobby's father. In fact, they never did.'

'I feel bad for the Revata,' I said.

'Yes, yes,' Hendrik sighed and put his hand to his face.

'My mother was a connoisseur of music and she told me to always respect the Gitanes. She said they'd given the world some fantastically influential music, and all they got in return was constant harassment and a one-way trip to the gas chambers.'

'Your mother was right,' Hendrik still had his face in his hand. 'Please stop this line of conversation, Martel. I already know I'm a scum bag exploiter of a persecuted minority. Don't make me feel worse than I already do.'

'Sorry, darling, I don't believe for one minute you're a scum bag exploiter. So how are things with you and Bobby these days?'

'Our relations are tepid, at best. I'm the one who puts him in rehab and sees that his teeth get fixed. He has a problem with his teeth. They keep getting knocked out in fights.'

'Yes, Willem told me he's not one to back down on a challenge.'

'He's usually harassed by drunken *gadjo's* who think they can play guitar. Bobby has to use a knife when he fights because he can't take the risk of hurting his hands. I'm trying to convince him to let his bodyguards take care of the assholes.'

'So, what's he doing for sex? With his appeal it sounds like he might be pansexual. You know, open to all.'

'As far as I know he just likes girls. He was married at sixteen. The whole charade was merely a sop to Revata custom. Bobby says it was a matter of form.'

'The way you talk he sounds like he's pretty sophisticated.'

'Why shouldn't he be?' Hendrik looked puzzled: 'He's been hanging with musicians and traveling all over the world since he was nine years old. He has lots of women, but his harem isn't enough for him; he still sees Venessa and only god knows what those two get up to when they're together.'

Poor Hendrik, I really felt for him, and only hoped that Bobby and Venessa were playing chess together or indulging in some equally innocuous, but mentally stimulating, activity.

'Venessa and Bobby are horrible little shits,' Hendrik grimaced and poured another shot. 'Those two idiots were fucking without protection and Venessa managed to get herself knocked up. As she explained to me later, she knew it was genetically bad to have Bobby's child, but she couldn't bring herself to abort because the baby might be a genius like his father. She didn't know what to do, so, using adolescent logic, she took an overdose of pills.

'She was supposed to go to work with me in the morning, and when she didn't come down for breakfast I went up and knocked on her door. There was no answer, so I went in and found her lying on the floor next to the bed. Fortunately, I got her to the hospital on time. She survived, but the fetus didn't.

'Bobby didn't know about the pregnancy, and when he learned, Venessa was in the hospital recovering from a miscarriage; he went on a binge and ended up in jail.'

A few tears slid down Hendrik's face: 'When Venessa was fully recovered, I told her there were doubts about her parentage, and that it was possible that she and Bobby were not related by blood.' He shrugged: 'That's it, Martel, now you know everything. There's nothing left in the closet.'

'Let's go upstairs,' I said.

We went to Hendrik's room and laid down on the bed with our clothes on and I held him in my arms and his body shuddered and he started to sob and I could feel his tears wet on the side of my face and it was like he was expelling a huge cancerous mass that had been eating his body and I held on tight until he was through.

In the morning Hendrik was pale and subdued. Dredging up memories of his children and their problems had taken its toll: 'I feel like I'm all emptied out,' he said.

'You are, darling. You're empty because you purged yourself of deep pain and emotional blockage.' I smiled: 'You'll feel better after you drink some coffee.'

'I hope so,' he managed to give me a wan smile. 'Bobby wants to meet you,' he said.

'Yes, Willem told me.'

'Will you see him?'

'That's up to you.'

'You might as well. The kids a real experience. He'll charm the shit out of you.'

'I'll meet him,' I said, wanting to please Hendrik and secretly excited at the prospect of an encounter with the wonder child. 'You set it up. Make it some public place where I can exit gracefully if things start to go bad.'

'I'll talk to him tonight,' he paused, 'Now that you know all my dark secrets, why not be my wife?'

'You mean legally?'

'Yes, I mean legally. Do you have any objections?'

'I think that's way too complicated. Venessa would get pissed because she'd think I was after her share of the loot. Why don't we have a private ceremony, just you and me, we can write up some documents and sign them in blood. After that we can throw a big party to announce the event.'

'Are you serious? A blood ceremony sounds like a Faustian pact. What do I have to give you?'

'Nothing but your body and soul.'

'You've already got that.'

'Yes, but signing in blood will make it official.'

'And what do I get from you?'

'My heart, liver, and lungs.'

'I can get organ meat at the butcher's.' He laughed. 'Why don't you give me your pussy?'

'We don't have to wait for the ceremony. We can do that right now.'

I met Bobby at The Bald Hyena, an old style coffee shop in the De Pijp. It was only a block from Venessa's apartment, and it seemed pretty obvious that he'd spent the night with her. He was comfortably ensconced in an armchair, nursing a beer and smoking a fat joint. Two tough-looking Revata dudes sat at the table with him and when they saw me approach they scattered.

The first thing I noticed about Bobby was his golden glow. He had some kind of a radiant thing going on with his skin. It may have been the light coming in from the window behind his back and making an optical illusion, but he looked like he was surrounded by tiny, shimmering vibrations. You could say that the light around him looked like a halo. The fucking kid looked like a Bodhisattva and for a moment I wanted to offer him some fruit, or sink to my knees and touch my forehead to his feet. Instead, I ordered a beer.

Bobby offered me the joint and I took a hit. At that moment, I almost lost the thread that attached me to reality. My eyes focused in on his hands. They looked so strong, it was as if they could break your neck and wring your heart at one go. Aside from great strength his hands radiated the golden glow, and his tensile fingers seemed to stretch into infinity.

'I never knew Hendrik to have a steady woman before.' His voice was oddly pitched and had a vaguely hypnotic effect.

'We knew each other a long time ago. It's a recycled affair.'

Bobby smiled. His teeth were white, but not dazzling. They were fairly even, but not oppressively so. Hendrik had found him a good dentist.

'Recycled, I like that,' he said. 'When you think about it everything's recycled, isn't it?'

'Yes, it seems that it all just keeps going round and round.'

He passed me the joint again: 'Smoke some more weed, Martel.' The words came out sounding like a command and I obeyed.

After I took a couple of big tokes I said: "So, what's it like to have everybody kissing your ass and telling you how supernatural you are?'

'It's not easy,' he sighed, covering his face with one hand in a gesture that was eerily similar to the one Hendrik used when the world was getting him down.

'Why don't you forget all this Michael Jackson shit and give your father a chance?'

'I'd like to, but in case you haven't noticed the man's a fucking *gadjo* and I'm Revata to the core. His blood is like poison in my veins and sometimes I'd like to kill him. The father-son relationship is a huge conflict. I love him and I hate him and I look just like him.'

'Darling, you've got to give it a try.' I sounded like a school mistress, but I didn't care. 'If it's any comfort he looks a lot older than you.'

'He's a decrepit old bastard but he's still got enough stuff to rein in a woman like you.'

'Don't talk about me like I'm a horse! He didn't rein me in. I'm with him of my own free will.'

'Do you find him lovable?'

'Intensely so.'

'Yes, Hendrik inspires intense feelings. I often feel intense hatred for him.'

'You're a real bullshitter, Bobby.' I gave him a snarky smile.

He snarked me right back: 'If you and Hendrik get on so well together, how come you're not married?'

'We're thinking about it. Not a legal ceremony, but a personal one. Then we'll have a big party afterwards and celebrate.'

'I don't believe it!' Bobby laughed like I had just given him hilarious news: 'Hendrik, the dashing scion of the Van der Saar dynasty is giving himself up to a woman in a Commitment Ceremony. That is so tacky and middle class. I really thought better of the both of you.'

'Who said anything about a Commitment Ceremony? We're just signing a contract and having a party. What do you know about Commitment Ceremonies anyway? You sound like you're the one who's been hanging with the middle class.'

'I know about them because some rich asshole paid me a hundred thousand euros to play at his dismally pretentious mock wedding.'

'Well, I can assure you our party will be neither dismal nor pretentious, and we won't even expect you to play.'

'Who says I'm coming to your party?'

'Venessa will be there,' I said, giving him the sly eye.

'How do you know about me and Venessa?'

'It doesn't take a detective to figure that one out. In case you haven't noticed, The Bald Hyena is only one block from her flat.'

'You talk like you don't object.' Bobby seemed surprised that I was cool with the relationship.

'I'm neutral on it, but Hendrik isn't. The thought of you and Venessa fucking drives him insane. Is that why you do it?'

'We don't have sex that much anymore. It was a thing we did when we were kids. She was so soft and pretty I wanted to be in bed with her all the time. Now I'm not so obsessed.'

'But you do knock off a piece once in a while for old time's sake, don't you?

'I guess we do it to keep Hendrik in line. We both know he hates us being together.'

'I think your relationship with Venessa is indicative of deep psychological issues. You two belong in a Freudian case book. You're living examples of his most bizarre theories.' I paused to drain off my beer: 'You are coming to the party, right?'

'I wouldn't miss it for the world.'

I stood up and prepared for my exit, but before I left I told him he had to tone down his halo when he came to the party.

Hendrik and I had our ceremony. I thought it was a powerful one, but he seemed to think it was a bit of charming idiocy. We dressed in our favorite clothes. Hendrik wore a black cashmere sweater and his favorite Japanese jeans. I wore the turquoise silk with the magenta trim that I'd bought at the flea market in Ghent.

We needed background music for the event and I was damned if I was going to play anything by Bobby. I didn't want that little shit horning in on our intimate ritual. We settled for Dinu Lipatti's sublime interpretations of Chopin. Maybe Dinu wasn't such a great choice – he died tragically young, and people venerated his memory like he was a great saint or Bodhisattva. It was surely a tribute to his genius that eighty years after his death he still had a fan base worldwide, and an American rock group had even written a song about him. Dinu's legend was immense, and it was much like Bobby's. Fuck, Dinu was Romanian, and that meant his genes were suspect. He'd sure as hell looked like a gypsy with his slick black hair, big nose, and liquid eyes.

As Dinu exuded purity on the piano I cut into Hendrik with a bone-handled knife he'd sharpened especially for the occasion. I went first and cut him between the thumb and forefinger as agreed. Talk about intense, when the blade sliced into his flesh I felt like my brain was going to pop. I withdrew the knife and was astonished to see black blood flowing rapidly out of the wound.

'I didn't know I had black blood. The last time I looked it was red,' he said.

'It probably has something to do with your diet,' I said, mentally dismissing the thought that Hendrik might be a demon or a creature from outer space. 'You better hurry up and do me before you bleed all over the table.'

When he cut me I didn't even feel it. I just stood there and watched my blood, which was dark red in color, flow into a large goblet and mingle with his. The sight was really quite magnificent.

After we'd bound up our wounds, Hendrik produced an antique pen he'd taken from the studio. He dipped it in the blood and filled it and then handed the pen to me. I signed and then Hendrik followed. The blood soaked into the heavy parchment paper leaving an imprint of darkest red. When Hendrik finished, he kept the pen and surprised me by doing some Arabic calligraphy below our names.

'That sign is exquisite. What does it mean?'

'I think it has something to do with eternity.'

We let the paper dry and then stashed it in the wall safe in Hendrik's bedroom. During the next stage of the ritual we smoked some pot and drank some champagne. When we were stoned enough to enjoy the process, we slowly plucked the petals from two dozen pink roses and scattered them on the bed. When we finished the duvet looked and smelled like the paradise of ten thousand virgins. We jumped on the bed and rolled around on the rose petals. The sensation was that of being enveloped in a big, sweet smelling cunt. At some point we took off our clothes and sealed the deal.

We spent the next day getting ready for the party. The guests were coming at 7pm, so we had plenty of time to put together a five star presentation. In the morning Hendrik placed bottles of vodka and jenever into rubber molds and added stems of lavender and roses. After that he added distilled water to the molds and put them in the freezer. Years ago, I had tried to make one of these gorgeous, decorative blocks, but I'd used a milk carton for the mold and filled it with tap water. The block didn't come out clean because the paper from the carton stuck to the ice. Even more disappointing, the flowers didn't show through because the ice was cloudy. When I told Hendrik about the mishap, he said the secret was in the distilled water.

I'd insisted on serving up a Russian buffet and Hendrik did not oppose me even though he preferred Indonesian. I found a chef who had just arrived from Moscow and claimed to have recipes direct from the kitchen of Vladimir Putin. He and his staff whipped up and laid out a delectable feast of all the classics. While the caterers fussed with the food and stuck bottles of champagne in tubs of ice, Hendrik busied himself making a huge bouquet of red and white striped tulips. It was getting late, the guests would be arriving soon, and I finally dragged him away from his tulips, and we went to our respective rooms to dress in our finery.

I wore a deceptively simple Mariano Fortuny gown made of silver fabric trimmed with gold at the neck and sleeves. The dress had tiny pleats that flowed over the body and down to the floor like waves in a shimmering sea. The day I found the Fortuny at a junk shop in Chicago was an unforgettable memory. It was stuffed in a box of old curtains and I grabbed it, clutched it to my chest, and hurriedly paid the proprietor ten dollars. I ran out of the shop before he discovered he'd just been robbed of an item worth many thousands of dollars. The gown was one of my great prizes, surely the most exquisite garment I'd ever owned. When I put it on and sprayed myself with Guerlain's *Mitsuko*, I felt like a grand enchantress from the days of Art Déco.

I met up with Hendrik in the hall. He looked surprised and delighted when he saw me in the dress. I guess he'd never thought I could look so beautiful. I smiled and put my cheek to his face because I didn't want to smear my red lipstick.

'You overwhelm me, Martel,' he said.

'You don't look so bad yourself,' I said, eyeing him up and down. He was wearing a black suit from some tailor in Naples who'd fashioned it out of wool so fine it looked like a cloud of black ink. The jacket hung open and underneath was a forest green shirt of dull, heavy silk. He hadn't bothered to close the top two buttons on the shirt and that made just the right effect, vaguely titillating, but not overtly sexual. For an added, foppish touch, he'd put a loose bracelet of solid, silver links around one of his wrists. I touched the bracelet and said: 'I'd like to chain you up in this.'

He smiled: 'Perhaps later.'

We stood there in our perfection and then the perfection faded and we went to greet our guests.

The party was a huge success, the decor was beautiful, and the food and drink were of spectacular goodness and quality. Venessa got a little drunk and started playing tinkly background music on the piano. I looked for Hendrik, and he was talking to a good-looking guy that didn't look like he belonged at the party because he was wearing a scruffy brown suit. Aside from Willem, who was attired in his usual faux Viking gear, the stranger was the only bum in the crowd.

I caught Hendrik's eye and he motioned for me to join him. I walked over and he introduced me to his old buddy, Detective Nikki Gripsa of the Amsterdam art squad. I looked Gripsa over carefully – who knew, he might be Venessa's blood father – but all I could see was a lot of muscle under the wrinkled suit and a hard rock of a face with prominent cheekbones. The only thing that softened his features was the longish shock of dirty blonde hair that fell across his forehead and threatened to obscure his left eye.

Although he looked forbidding, Nikki seemed to be friendly enough, and when I questioned him about his job as an art cop he laughed and said that it wasn't as glamorous as people thought. Right now he was on the hunt for a fake Picasso that was being used as payment for a truckload of cocaine. Apparently, various world mafias had got onto the idea of using fake or stolen art to finance their operations. Nikki confided there were rumors that a couple of guys from the New Jersey mafia were lurking around town. Word had it they were trying to recover a stolen Rembrandt.

'Anything we should be worried about?' Hendrik asked.

'I doubt it, but it wouldn't hurt to keep your eyes open. Right now it's all rumors and innuendo,' Nikki said.

I could see that Hendrik wasn't comfortable with the information that Nikki had just given him. I got the feeling he wanted a few words with the cop in private, so I made my goodbyes and went back to my hostessing duties.

I was standing at a window overlooking the canal, drinking champagne and chatting with a woman who was a curator at the Stedelijk museum when Venessa launched into a loud and attention getting version of *Lover Come Back to Me*. People stopped talking and began to listen to what she was playing. Just then I looked out the window and who did I see approaching, but Bobby and two Revata guys. I was glad Bobby had decided to drop by, but when I looked at him there was a problem: he was dressed exactly like Hendrik in a black suit and forest green shirt. I didn't have to look at his wrist to know there was a silver bangle dangling from it. Fuck, things had been going way too well, but now they were heading for disaster what with Venessa acting up and Bobby appearing as the evil twin.

I excused myself and ran out of the salon and down the front hall. In honor of the occasion I was wearing five inch heels and could barely walk, let alone run, but I was so freaked-out I practically flew. When I got outside Bobby was just coming up the stairs and the bodyguards were turning back towards the canal.

'You're looking slick, Martel,' Bobby smiled.

'So are you, darling, but there's one big problem, you're dressed exactly like your father.'

Bobby blanched, and you could see his golden glow fade into the atmosphere. There was no way he could account for this faux pas.

'Just stay right here and take off your jacket and shirt. I'll go get one of Hendrik's sweaters.'

I slipped into the house without being noticed and went directly to Hendrik's room. I opened his top drawer and grabbed a black cashmere. It looked like the one he'd been wearing at our private ceremony.

When I got back outside Bobby was half naked. His bodyguards had returned, and one of them was folding his shirt and the other was holding his jacket. I tossed Bobby the sweater, and he started slipping it on over his head, but not before I got a good look at his chest and arms. There were no needle marks on his arms, but that didn't mean anything – he could have been shooting up in his groin. He was junkie thin, but his body was still attractive because of the radiance of his skin and the length and heft of his bones. He even had Hendrik's trademark strip of dark hair running down his chest and into his trousers.

A jagged bolt of quicksilver flashed through my brain: 'I wonder what it's like to fuck him.'

Bobby had the sweater on and was smoothing it down over his body. He must have read my mind because he said: 'We could give it a go if you want.'

'It was just a random thought. Anyway, I've already experienced it with Hendrik.'

'Yes, but with me you'd get more vigor.'

'Granted, but Hendrik has more skill.'

'I guess we'll never know,' Bobby said, grinning and putting his arm around me in comradely fashion. We laughed, and the Revata guys, sensing everything was OK, drifted back toward the canal.

'They don't need to leave. They can come to the party.'

'It's not their kind of thing, they wouldn't be happy mixing with all the *gadjos*. Besides, they're working. They have to keep an eye on that guy who's lurking down by the canal. Do you know you've got a tail, Martel?'

It was my turn to blanch and lose my composure: 'Is the tail an American who looks like a clone or a robot?'

'That's the one. Benno spotted him the other day outside the coffee shop. The fucker followed you home.'

'Don't tell Hendrik,' I said. Although I'd mentioned the robot to Hendrik when we were in Ghent, I didn't want him to know the Greylander clone was hanging around the Herengracht. If he found out, he'd probably blow the fuckers head off, and we didn't need those kinds of complications.

'Are you in trouble, babe?'

'Bobby, please don't call me babe.'

'Why not, am I being too intimate with you?'

'Stop flirting, you little shit. This is serious business.'

'I can have the boys rough him up if you want.'

'No, he comes from bad people. They'd just send somebody else in his place.'

We were at the top of the steps, and I looked back towards the canal. I could see the bodyguards but there was no sign of the clone. 'He's gone,' I said.

Inside Venessa was still pounding away. Now she was playing *When Your Lover Has Gone*.

'Jesus what a noise,' Bobby said, shaking his head, 'Maybe I should have brought a guitar.'

'She'll stop now that you're here.'

'Venessa's getting to be a problem. I want to end the physical stuff but she's totally hung up on consuming my body.'

'Sweetheart, please try not to think about it, go check in with your father and I'll bring you a drink.'

Hendrik had been talking shop with a group of art dealers, but when he spotted Bobby he cut the conversation short. They walked toward each other and met in the center of the room where they embraced. The music stopped and the chatter died down and all eyes were on father and son. Bobby slumped and rested his head on Hendrik's chest. His body language suggested extreme weariness and complete surrender. Hendrik held him and began to gently stroke his hair. The whole scene was too intimate to continue watching so everyone went back to the buffet. I found Willem down at the end of the table filling up on *pirogi* and *Stroganov*.

'What's going on with Bobby and Hendrik?' he asked. 'It looks like they've finally been reconciled. Is this due to your good influence, Martel?'

'I doubt I have any influence on either of them. Right now I'm going to bring Bobby a drink. After that we have to tempt him with a plate of food. The little fuck doesn't eat.'

'That's because he's a junkie.'

'Tell me something I don't know,' I snapped.

I picked up a small block of ice, there was a sprig of lavender and a bottle of vodka suspended inside it. I tipped the block and poured vodka into a glass. Then I started across the room. Bobby was still clinging to Hendrik, and Hendrik was still stroking his hair. They were so wrapped up in each other they barely noticed my arrival. When they finally broke apart, I noticed they both had red eyes. I handed Bobby the vodka, and he drank it down in one gulp.

The magic of reconciliation seemed to have worn off because Hendrik was staring dubiously at Bobby's torso. 'Are you wearing my sweater?' he asked.

'Yes, and it stinks to high heaven of roses. I didn't know you wore such a girly perfume.'

Hendrik chose to disregard this comment, there was no way he could explain the heavy scent on his sweater. 'Just make sure I get it back.'

'I'll have it dry cleaned and returned to you, although I doubt the cleaners will be able to get rid of the smell.'

'All right you two, cut it out.' I thought the truce might be a fragile one and that the bickering could turn to hostility at any moment.

'We're just playing,' Bobby assured me.

Hendrik nodded at me like he was sharing a secret, and then turned away and guided Bobby over to the buffet table. They left me alone tottering on my high heels. My body had been high on adrenaline and emotion, but when the two men walked away, the tension that had been holding me up slipped away, and I felt weak kneed and ready to fall. Just as I was about to let go, somebody grabbed my elbow: 'You need to sit down, Martel.'

Venessa had come to my rescue and steered me over to a loveseat near the windows. She looked like Ophelia, with tendrils of her long, blonde hair falling around her pale and ethereal face. She was wearing an ice-blue gown, and for a moment I thought she had a shiny dagger in her hand. On closer examination the dagger turned out to be a highly designed vodka glass. She had her eye fixed on the buffet where Hendrik was filling plates for himself and his son.

'Look at those two, they really are disgusting. The next thing Hendrik will do is start hand feeding him.'

'They're not disgusting. They love each other.'

'Yes, but what kind of love? Surely you don't believe it's a normal father-son relationship,'

'Knock it off, Venessa. In this family, you and Bobby are doing the incest.'

'I doubt we're related by blood, everyone knows my mother slept around.'

'In this case blood doesn't matter. It's psychological incest.'

'Spare me your cheap theories, Martel. You have no idea what's going on between Bobby and me.'

'I know he doesn't want to sleep with you anymore, so why don't you show a little class and let him go?'

'He needs me. I help him keep the demons at bay.'

'Yeah, you and the heroin.'

'Maybe he needs us both. You see, Bobby's got a problem with being part *gadjo.* He comes from a persecuted minority of entertainers and outliers, and he was totally invested in that identity. When he found out Hendrik was his father, it plunged him into confusion and despair.'

'I know it was incredibly hard on the poor kid,' I said, 'but you have to admit he was taking heroin before he ever knew that Hendrik was his real father.'

'That's what his mother claims, but Bobby says she's full of shit.'

'Is that true?'

'Yes, she was running a con on Hendrik because she couldn't handle Bobby and wanted him to take over while Zonzo was in prison. Bobby was wild, but he wasn't shooting smack, he was going out with his friends and getting drunk. They smoked weed, and did a little molly. His mom didn't think he was practicing enough, so she went all hysterical and blew everybody's life apart.'

'Oh, fuck!' I said.

'When Bobby found out he was part Van der Saar, he took a look at the family tree and learned the ancestors were Nazis.

He went totally insane and that's when he started doing heroin.' Venessa gave me a hard smile. 'Did you know that during the Hitler war two thousand Revata went to the Kulmhopf Extermination Center? The rest were sent to Auschwitz. When that war was over, there were only thirty six Revata left alive in the world.'

'Oh, god,' I moaned. 'Did Bobby confront Hendrik when he found out?'

'No, he kept it to himself. I was the only one he confided in. Daddy hasn't a clue.'

'Well, I'm not going to tell him,' I said. I felt lower than whale shit. This was supposed to be a happy day, but all I wanted to do was curl up and die.

'Good, Hendrik doesn't need to know. It would probably kill him if he found out Bobby was aware of the Van der Saars' Nazi past. I only told you because you were acting like a condescending bitch with all that incest crap and I wanted you to know what the score really was.'

'I'm sorry, Venessa. Can you forgive me?'

'I'll try,' she said, pointing her vodka glass at me like it was a weapon.

I looked away. By this time, most of the food and drink was gone and the guests were starting to leave. A young, good-looking dude who ran a design shop in the Jordaan stopped by to pay his respects to Venessa. She stood up, took hold of his arm, and damn if they didn't sail out the door together. I took this for a good sign and naively hoped it might be the start of a new romance.

Hendrik and Willem and Bobby and Nikki were all drunked-up and hanging out in a corner smoking cigarettes and making a lot of noise. The salon was practically empty, and Willem brought out the weed. I felt very tired and very sad. I didn't care to join the men in their revels, so I took off my shoes and went up to my bedroom. After carefully folding my Fortuny gown and taking down my hair, I got into bed and tried to stop thinking about poor little Venessa and poor little Bobby and the robot-clown who was lying in wait down by the canal.

I woke up at 4 a.m. because Hendrik was sitting on the side of the bed, staring at me. He still wore his fabulous suit, but now it was soiled and wrinkled. The fabric must have picked up the odors of liquor and smoke because he stank to high heaven, and this time it wasn't of roses. He looked like a broken down tramp, who was trying to find a place to crash.

'Can I get into bed with you?'

'Of course, darling, but before you do go into the shower and rinse off.'

When he got into bed he was naked and smelled of lemon soap and antiseptic mouthwash. I was on the far side of the bed, but he grabbed hold of me and hung on like he was a drowning man and I was a life raft.

'Are you still straight with Bobby?' I asked.

'Yes, it's as good as it ever will be.'

'Is he here?'

'He left about an hour ago. His minders came to pick him up. They said they were taking him to his mother's.'

'What about Willem?'

'He's sleeping it off in his old room.'

I kissed the side of his face: 'Go to sleep, darling, I'll be right here beside you.'

I was first up in the morning and hurriedly dressed in jeans and a sweater, went outside and took a brief stroll down the canal. The robot was nowhere in sight, so I went back in the house and made a pot of coffee. I spent the morning sitting at the kitchen table looking at Taschen books on contemporary design and wondering what had gone down between Bobby and Hendrik last night. Willem joined me and drank some coffee before he took off for the shop. He didn't have much to say about the party and I didn't press him.

Hendrik had still not emerged from my bedroom by noon and I thought it was time to wake him. I made a fresh pot of Italian roast and put two cups on a tray. I knew he was going to be dehydrated so I grabbed a chilled bottle of mineral water and took it along too.

He was in the shower when I walked in. I put the tray on the table and sat down to wait for him. When he came out he was naked, and I told him to go back and put a towel around his waist. He looked perplexed, but did as I asked. The truth was I didn't feel like looking at his dick while I was talking to him.

When he was safely wrapped in the towel, I gave him the bottle of water and he glugged it down. After that he drank two cups of coffee and was finally able to engage in conversation: 'I'm sorry if I neglected you last night,' he said.

'Don't worry about it. I realize you had to help Bobby. I know how fragile he is.'

'He lost it, Martel, he just fucking fell apart in my arms.'

'You were both crying.'

'I suppose we were. There's a lot of sadness between us.'

'Hendrik, I have some strange feelings about Bobby. Sometimes I think he's a Bodhisattva.'

'He could be a Bodhisattva in the sense that he has taken on the sufferings of his people. He lives in torment because of the persecution they've suffered over the years, and he's confused by the adulation heaped on him by the *gadjos*. It's a difficult situation for him, the *gadjos* claim to adore him, even press divinity upon him, but they despise the tribe he comes from. He's agonized over this dichotomy for years. I can barely imagine the devastation he felt when he learned his father was a non-Roma. The only thing that keeps him alive is the music.'

'Venessa's been trying to keep him alive.'

'Maybe, but she also fucks him for her own selfish reasons. Forgive me, but at the moment I can't locate any compassion to give to that poor girl.'

'You're a bastard, Hendrik. Venessa needs your love just as much as Bobby does. She's killing herself over that boy.'

'For god's sake, Martel, of course I love her, it's just that I can only take one of them at time.' He glared at me: 'Will you please stop prattling on about those obnoxious brats! Don't you understand that they've been driving me insane for years? Right now I've got a hangover and I need a beer, so let's stop this discussion and go down to the kitchen.'

'I could use a beer myself,' I said.

On the way downstairs I asked him if he could see Bobby's halo.

'Only too well,' he said grimly.

'So what do you think the halo means?'

'I suppose it means he's a Bodhisattva.'

He reached out and put his hand over my mouth: 'No more,' he said.

PART THREE

Bobby called a couple of days after the party and said he had information about the robot-clone and we agreed to meet at the Bald Hyena coffee shop. When I got there Bobby hadn't arrived, so I located an empty table and sat down and waited for him. I didn't wait long, he must have been lurking somewhere close waiting for me to show up. The kid presented a different image than the one I'd seen before, and this time there were no shiny vibrations or halos in sight. Bobby looked scruffy and unkempt in a grungy leather jacket with a long scarf hanging around his neck. His legs were encased in tight, drainpipe jeans, and his height was accented by cowboy boots with pointed toes and Cuban heels. All things considered, he was a nice bit of rough, and the boots were absolutely amazing.

As soon as Bobby sat down, a wait boy hurried over. That was odd, because the place was self-service, but I suppose celebrity must be served. The kid obsequiously took our order and got it back to us in record time; two drafts and a packet of Afghan kush.

Bobby rolled a spliff and smiled: 'This is some wicked shit, Martel. Are you sure you can take it?'

I could smell the weed across the table, the bud positively reeked of earth and resin. 'Of course I can take it, I've been smoking for years.'

He snickered: 'This is a lot stronger than that Mexican ditch weed you Americans grew up on.' He smirked like a know-it-all, which pissed me off. If it hadn't been for us pioneers, these kids wouldn't know dick about cannabis.

Bobby lit the spliff and took a hit. The smoke was sweet and smelled of pine forest. 'Maybe we shouldn't get high. I thought we were here to discuss important business,' I said.

'You need to be relaxed when I give you the news.'

'Is it that bad?'

'It's bad enough,' he said. 'My crew has been keeping tabs on the little bastard that's tailing you, and they think he might have some associates. What the hell did you do to get these guys on your ass?'

'Guys?' I repeated. 'You mean there's more than one? I thought it was just the robot-clone.'

I took a hit from the spliff in my hand. Bobby was right, it was strong stuff, and I hoped it would help quell the bursts of pure panic that had suddenly attacked my body.

'We don't know for sure, but Benno has seen two tough-looking American dudes hanging around the Van der Saar shop. They look like gangsters from some American mob.'

I held on to the joint for dear life. The smoke seemed to have a narcotic effect rather like heroin. After a few minutes in which both Bobby and I sat in contemplative silence, I felt a lot better. The weed made me think I could deal with a trio of Greylander assassins and come out alive.

'That's enough, Martel!' Bobby held out his hand and I gave him the joint.

'This stuff is like smack,' I said.

'Yes,' he smiled, 'that's why I like it. Now tell me, what the hell did you do to get all this surveillance?'

'I helped kill Preston Greylander. They probably work for his outfit.''

'Who's Preston Greylander?' Bobby didn't seem surprised that I'd just admitted to killing someone. Maybe the Revata were so inured by the crimes the *gadjos* had committed against them they thought we were all killers at heart.

'Preston Greylander was the CEO of a giant agri-business combine,' I said. 'Greylander International is trying to gain control of the world's food supply.'

'That sounds familiar,' Bobby nodded thoughtfully, 'Isn't Greylander the corporation that's causing the trouble in Africa?'

'Yes, in Africa and other places. The group is expert in deforestation and chemical burns. They also specialize in genocide.'

When I said 'genocide' Bobby winced. He was probably remembering back to the big kill-off of his ancestors in Nazi times. Not all the weed in the coffee shop could make him forget that.

'Was Hendrik involved in the murder? These American punks seem to have an interest in him.'

'No, Hendrik and I hooked up after the murder. He didn't know anything about it. I had to tell him when we got serious.'

'I think the clone is after you, and the New Jersey people are looking for something, or someone, else. It's two separate issues, but they must be working for the same people.'

I thought back to the party: 'When I met Detective Gripsa, he said something about rumors of American mob guys invading the city and looking for a mystery painting. He said it in passing and didn't offer any detail, just that the painting is a Rembrandt.'

'Come on, Martel, if it's a Rembrandt, you've got to know Hendrik's involved, and probably Willem too,' he paused, 'maybe even Venessa. Are you sure you don't know anything about this picture?'

'Not really. I brought the Van der Saars a painting from Preston Greylander's collection. He wanted it restored. Preston thought it was a Rembrandt, but it was no such thing. It was of the period and probably done by one of Rembrandt's circle. As far as I know, Willem cleaned it up and after Preston's death the painting went to his aunt, Madame Pookie Greylander, a collector who lives in Switzerland. We never did find out who painted the dam thing.'

'I think you should talk to Hendrik about this. Maybe the painting never got to Madame Pookie.' He paused for a moment: 'Venessa usually knows what's going on down at the shop. I'll talk to her about it tonight.'

'I hate to think Hendrik is hiding something from me.'

'Don't act so naïve, everybody lies, everybody hides, even from their nearest and dearest.'

'I hope you don't really believe that,' I said, taking the spliff out of his hand. 'Are you staying with Venessa? I thought you wanted to get away from her.'

'I do, but I can't seem to stay away, she always pulls me back. When I play music I see her in my mind's eye and I start to want her again. I see us in the past, we've been together through many lives and we make each other complete.'

'I didn't know you believed in reincarnation, let alone that you were able to see your past lives.' We seemed to be getting off the subject of the Rembrandt and the thugs from America – maybe it was the grass.

'I'm a Revata,' he declared, 'we come from India, so of course I believe in reincarnation.' Bobby smiled: 'Venessa and I have even changed genders and a couple of times we were gay.'

'Well, isn't that charming? You must know each other extremely well after all those lives together.'

'Yes, but sometimes there are problems. This time Venessa is suffering a lot. It's because she was raised by those two idiots, Hendrik and Willem. There were no women around when she was a kid, and she missed out on warm breasts and tender love. Venessa says Dries, Willem's kid, is fucked up too. I guess he really needs a mother.'

'Don't be so hard on Hendrik and Willem; they did their best. A lot of women are lousy mothers and don't give out tender love. What's yours like?'

'Anoushka is a tough Revata Mama and I got plenty of love from her. When I was a baby, I never left her side, she nursed me until I was almost four years old. When I was four, I left the breast and took up the guitar and went with Zonzo and the boys. Now that I'm a big player she still tries to run my life. '

'Was Anoushka the one who made you get married?'

'No, that was the whole group. It's our custom to marry young and to have lots of children. We have to make up for the loss.'

'Do you have any kids?'

'Yes, a boy and a girl. The girl came first and we called her Luz, she also goes by Lucia. The little boy is Sebastien. My wife is Mouchi. She's very cute with black, curly hair and a smart mouth. I love my family, but our relations are different than the ones in a *gadjo* family. Mouchi and the kids hang all day with the women in the clan. They seem to like it that way. When I'm around, I am with the men. It's a segregated system and it works for us. A lot of people in the world do it the same way, but the *gadjos* don't like it. They think it's sexist.'

'I wouldn't worry about what the *gadjos* think.'

'I'm not having any more kids.'

'That's probably a wise idea.'

'Martel, did you know the human race is going extinct? The Revata saw it coming. When you live on the outside for a thousand years, you can always see the signs. We thought we might survive, but now I'm not so sure. The earth is so damaged, it won't support humans much longer,' he paused and took another hit, 'I'm sorry the Revata made me marry and have kids. Now that my children are here, I love them and I don't want them to suffer some horrible end.'

'Oh, Bobby,' I sighed. He was only twenty years old and he was carrying such a heavy load he made my hard old heart break for him. 'Maybe the Revata will survive. It seems that outliers and nomads have a better chance than most.'

Bobby shook his head in the negative: 'It's gone too far. The adverse elements have been set in motion and they cannot be controlled or stopped. The rats are going to take over. They will become as big as elephants and they will rule the earth.'

'Are you fucking serious?' I laughed, but it was a nightmare image and I didn't want it showing up in my dreams. Rats the size of elephants… Jesus and Mary, help us.

'I'm afraid so.' Bobby's head dipped and he closed his eyes. I hoped he was just nodding out and not going into a serious depression.

'So what will happen to our immortal souls and our monkey minds once we become extinct? Will we just float off into space and become part of the great big engine that runs the universe?' I asked.

His head came up and his eyes opened: 'That was explained to me by a Buddhist monk in Thailand. I was doing an early morning practice at a club in Bangkok and this monk came in with his begging bowl. He was a jazz fan and we got to talking. He told me that when it was all over on earth this human form would go on to another planet and continue to work out its collective karma. He was quite a jolly monk and seemed to think we'd go on wrecking planets until we got it right.'

'Well, there are certainly enough planets out there. The universe is so immense. I've never been able to figure it out.'

'The learned people say the meaning of the universe is in the Bhagavad Gita, but nobody can read it anymore, the language is too antique.'

'Jesus, Bobby, you know a lot for a twenty-year-old. Are you sure you didn't play a flute in one of your former manifestations?'

He laughed: 'No, I never played a flute, but true musicians all carry a glimmer of Lord Krishna's light in their souls.' He gave me a broad, flirty smile: 'That's why we get all the girls.'

At first I didn't understand what he meant, but then I recalled that Lord Krishna had a large number of female fans that followed him around and received his sweet love. The antics of Krishna and his girls was probably the first documented rock star and groupie bang-off.

I noticed that the spliff was laying in the ashtray, dead and burned out, and I suddenly realized I was so high I could probably float out of The Bald Hyena and all the way back to the Herengracht without touching the ground. I got panicky: 'Do you have a car, Bobby? I don't think I can make it home on my own.'

'Yes, Benno's waiting outside. He'll take you back to the Herengracht. I'm going over to Venessa's.'

'Do you think I should talk to Hendrik about the Rembrandt?'

'No, hold off on that. I'll see if Venessa knows anything. I'll call you tomorrow and we can take it from there.'

'What about the robot-clone?'

'Don't worry about him,' Bobby smiled, 'he won't bother you for a while. I heard he got mugged last night in the Red Light district and that he'll be in the hospital for a couple of days.'

Bobby stood up and came over to my side of the table, he pulled out my chair, and helped me to my feet: 'I told you that weed was strong,' he said.

Bobby called around ten the next morning; his voice sounded husky and full of sleep, but his message was urgent: I was to meet him at Venessa's apartment ASAP. I left immediately and biked over to the De Pijp. When I got to Venessa's building I ran up the two flights of stairs to her apartment in record time. She opened the door and I walked inside.

It was a weekday, and Venessa should have been down at the shop, but apparently whatever information she had was important enough to make her stay home from work. Venessa led me into the living room. Bobby was sitting in a corner with an acoustic guitar in his lap. Both Bobby and Venessa looked strung out and sleepy, they were unwashed and uncombed and still wearing their nightwear, which in Bobby's case was a pair of boxers and a wife beater T-shirt with a silk screened portrait of the youthful Dimitri Shostakovich on the front. It was a terrific image, young Shosty was casting a belligerent glance and wearing heavy, horn rims on his cute, little nose. Venessa, on the other hand, was not carrying any artistic messages on her nightgown. She wore a faded pink extra-large T that hung to her knees. The faint color complemented her skin and gave it the sheen of a natural pearl. Bobby and Venessa, even in a rumpled and unadorned state, were mouth-wateringly lovely and frighteningly remote. They seemed to exist in a different time-space than the ones we normal humans inhabit.

Instead of making coffee Venessa handed out large cans of Red Bull: 'Do you want vodka in that, Martel?' she asked.

'No, thanks, darling, I think I'll go *au naturel* this morning.'

'That's probably a good idea,' she said, taking a big slug out of the Red Bull and then pouring some Absolut in the can.

Bobby watched her affectionately before he lit up a joint; apparently he was off the smack for the time being. 'Hey, baby, why don't you explain to Martel about the Rembrandt? Tell her what you know.'

Venessa looked at Bobby and smiled. They did seem to be totally in synch, and I was tempted to believe that, just as Bobby said, they had been lovers through many lifetimes. They broke their communion, and Venessa gave me her attention and started a mini-lecture:

'After you left town, Willem got down to work on the painting, and the first thing he found was the famous RHL initials and the date, 1632. It was a transitional painting; Rembrandt used the initials before he went to the full signature. Willem called Daddy and me into the studio and showed us the signature, after that he demonstrated the authenticity of the painting to our satisfaction.

'For once, my Dad and my uncle were confused and unable to think of a plan of action regarding this unknown work by our most revered, and highly priced, Dutch master. After considering our options, we took a vote and decided that the painting should eventually go to the Dutch state and that we were going to fuck the Greylanders out of their trophy. While we were making the plans, Daddy suggested we let you in on the secret, but neither Willem nor I wanted you involved. We thought you were a loose cannon and that you might not be able to keep your mouth shut. Eventually Hendrik agreed.'

'Gees, thanks,' I said, 'I was the one who risked my ass and brought you that picture. The least you could have done was keep me in the loop.'

'I apologize, Martel. I can see now that we were wrong.'

'Apology accepted,' I said grudgingly. I was still fuming about the Van der Saar's appropriation of the painting and their lack of trust in me, but I decided to keep my anger to myself for the time being, knowing that eventually I would take my beef to Hendrik and make him pay for the disrespect.

'Willem made a copy of the painting and after two months of aging and drying it was sent on to Madame Pookie.'

'I guess old Pookie wasn't as dumb as you guys thought. She must have had suspicions about the piece and called in an expert who identified it as a fake,' I said.

Venessa was seriously uncomfortable: 'That must have been what happened,' she admitted.

'So where is the Rembrandt now? Did you guys stash it in a salt mine in the Ukraine?'

'I don't know where it is. Hendrik and Willem took it away one day, and I haven't seen it since.' She drank some more Red Bull and looked helplessly toward Bobby, but he was doing something with his guitar strings and wasn't offering any support.

'It shouldn't have happened like this,' she wailed. 'The painting Willem sent to Switzerland was brilliant. There are only a few people in the world that could have identified it as a fake.'

'Well, the Greylanders have an unlimited budget, so they must have got hold of one of those people. Now we've got these goons from the USA running all over town looking for the real item. You better hire some protection, Venessa, just in case.'

Bobby looked up from his guitar, 'She'll be OK because the Revata are looking out for her.'

'Well, that's a relief. You guys seem to be pretty good at surveillance.'

'Yeah, it's in our blood. We've became preternaturally alert because of our centuries on the run.'

'Am I indebted to you and the Revata for putting the robot-clone in the hospital?'

'You're not indebted, Martel, you're part of the family now.'

'Thanks, darling, you honor me.'

'You know, Martel,' Venessa said slowly, verbally intercutting between me and Bobby, 'I think the Rembrandt may be stashed at Uncle Nikki's house.'

'Uncle Nikki? Do you mean Detective Gripsa, the art cop?'

'Yes, I've known him since I was a baby and I always call him Uncle.'

I nodded at Bobby: 'More family?'

'Yeah, Nikki's okay, he and the Revata have worked together on occasion.'

I turned back to Venessa: 'What makes you think the Rembrandt is with the detective?'

'Just a hunch, Willem and Daddy and Nikki go way back to University and the time of political rebellion. They have a lot of history between them, and I know they trust each other. Nikki has a small collection of good paintings in his house in the Noord and he keeps the rooms at museum temperature and has maximum security. It would be a good place to stash a hot painting.'

'How do we get in?' Bobby asked.

'It should be easy,' Venessa said. 'His mother lives there and she's usually at home.'

'If we get in and the painting is there, what do we do?' I asked.

'We'll worry about that later,' Bobby said.

I wasn't terribly anxious to go; even if the painting was at Gripsa's house, it wouldn't be out in plain sight. What were we going to do, tie up some old lady and search the house?

'Why don't we just smoke some more of that Afghan kush and drink some vodka and Red Bull and listen to Shostakovich Symphony Number Five and think about the rest of it tomorrow?' I said.

'Fuck that, Martel, we are now on the case,' Bobby said, he looked eager to travel. He handed me the joint he'd been smoking and I took a hit: 'Did you ride over on your bicycle?' he asked.

'Yes, I did,' I said dreamily, knowing we were all going over to the Noord on our bikes and visit.

Nikki's mother.

'Should we have a gun for protection?'

'Martel, stop being a fucking American,' Venessa said. 'We've got knives, so don't worry about it.'

'Okay, I won't,' I said and took another hit off the kush.

We rode our bikes to Centraal and then caught a ferry across the river to the Noord. The Noord is a piece of land that is separated from Amsterdam by the river, and once you cross over, you find the area round the wharfs is quite touristy, picturesque, and artistically inclined, but when you get away from the landing, a small town, semi-rural vibe develops.

It only took five minutes to cross the water, but by the time we docked, the weather had changed, and we were in heavy mist and light rain. We got on our bicycles and followed

Venessa out past the restaurants and the shops to a smart little village comprised of wooden houses that were nicely painted in pastel colors with roofs of orange tile and grey slate. She stopped in front of a lovely little house that looked like a marker in a board game.

'This can't be it,' I said. The fucking house was a two-story affair with windows fronting the street. It in no way looked like a fortress where you'd stash a painting worth millions of Euros.

When she saw my doubtful look she said: 'It's Nikki's house. I've been here lots of times for parties and dinners.'

'Do you think he's home?' Bobby asked, wiping the mist from his face with his scarf.

'I doubt it,' Venessa said, 'he spends most of his time in the city.'

She pulled her phone out of her sleeve and started to call.

'Jesus,' Bobby said, 'we're standing in front of the fucking place, let's just go knock.' He walked up to the door and started banging on it.

He didn't bang long because the door was soon opened by an older woman with dyed black hair and a heavily made-up face that made her look like the old time TV diva, Joan Collins. After I got over the face, I saw there was a black dog the size of a Shetland pony standing discretely behind her.

Venessa stepped quickly in front of Bobby and said: 'Hello, Madame Lillian, is Nikki around? My friends and I are touring the Noord and thought we'd drop by on the off chance he'd be here.'

'Why, Venessa, darling, I barely recognized you it's been so long. I'm afraid Nikki's in town, but bring your friends and come in and have a chat with his old mum.' She made a hand gesture to the dog and said, 'It's all right, Rowley, these humans are friends.'

We all smiled at the lady and watched as the dog, a Bouvier des Flandres, came out from behind her. He moved onto the doorstep and began to herd us into the house. The detective's mother smiled indulgently while the big animal gently nudged us toward the sitting room.

'When did you get the dog, Madame Lillian?' Venessa asked.

'Nikki brought him home a few months ago. He's a retired police officer and Nikki wanted to give him a good home in his old age.'

'But doesn't he require a lot of maintenance?'

'Oh, yes,' the old lady said breezily, 'a colleague of Nikki's comes every morning at six and takes him for a two-hour run. After lunch he works out on the treadmill, and in the evening he plays on the obstacle course we've installed in the garden. Rowley really is a dear, in his spare time he helps with the housework.'

By this time Rowley had us all in the sitting room and was directing us to our seats. Bobby and Venessa were led to a love seat and I was given a comfortable chair upholstered in faded chintz. When we were seated, the dog came up and formally ran his nose over each of us.

'Don't pet him,' Madame Lillian advised.

When Rowley finished his ritual he retired to the hearth rug and relaxed. The handsome beast and his dog-like activities had been an amazing distraction, but when the novelty was over and I looked around, it registered that we were in a Dutch sitting room with Delft plates on a rail and old master type paintings on the wall. One of the paintings appeared to be a portrait of a Dutch burger and his wife done in the style of Rembrandt.

'You kids,' Lillian gave me a questioning look, probably wondering what a middle-aged woman was doing biking around in the rain with a couple of juveniles, 'look like you could use some tea. It will just be a minute,' she said, and left the room.

'Is that it?' Bobby whispered, glancing surreptitiously at the Rembrandt.

'It looks like it,' Venessa said.

'I think so,' I said. Venessa got up off the love seat. Surprisingly, Rowley didn't growl or move from his place on the hearth rug. She walked over and examined the painting. I could see her eyes lingering on the black areas and the gold jewelry.

'It's the real thing,' she said. Her voice was hushed, almost awestruck.

Just then Madame Lillian walked in carrying a heavy tray that was overloaded with a teapot, cups, and a platter of scones and sweeties. I was surprised she got it to the refreshments table without dropping it smash on the carpet. She set the tray down quite smartly on a round table and went over to a cupboard and pulled out a bottle of rum: 'I expect you lot will be wanting a drop of the hard stuff after your bike through the rain.'

'That would be wonderful,' Venessa said.

She introduced Bobby, but Lillian was sharp, she already knew who he was. It turned out she was a jazz fan and had all his CD's. Venessa explained my presence by saying I was Hendrik's girlfriend from America and that she and Bobby were showing me the sights. Lillian said Hendrik was a bit of a rascal, but she was sure he'd calmed down and reformed since the old days and she knew I'd able to handle him.

Madame Lillian poured the rum into tiny shot glasses and handed them around. We slammed the rum and put the empty glasses back on the table. Lillian filled the glasses again. After that she poured tea and gave us little plates full of pastries.

'Did you see Nikki's new picture?' she asked brightly. 'I swear I can't keep up with that boy. I think he has a collecting mania. He came home with this lovely false Rembrandt about two months ago. He said Willem gave it to him because the Van der Saars couldn't sell such an obvious fake.' She gestured toward the painting, 'I'm no expert, but it looks real to me.'

I reached for my tot of rum and tossed it down. I couldn't figure if the woman was just making conversation or playing around with the fact that she knew the picture was real.

'Well, Lillian, I can see from here that the painting is not right,' Venessa said smoothly. Her voice was slick as glass, she sounded like a true Van der Saar. 'It looks nice on your wall out here in the Noord, but it would never pass in Amsterdam. I hope you and Nikki enjoy it. Has anyone else seen it?'

'I had a party last week and the neighbors dropped by. They knew it was a fake but they liked it anyway.'

'Madame Lillian, your apple cookies are superb,' Bobby said, helping himself to another. He really must have been off the heroin because he was gobbling the pastries like crazy.

'Why, thank you, darling, I made them myself. I used to be a pastry chef years ago, and now I've gone back to baking since I've been living out here. Nikki's not home much, he has an apartment in town, and I need something to occupy the time.'

Bobby glanced admiringly at Lillian's figure which was pretty decent for a woman who looked to be in her late seventies: 'Surely you can't be eating all these rich pastries yourself?' he asked.

'Oh, no, I distribute them at the local schools. I use only fresh, organic ingredients and the kiddies all love a wholesome treat. Now that Rowley is here, we distribute them via dogcart. The kids love it when Rowley pulls up in his cart full of goodies.'

The pastries were delicious and I found myself happily sampling a number of delicate treats. It must have been the last of the kush kicking in.

Madame Lillian went back to the kitchen and made another pot of tea, and we all chatted pleasantly for an hour or so. When it was time to go, Bobby and Lillian exchanged phone numbers. He was going to comp her a couple of tickets to an upcoming gig at the Paradisio. All the while we were taking our tea Rowley was dozing on the rug. Unlike many dogs, he had shown no interest in the pastries. Lillian said he only liked raw meat and boiled vegetables. When we stood up, he jumped to attention and briskly escorted us to the door.

Outside, it was still misting and the land was covered by a light that reflected smoky greens and browns similar to the famous *Sfumato* seen in the paintings of Leonardo da Vinci. As we traveled through the marvelous light to the ferry, I began entertaining all sorts of unusual thoughts about our recent encounter. It seemed to me that we had been kicked out of the twenty-first century and back into some timeless fairytale. We had entered an enchanted cottage and met with a benevolent witch and a magical beast that were guarding a precious treasure.

When we arrived back in Amsterdam proper we stopped at a café across from Centraal Station to discuss the situation and review our visit with Madame Lillian and Rowley. Fanciful ideas aside, I was totally flummoxed by the meeting and drank an espresso in the hopes that the caffeine would help me puzzle things out.

'That fucking dog didn't look like he was some broken down, retired cop,' Bobby said.

'He's a killer posing as a sweet and lovable companion,' Venessa said. 'Did you get that bit about him pulling the cart full of pastry around the Noord to the primary schools?' she sniggered.

'Yeah, that was pretty cute,' Bobby said, stirring sugar into his espresso. 'Vennie, I thought you said the house was wired. Why do they need a dog?'

'I really don't know, baby. Maybe he's there to put a scare into people who come snooping around.'

'Do you think Madame Lillian is in on the plot?' I asked.

'I doubt it,' Venessa said. 'I think she's glad to have Rowley around for companionship, and as far as the painting is concerned, she seems convinced it's a copy. The idea that it's a genuine Rembrandt wouldn't even enter her mind.'

'You know,' Bobby said thoughtfully, 'Nikki is a pretty callous dude putting his mother into a situation like this.'

'Don't forget Daddy and Willem, they're in it too. They're letting the old lady take all the risks!' Venessa was indignant.

'We have to protect Madame Lillian,' I said, trying to dismiss the fact that my lover was a rotten, lying bastard who was hiding behind the skirts of an elderly woman.

'So far, the guys from the American mob haven't copped to the fact that the picture is out in the Noord. Right now they're focusing on Hendrik and sniffing around town looking for the painting,' Bobby said.

'Well, thank god for that,' I said.

Venessa took out her phone and looked at it: 'Shit, Hendrik's been texting me all morning. There's an emergency at the shop and I have to get down there right away!'

'Did he say what's wrong?' I asked.

'No, that's what puzzles me. If it's something important he usually tells me.' She stood up and put on her jacket.

'I'm going with you,' I said. 'How about you Bobby, do you want to come along?'

'No, I've got a gig in Rotterdam tonight and I have to get ready for it.' He turned to Venessa: 'Call me if there are problems.' She bent over and kissed his cheek: 'When will I see you again?' she asked.

'Not for a couple of days. I have to spend some time back at the camp.'

Venessa nodded. I figured he had to be with his wife and kids and his mother and Zonzo and the rest of the tribe. Surprisingly, Venessa seemed OK with that. I guessed she was used to sharing.

'Don't you guys do anything stupid,' Bobby advised. 'If there's trouble, call me and I'll put Benno and the boys on it.'

'Okay, Bobby,' I said, and followed Venessa out of the café.'

When we got to the shop, the blinds were drawn and there was a closed sign stuck on the door. Venessa took out her phone and called, and after a minute or so Hendrik came to the door. He took one disgruntled look at the both of us and then let us in.

'Where the hell were you?' he asked Venessa.

'I took Martel on a bike ride this morning. I didn't think you needed me till this afternoon.'

'Fucking hell,' he said. 'Willem had a rush job and decided to come in early to finish it off. He arrived around six this morning, and two thugs were waiting for him in the street. They stuck a gun to his head and forced their way in.

Once inside, they pistol-whipped him and made a search of the workroom and my office. Now the place is a shambles and Willem's in the hospital.'

'Is Willem going to be alright?' Venessa asked. Her demeanor was cool, but I could see the worry lines around her mouth and eyes.

'Yes, he's vaguely coherent and claiming his attackers had New Jersey accents. He says they looked like actors in an American TV series about gangsters.' Hendrik winced and scratched his head. He really was upset. 'The medical team says no damage was done, but Willem has to rest for a few days. Dries is down at the hospital, holding his hand and looking after him.'

'Dries really loves his dad,' Venessa commented as she walked toward the studio. 'Is anything missing?'

'I don't believe so. There's millions of Euro's worth of art in here, but they just hurt your uncle and made a huge mess.'

'I suppose they were looking for the Rembrandt,' I said sharply.

Up until now Hendrik had barely registered my presence, but when I mentioned the Rembrandt, I finally caught his attention: 'Oh god, Martel, don't go off on me now. I didn't tell you because I wanted to protect you. Please understand.' He looked surprised and sounded defeated.

'You wanted to protect me, yet you include your own daughter in your dangerous schemes. What about her welfare?'

'Give it a rest, Martel,' Venessa said, 'He's crazy about you, but you're not really a Van der Saar. That's why he wanted to keep you out of it. He only trusts his own blood.'

'That's not true, Venessa. You know I'd trust Nikki Gripsa with my life,' he paused, 'and as for Martel, she'll soon be a real Van der Saar. We'll be getting married in the near future.'

'That's the first I've heard about it!' I wondered if the assault on his brother and the wreck of the studio hadn't scrambled poor Hendrik's brains.

'Well, you've heard about it now,' he snapped.

'Jesus, you're worse than children,' Venessa said. 'Work it out later when I'm not around.'

By this time we'd reached the studio, and Venessa and I got our first view of the chaos. It was a real mess: equipment and work tables were overturned, bottles were spilled, pigments were smeared, brushes and tools were thrown about, but, amazingly, none of the pictures that were waiting for restoration had been damaged.

'They didn't hurt anything important,' I said.

'It's the same in my office,' Hendrik said, 'everything is thrown around, but I don't think anything has been taken. They were after the Rembrandt and nothing more.'

'Has Uncle Nikki been here?' Venessa asked.

'Yes, I called him right away. He brought a team over and they dusted the place for prints. It's an art related crime so Nikki will be handling the case.'

'Let's hope he takes the Rembrandt out of the Noord. I doubt that he wants his mother to get hurt.' I said.

'You know about that?' Hendrik was startled.

'Yes, daddy, we know everything,' Venessa said. 'We went over to the Noord this morning and met Rowley and had tea with Madame Lillian.'

'We also saw the Rembrandt.' I said. 'Lillian told us it was a fake and that Willem couldn't sell it so he gave it to Nikki.'

Hendrik put his right hand to his head and sighed: 'The gangsters won't figure it out, and if they do, Rowley will rip their livers out and eat them for breakfast,' he paused. 'Nikki would never put his mother at risk; the house is wired, state of the art. I saw to it myself.'

'Keep telling yourself that, buddy,' I said.

Venessa looked around disgustedly: 'Who's going to clean up this mess?' she asked.

'I gave everybody the day off.' Hendrik said, 'I was hoping you'd help me, Vennie.'

'I will, Dad, don't worry.'

'Seeing as I'm here I might as well help too,' I said.

'Thank you, darling,' Hendrik said, and handed me a trash bag.

By the time we finished clearing the mess and putting things back in order it was almost midnight. Venessa came home with Hendrik and me: she had a fear of going to her apartment alone, and who could blame her? Who knew what those thugs were going to pull next? When we got to the Herengracht, we were all hungry and went to the kitchen to make ham and cheese sandwiches. We were subdued, seemingly deep in our own thoughts and after consuming our food we went quietly to our separate beds.

The next day, I picked up a bouquet of cream colored tulips at a flower stall and went to visit Willem. I made my way to a private hospital, discretely hidden in the back streets of the Ould Sud section of town, where a crisply starched nurse in a white cap greeted me and led me to Willem's room.

The room itself was light and airy, but the two inhabitants inside were grimy and dim. A pale, wraith of a boy whose extreme slenderness hinted of an eating disorder was seated next to the bed hunched over an iPhone. He didn't bother to look up when we entered and he did not verbally acknowledge our presence. It was possible he was mute, but it was more likely he was suffering some form of autism. I assumed that the young man was Willem's reclusive son, Dries. Like Venessa, he had grown up without benefit of a mother's love. In Dries' case, his mother had suffered a post partum depression and killed herself by driving her car into a canal shortly after his birth.

Willem was laid out on white sheets and his head was propped up on white pillows. His skin had turned gray green and was spotted with purple bruises. The fabulous Viking braids that had been Willem's trademark were gone and his head was shaved. I had never seen him without his glorious, golden hair and it was a terrible shock. Without the hair, his gaunt and hollowed face could have passed for a death mask. I handed the tulips to the nurse and leaned over and kissed Willem's cold face. He acknowledged my presence by taking my hand and holding it for a moment, but there was no energy in his grasp.

The nurse put the flowers in a vase and brought it to a table at Willem's bedside. He looked at the flowers and moved his lips in a weak smile: 'Those are my favorites, Martel, thanks.'

'You're very welcome, darling. How are you feeling? It's a terrible shame about your hair.'

'I'm feeling OK. The hair is the least of my worries.'

The nurse walked out of the room and the boy looked up from his iPhone: 'You were right, Dad, those bastards are working for Greylander International. The Viper followed the trail to a bank in London. He couldn't go any farther because there's black ice protecting the rest of the transactions.'

'Good work, son. Thank the Viper for me.'

Willem turned to me: 'Martel, I don't believe you've met my son, Dries. He and his mates are gathering information on my assailants.'

'Hello, Dries,' I said. The kid looked at me with wide, bloodshot, eyes: 'I've heard about you. You're Uncle Hendrik's new woman.'

'You could put it that way,' I said.

Dries nodded, lowered his eyes, and went back to his iPhone.

'Willem, shouldn't you wait until your head clears before you start an investigation?' I asked.

'It doesn't matter about my head, Dries and his crew are doing all the work.'

'What about Detective Gripsa? Isn't he on the case?'

'Yes, but these kids are able to access information the cops can never get to.'

I was standing next to Dries and he handed me his iPhone: 'Hang on to this, Martel,' he ordered. He pulled a tiny, throw away cell out of his pocket and made a call. He spoke in a few syllables of code and then terminated. He took the iPhone out of my hand and went back to work.

I spoke to Willem: 'Venessa's coming down to visit later. She says Bobby will be back from Rotterdam around four and will drop by as soon as he hits town.'

'Bobby's coming in?' Dries head jerked up from the phone.

'Yes, he should be here in an hour or so.'

'I've never met him,' he said.

'Well, you will now. He's a great guy, I'm sure you two will really hit it off.'

'Now that Paco de Lucia is dead, Bobby Janacek is the world's greatest guitar player,' the kid declared. He sounded like a recorded message.

'I love Bobby's music, but no one will ever replace Paco,' I said.

It was true, when Paco de Lucia died he left a great hole at the heart of the world.

'You listen to Paco's music?' the kid asked, and for the first time I saw his face brighten.

'For twenty or thirty years,' I smiled. "Maybe we can listen together some time.'

'Maybe,' Dries said warily. He went back to his iPhone giving me the distinct impression that I had overstepped my bounds.

The nurse came in and gave Willem a cursory glance. He had closed his eyes and was breathing heavily.

'Is he alright?' I asked.

'He's sleeping. He goes in and out,' she said. 'That's how it is with head injuries.'

'I'll let him get some rest.'

Dries looked up from his phone. 'What should I say to Bobby when he gets here?'

He sounded confused: apparently, meeting a musician of Bobby's stature was more than he could handle.

'Forget about the music, talk to him about the research you're doing on those goons from New Jersey. He's interested in that. He wants to nail those guys too. Tell him everything you know'

Dries processed the information I had just given him and then he smiled. His teeth were stained, but they didn't appear to be decayed: 'Thanks, Martel. You've given me a good idea. I will talk to him. Maybe he can help us catch those guys.'

'Maybe,' I said, wondering just what the hell Dries and his gang of mutant game boys were up to. From what I'd been told, these skinny little shits were no-hope nihilists who slept all day and gamed and hacked all night. They were totally unhealthy and subsisted on Red Bull and ramen noodles. Lately, a few were coming out of their lairs and traveling to Russia to learn the deadly art of Free Climbing. I wondered if Dries would tackle that next; I could just see his skinny frame crawling to the top of the Moscow Bridge or the Shanghai tower. He'd be perfect for the art.

Dries was still hunched over his phone as I left the room. I was in a hurry because I had to meet Hendrik to discuss our wedding.

When I got home from the hospital I found Hendrik in the kitchen arranging an extravagant floral display that was taking on the form of an old fashioned *nature morte.*

'That looks like good therapy,' I said, watching him fill a large, glass vase with red and white striped tulips, pale pink old fashioned roses, and large rust colored carnations. The flowers were all in high bloom and wouldn't last more than a day before their heads began to droop.

'It is,' he looked up and smiled. 'The flowers got misplaced in the confusion down at the shop. By the time I found them, they weren't fit for public display, so I thought I'd bring them home. We can enjoy them for a couple of days.'

'You've got a beautiful design going there. I think we have a couple of stems of tiny lemons in the refrigerator. They might work if you want to add them.'

'Sure, I'll give it a try. Why don't you get them for me?'

I went to the fridge and retrieved the lemon stems from the vegetable bin. The leaves were green and shiny, but the baby lemons were shrunken and slightly withered with just the right amount of implied decay that went perfectly in a Dutch still life. I handed Hendrik the stems and said: 'I was just at the hospital. Willem looks pretty beat up.'

'Don't worry about him. I talked to his doctor this morning and he's doing fine.' Hendrik snipped the stems of the lemon branches with a sharp instrument.

'Do you know Willem's got Dries and his hacker friends running around the internet looking for information to tie the attackers to the Greylanders?'

Hendrik looked surprised, his forehead wrinkled, and then his mouth broke into a big grin: 'They'll probably do better than Nikki and the cops. Dries is a smart kid. Have they come up with anything?'

'Apparently they found some financial information that ties the Greylanders to the New Jersey mob.'

'Oh, great, now we're not only fighting the Greylanders but some TV gangsters. I didn't think they existed in real life.'

'Darling, you are so naïve,' I said, and kissed his cheek.

He finished placing the lemon stems in the vase. 'Where should we put the flowers? Do you want them in your rooms?'

'No, they're much too grand for my little space. They might look good in your study.'

'That's an idea. I'll take them up now."

'Do you mind if I join you for a moment.'

'No, not at all, but there'll be no fooling around. I have work to do.'

When we got to the study Hendrik put the bouquet on a table between a pair of casement windows. He adjusted the windows to let in light and air: 'Maybe a butterfly will come floating in and settle on the flowers,' he said.

'That would be wonderful.' I sat down on a chair opposite the desk.

'I've seen it happen,' he said. Hendrik unlocked his desk drawer and pulled out a semi-automatic weapon. 'It needs to be cleaned,' he explained.

'Is that a Glock?'

'Yes it is. How did you know?'

'It looks like what they use in the movies.'

He spread a cloth on the desk and opened a neat, leather kit that contained cleaning tools. I was reminded of old times back in the States when Terry cleaned his Sig Sauer and I sat beside him while we plotted the death of Preston Greylander. Terry had been on a righteous mission, but now it looked as though Hendrik was defending against his own crimes. He and Willem could have handed the picture over to Madame Pookie, but no, they made a forgery and gave that to her. They were deep into the repercussions of their crime, and I was not going to get caught up in guilt over their actions. I had helped kill Preston and would take full responsibility for that, but, as for the Rembrandt, that was on the Van der Saars.

I had come up to the study to talk to Hendrik about the wedding he had alluded to down at the shop. As I had told him before, a private commitment was all that was needed to keep us together, but he seemed to disagree with that. Hendrik was a tough negotiator, and for some reason he wanted us legally linked together. I had my doubts because I had seen my life as a free woman deteriorate since I became involved with him. In the first blush of our love I had been caught up in the enchantment of the moment and became a willing sex toy. When the high degree of ecstasy wore off, Hendrik had sent me out on a futile journey through the Netherlands and Flanders chasing the shadow of a phantom painter. He had duped me and excluded me from the truth about the Rembrandt. Now that the shit was coming down full force and I knew all about his double dealing, he was repentant and thought marriage would make everything right between us. To me, his male logic was totally incomprehensible and I wanted to make him understand I wasn't going to allow him to rush me into a union based on deceit and fear.

Just as he was sticking a swab into the barrel of the gun, I asked him why he wanted to get married. Naturally, that set him off and we got into a slam bam fight. We were both frazzled and angry, and he was waving the barrel of the Glock at me. I was utterly pissed and wanted to kill, or at least maim. I was about to go for his throat when I looked over toward the windows and saw a large, electric blue butterfly fly in and light on one of the roses. The sight was so lovely and unexpected that I forgot about strangling Hendrik and stared at the vase of flowers and the exotically colored insect. He saw the butterfly, too, and put the gun down on the table. It was a highly significant moment – you might even call it magical – and we gravitated toward each other and he put his arm around me. Later, after the butterfly had flown out the window, I agreed to consider a marriage in the near future.

Hendrik was not the only one who had been deceptive. Neither Bobby nor I told him about the robot-clone. We figured he had enough on his plate with Willem still in the hospital and the New Jersey duo lurking around town. I knew something was afoot because Hendrik was walking around with the Glock in a shoulder holster and having multiple conferences with Detective Gripsa.

One evening, Dries and his friend, the Viper, showed up at the house for a meeting. I was amused to see that the Viper actually looked like his namesake and moved with a slightly slithering gait. I offered the boys some Red Bull, but they turned me down. They had brought a four pack of Monster energy drink and a giant bag of chips and didn't need further refreshment. Hendrik took them to his study, and they were there for almost two hours.

The next day, Benno, Bobby's chief of staff, called and told me the robot was on the move. The clone's injuries from the beating were minor, a couple of broken ribs and a swollen face. He'd released himself from the hospital and gone back to the Marriott City Center where he spent the night. Now, like a typical tourist, he was on his way to the airport in a cab. Benno said the robot was registered at the Marriott under the name of Ashton Drecker, and that he was a US citizen from Dallas, Texas. He and the boys were trailing Drecker to the airport, and Benno wanted to know it they should detain him in the lobby before he went through the departures gate. He thought I might want to question the nasty little fucker. I told Benno to hold him. I'd be out on the next train to Schiphol. He told me to get off at the KLM terminal and that one of the boys would be waiting for me at the train stop.

On the way to the airport I thought about the information I wanted to get out of Drecker. First and foremost, I needed to know who he was working for. Whether he'd give out that information was a big question. If he was a real professional, we'd have to cut his balls off before he admitted to anything, and ball cutting wasn't possible in the KLM lobby.

I got off the train and was surprised to see Bobby standing back by the escalator, watching the passengers disembark. We caught sight of each other at the same time, our eyes locked, and I hurried towards him.

'I didn't expect to see you here. I thought you were in Rotterdam,' I said.

'It was only two nights. I got back this morning.'

We got on the escalator and he told me the robot was being held at a Starbucks in the lobby. Bobby laughed when he told me the robot was scared shitless and drinking a thirty-one-ounce Caramel Macchiato to soothe his nerves. When we got to the Starbucks, the Revata crew spotted us and got up off their chairs and went to another table. Bobby and I sat down and Drecker said: 'I'm innocent!'

Ashton Drecker no longer looked like a robot-clone; up close he was all too human. His face was bruised and swollen and he was wearing a neck brace. Still, I didn't have any pity for this bruised wreck of a man: 'Don't give me that bullshit; you were tracking me for weeks,' I said.

'I was tracking you because that was my job. I was told to follow you around and be very obvious about it. I was supposed to let you know you were being tailed and to scare the hell out of you.' He gave me a pleading look and took a big slug of his Caramel Macchiato. 'My plane takes off in an hour. I have to be on it!'

'Hey, no problem, man,' Bobby said, 'just tell us who you're working for and you can be on your way.'

'I was never told who the client was. My boss gave me the details and sent me on my way.'

'What's the name of your organization?' I asked.

'I work for Tin Badge Investigations out of Dallas, Texas. We mostly work on high-end divorce and custody problems, so I was happy to catch this case even though it was a weird one.'

'In what way was it weird?'

'Because they didn't want to punish you, they just wanted to scare you. In my work it's usually a situation where both parties are out for blood and nine times out of ten they end up destroying each other. This case was different in that it wasn't personal.'

'Give us the name of your client,' Bobby said. He gave Drecker a mean look and I could see the poor guy quake in his chair.

'I can't! I told you I can't,' Drecker wailed, 'The assignment was given me by one of our executives. It was an unusual job, but I didn't question it.'

'Who was the guy on top that gave you the order?' Bobby asked.

'I can't reveal that information,' Drecker said.

'That's OK,' I said, knowing that if I put Dries on the case, he could probably find the name of the executive and all his information in a couple of hours, 'we'll respect that.'

'Are you working with a couple of goons from the New Jersey mob?' Bobby asked.

Drecker was offended: 'I don't know what you're talking about. Our organization does not work with the mafia or any other gangsters. We are an elite organization of former FBI members.'

'Just checking,' Bobby said.

'Why don't you go to the departures area?' I said. 'We won't trouble you any further.'

Drecker grabbed his huge cup of Starbuck's and took off. I noticed that he didn't bother to look back because he was running towards the gate at a ferocious clip. Suddenly, I was sick of the whole scene: 'Come on, Bobby, let's get the fuck out of here and try to find a decent cup of honest coffee.'

'I'd settle for some ganja,' he said.

'We have to go into the city for that.'

'Maybe not, I know a place that has terrific coffee and some pretty good dope. It's not in the airport, but its close.

'That's fine by me. Let's go,' I said.

While we were having coffee and kush, Bobby mentioned he was playing a gig at a jazz club in the Leidseplein tonight, and said Hendrik and I should drop by. I was eager to go because I'd never seen Bobby perform live. When we got to the club I noticed the entrance fee was a hundred Euros a head, but Bobby had thoughtfully put our names on the guest list and we got in without paying. Even at that high price the club was crowded, and people were in an excited, almost ecstatic mood; they were expecting a great performance by a brilliant musician.

After we were seated at a small table in the rear, I noticed Madame Lillian and a handsome man about thirty years her junior at a table down front. Lillian was wearing a dress that was covered in red sequins and her raven hair was dressed in a lively bouffant. She looked very much like Joan Collins, and the people at the table next to us had spotted her and were thrilled that the fabulous Joan was in the house. I wanted to go down and talk to Madame Lillian, but the quartet, consisting of a bass player, two rhythm guitarists, and Bobby on lead, arrived on stage. The group all looked to be Roma and were dressed in dark suits. The young maestro was done up like a real Andalusian in a black suit of an entirely different cut and style than the one he'd worn to the party. The suit was austere, almost priestly, and with it he wore a black shirt buttoned all the way to his neck. With his hair slicked back and tied in a matador's pigtail he exuded *duende*, that untranslatable quality so prized by Spanish musicians, artists, and bullfighters. For a moment I thought we had slipped into a flamenco concert by mistake.

When the music started it was definitely not flamenco, but swinging Roma jazz, heavy on mathematical structure and played at an unbelievable rate of speed. The Rhythm guitarists were strumming so fast their hands were blurs of light, and Bobby was throwing out ornaments faster than the ears could absorb them. It was a pyramid of sound with the bass holding firm on the bottom, the rhythm guitars in the middle, and the lead flying so high on top that it sounded like it had got loose of the earth's atmosphere and was throwing notes back from the stars. At precisely the correct moment they all stopped cold and let the silence take over.

I don't think anyone in the crowd applauded, they were stunned by the creation of a jazz masterwork and probably didn't know they had hands to clap with. The musicians seemed to be exhausted, the Rhythm guitarists slumped in their chairs as if they had passed out, and the bass player drank two bottles of beer in rapid succession. Bobby got up from his chair and did something with his hands. I believe he was just shaking them out, but the crowd misinterpreted his gesture perhaps thinking he was beckoning them to come to him and they surged for the stage. The mob was pushed back by a combination of house security and Bobby's Roma crew. The professionals were none-too-gentle with the out-of-control fans, and somebody went down and was trampled on.

Bobby ignored the fracas in front of him, and an assistant handed him another guitar. While he made some adjustments to the guitar, I looked across the room to Madame Lillian's table. She and her younger companion were in full party mode, festively consuming a bottle of Dom Perignon and chatting gaily away. At the table directly behind them, two burly tourists in brightly colored leisure suits were sipping glasses of whiskey and observing the carefree revelers in front of them.

I turned to Hendrik: 'Did you notice that Madame Lillian is in the house?'

'No, where is she?'

'She's down front with a much younger man.'

Hendrik laughed, 'That woman always was a *femme fatale* and even at her advanced age she's still pulling the men.'

While Hendrik was having his little chuckle, Bobby stepped to the mike and said: 'This one's for Venessa.'

That statement caught Hendrik's attention and he sat up straight in his chair with his ears perked while Bobby launched into an ultra-smooth and deeply felt ballad that went from the heaven of romantic love to the hell of a broken heart in about five minutes time. The music was so tender and passionate that even Hendrik became all misty eyed and sentimental. Half-way through the song he reached for my hand and held it.

The men seated behind Madame Lillian were the only ones who didn't seem affected by the dramatic musical exposition of love and loss. When the song ended there was an explosion of sound as the audience went nuts with the hand clapping.

'It sounds like he really loves her,' Hendrik commented.

'Oh, he does, darling, and you'll just have to accept it. They're seeing each other again and Bobby's off the smack. I have no doubt we can attribute that to Venessa and her presence in his life.'

'You can't expect me to approve! My daughter will never have a normal life if she sticks with Bobby.'

'Do you think she's had a normal life with you?' I said, stating the obvious. 'Just leave those two alone and let them live in peace without your interference.'

'He's married and the father of two kids!' Hendrik sounded like some shocked old codger who'd never heard of an adulterous relationship.

'That's a tribal thing and none of your business. The Revata work things out differently than we do.'

'And how do you know all this, Martel? Hendrik glared at me. The tender moment when he held my hand was long gone.

'I know because I've made friends with both Bobby and Venessa. I've gained their confidence and trust because I don't pass judgment on them. You ought to try it sometime, maybe you'd find out that they are both great human beings who deserve a little happiness.'

Hendrik's mouth was agape. For once in his life he didn't know what to say, which was fortunate because Bobby and his mates started up with the virtuoso part of the program where they played jazz standards faster than they'd ever been played before. Even with the dazzling technique, the music was not just a shallow display of finesse. There was always a spirited and definite Roma feeling at the center of each song. At the end of the set the band left the stage, and even though the applause was loud and raucous, they did not come back for an encore.

Hendrik was still brooding over the dressing down I'd given him about Bobby and Venessa and said he wanted to leave.

'Let's go speak to Madame Lillian for a moment,' I said.

'Why not,' Hendrik was suddenly amiable. 'I always enjoy a chat with the old girl."

He led the way down to the front table, and I noticed the heads of the two tourists turn towards him when he walked by. The men seemed to be interested in Hendrik. They were looking him up and down and whispering to each other. I had to assume they were the gangsters from New Jersey who had put Willem in the hospital.

Madame Lillian was pleased to see us and introduced us to her escort, a dog trainer named Piet. I asked after Rowley, and Lillian eagerly confided that he was entertaining some of his old comrades from the Canine Corps this evening. Piet had brought over three dogs from the pack to keep Rowley company while the humans went out. I smiled at Piet; he was a cute blond with a strong body that had probably been developed by running dogs for hours on end.

'Do you ever watch Cesar Millan on TV?' I asked.

'Oh yes,' Piet beamed back at me, 'the Canine Corps is devoted to Cesar and his theories. Last year he came by and spoke with us. He's such an inspiring mentor.'

'I play Cesar tapes for Rowley,' Lillian cut in, 'He loves the activities of the dog pack, and I think he's quite taken with Cesar's number one dog, Daddy. Frankly, I had a poor impression of Pit Bulls until I met Daddy on TV. That dog is a veritable saint.'

'Daddy passed on last year,' Piet said sadly, then he brightened, 'but Junior is being groomed to take his place.'

Hendrik looked bewildered, I guess he'd never caught 'The Dog Whisperer' on the National Geographic channel. I attempted to explain: 'Cesar's a dog psychologist who runs a doggie rehabilitation center in California. He specializes in hard cases.'

Hendrik nodded, but I could see his attention was elsewhere. He was looking suspiciously at the guys at the next table.

Piet was still going on about the dogs: 'Right now, we've got two rehabilitated Pit Bulls and a Mastiff out at Lillian's place,' he said. That sounded like overkill to me. Those dogs, rehabilitated or not, would surely tear the hell out of any intruder.

Hendrik wasn't interested in the dog talk, he stood up and walked over to the next table. He pulled up a chair and sat down without being invited. The thugs stared at him wide-eyed while he pulled out his Glock and set it down on the table in front of him. There was some discussion, and then passports were provided and slid across the table towards Hendrik. He inspected the passports, nodded, and slid them back. The thugs stood up and hurried out of the club.

I quickly excused myself and ran to Hendrik's side. 'It was a false alarm,' he said. 'They may have looked like goons but they're legitimate tourists from Las Vegas.'

'They really gave you the once over when you walked by.'

'They were looking at my suit. They're thinking of doing business in the Netherlands and know they have to upgrade their image.'

'Is that for fucking real, Hendrik?'

'Yes,' he smiled, 'just as real as those fucking dogs and that trainer you guys are so excited about.'

'You should watch Cesar sometime. You could learn a lot. He's a master psychologist right up there with Jung and Adler.'

Hendrik laughed, he thought I was joking, but I meant every word. He put his hand on my back between my shoulder blades and started to steer me out of the club.

'Shouldn't we stick around and wait for Bobby to come out front?' I asked.

'He never comes out at half-time. He doesn't do the meet and greet. He has to stay backstage and keep his concentration.'

'Have you noticed he's not showing his Bodhisattva side so much anymore? He seems more like a regular human these days.'

'I haven't been around him that much lately. You know how he avoids me. I don't think I've seen him since the night of the party, but now that you mention it, he didn't seem so ethereal and other worldly when he was on stage. I think he's gained a little weight.'

'I think so too. You should have seen him gobbling the pastries at Madame Lillian's.'

'Bobby was at Madame Lillian's with you and Venessa? You didn't tell me that.' He sounded surprised and vaguely aggrieved.

'It didn't seem important at the time.'

'I suppose it wasn't,' he admitted. By this time we were out on the street. We walked all the way home to the Herengracht without any followers.

I asked Dries to check out Tin Badge Investigations in Dallas. He said he was up to his ears in the Greylander project but would do his best to fit me in. He called several days later, when I was down at the shop researching the provenance of a nineteenth century landscape that had just come in from Poland. Dries said he had information for me but couldn't divulge it over the phone and asked if I would come out to his Dad's place to meet with him. I was hoping we could meet in Centraal, but he said no, he was too involved in business to leave his room.

The provenance on the Polish painting was giving me a headache, and I decided to get some fresh air and bike out to see Dries. The Willem branch of the Van der Saar family lived out back of Central Station on a recently developed piece of land that was called Java Island. You had to bike over a sharply articulated bridge to get to the Island, and then you were in a residential area of crazy, post-modern Dutch architecture. Willem and Dries lived on the top floor of a lopsided building that seemed to be falling into the harbor. It took a moment to realize the building was not actually collapsing and that it was supposed to look that way. Very dramatic, I thought, as I locked up my bike.

I entered the building but couldn't find an elevator, so I walked up seven flights of stairs to the top floor. I was surprised when Willem answered the door. He looked to be in pretty good shape considering the beating he'd taken. His skin tone was back to normal and the bruising on his face had faded, it was only the loss of his golden hair that continued to shock. Still, he was sort of cute as a baldy; he looked sensitive and wide-eyed, rather than cruel and brutal like a neo-Nazi.

'I thought you'd be resting,' I said.

'I'm getting bored with the recovery period. I'll be at the shop tomorrow.'

'That's good, because your assistants are unable to function without you. They walk around looking forlorn and sad, not even Hendrik can get them to do any work.'

He smiled, and I could tell that he was pleased to be considered indispensable.

'Surely you exaggerate,' he said.

'You won't be smiling when you see the workload.'

I followed Willem into a large room whose walls were hung with exotic pictures done in an updated and slightly fantastic Gauguin mode. The paintings were of nude women posed in dynamic scenes of idealized nature. There was a lithesome blonde lounging on top of a mountain; a brunette frolicking in a field of wild flowers; an auburn haired goddess on her knees in foliage; and finally, an African woman surrounded by the vines and tendrils of the jungle.

'Jesus, Willem, these are amazing! You really ought to exhibit them.' I was serious: even though the work carried a faint whiff of Gauguin, the pictures were fresh and unique.

'I don't think so Martel. They are open to interpretation and the politically correct crowd will consider them sexist.'

'That's ridiculous and you know it!'

'I had a small party while you and Hendrik were in Ghent, and some of the guests, particularly the women, expressed their shock and dismay on seeing the work. One of the women called me a misogynist and left. She couldn't stand being in the same room with my paintings.'

'I think you're hanging with the wrong people, bro.'

'You may be right, but the truth is, I don't want the hassle and notoriety of exhibiting.'

I took his point: the Old Master business may be unsavoury, but the Contemporary Art scene is a total cesspool. 'Alright, darling, have it your way. It is possible that you're better off toiling in obscurity.'

Willem nodded his bald head in agreement and said: 'Dries is in his room. Don't be shocked when you go inside, it's a mess, but at least he doesn't have any nuclear waste hidden away.'

'That's reassuring,' I said. By this time we were walking down a long hall toward a door at the very end. There was a poster on the door, and as I got closer I saw it was a publicity still of Bobby Janacek playing an acoustic guitar. Bobby was doing the full Rimbaud, and it was an image for the ages. I wondered where Dries had picked it up and if the posters were still available. I would have liked one for my own.

We were at the door and Willem gave it a light tap right on Bobby's nose: 'Have Dries make you a cappuccino while you're in there. He makes excellent coffee, and if he's in a good mood he'll foam a little heart on the top.'

Dries opened the door a crack. 'Hello, Martel,' he said, and opened the door just wide enough for me to squeeze in.

'Talk to you later, Dad' he said, before closing the door in his father's face.

The room was pretty much as expected: the usual stacks of Japanese comics halfway to the ceiling, empty ramen containers scattered at random, cans of Red Bull and Monster Energy drink made into towers and pyramids like old time grocery store displays, and then of course there was the digital equipment. Some of the electronics were state of the art, but a lot of them looked homemade. Frankly, I couldn't identify anything but the laptops. Over in the corner was an Espresso bar with a cute, blue, espresso machine and below that a tiny refrigerator. The place wasn't exactly filthy, just messy, and so dusty that I started to sneeze.

Dries motioned me to sit down in a worn, red leather swivel chair with a rip across the seat. 'I'll make some coffee,' he said.

'Good, I could use some. Your Dad says you make great coffee.'

His wan little face broke into a bright and warming smile. Like most humans, Dries reacted well to praise. He turned toward the coffee bar and gave himself up to the ritual of the espresso: grinding and measuring beans, pouring water, steaming milk, and finally bringing the finished product to me in a sweet, little cup and saucer of Italian design. When I looked down into my cup I saw the pretty swirl of a heart etched in foam on top of the coffee.

'You're a real pro, Dries. This is beautiful.'

'Taste it,' he said. 'The beans are from Trieste, they make the best roast in the world. I want to go to Trieste. Aside from the coffee, the town has a fantastic name.'

I added a cube of sugar and stirred carefully, but the little heart broke anyway. I took a sip and savored the taste: 'It's perfect,' I said.

'Mine may be good, but the coffee is better in Trieste.' He seemed to have the ancient city on the brain.

'Did you know you can take the train from Venice to Trieste?' I asked. 'I almost went there one time, but the train wasn't due for an hour, and the people I was with couldn't find the time to wait, so we went to Padua instead.'

'Too bad you didn't wait for the train. You should have let those wankers go off to Padua without you.'

'They were friends, and I was outvoted.'

By this time Dries was sipping a cappuccino of his own. He was looking serious, the small talk and the refreshments were over, and he was getting ready to talk business. He put his cup on his desk and handed me a printout of several pages: 'That's all the information you'll need, Martel. The guy you want at Tin Star Investigations is the CEO, William Baron. He also goes by the name of Wild Bill Baron which relates back to his service in the FBI where he was severely reprimanded for whoring, drug taking, and heavy drinking. That information doesn't relate to your inquiry, but I thought you'd like to know. You can find the full details of Wild Bill's indiscretions in the document.'

'You're being very thorough, darling. I like that.'

'Wild Bill was contacted by Brendan Kennedy, a senior vice president of marketing at Greylander International. He was the man who requested the tail on you. There's nothing colorful about this Kennedy dude, he's strictly a company man.

'The digital security at Greylander International is pretty weak, I was able to look at both company and personal emails.

Right after Preston Greylander's death, Kennedy had some conversations with other senior staff. A lot of these guys didn't care much for Preston – apparently they thought he was a demented sadist who was ruining the company with his genocidal policies. According to Kennedy, Greylander had put his foot in it big time. He'd backed a war in Equatorial Africa that was so brutal it shocked even the French and the Belgians. Apparently, the UN was looking into the conflict and they were getting very close to exposing Greylander. His death was welcomed by most of the staff. '

'So why did they put a tail on me?'

'I couldn't get much detail on that. They knew Greylander was murdered by a paraplegic named Terry Volkov. Apparently, Volkov shot Greylander and then turned the gun on himself. It could have been a crime of passion – some of the executives thought the two men were lovers, or it could have been something else. The boys at Greylander International found out you were a longtime friend of Volkov's and that you were working with Preston on his art collection, so they thought you might be playing both sides of the fence.'

'So what if I was involved? They should have been grateful I helped get rid of Preston. Why did they put a tail on me?'

Dries shrugged: 'Even though they were against Greylander's policies, they're still corporate pigs. They were playing a little game, trying to scare the hell out of you. If this cowboy from Tin Star found out anything incriminating, they were going to send a professional assassin to finish you off.'

He finished his coffee and brought out an electronic cigarette. 'Do you want one? They're sort of fun.'

'Yes, if you've got an extra around.'

'I keep a whole box in the drawer. Nicotine to the brain helps me concentrate. It's good with caffeine.' He handed me a small plastic case that contained one cigarette. 'So, were you involved in the murder?' he asked.

'Maybe a little bit. I was helping Preston get the Rembrandt cleaned, and I invited him to a party at the house where he was killed.'

I didn't want to meet Dries eyes so I started struggling with the plastic case. When I finally got the case open, I extracted the cigarette and took a hit. It tasted of chemicals and plastic, but there was nicotine in it. You could feel the jolt go straight to your head. 'This is vile,' I said, taking another puff.

'They're made in China by a subsidiary of Greylander International. I checked it out.'

'Well, isn't that just perfect,' I said.

Dries actually grinned: 'Those fuckers are everywhere,' he said.

'So how's it going with the Rembrandt project?' I asked. 'Are you getting any information?'

'Yes, we're almost there. The New Jersey dudes were hired by somebody in Switzerland. It's one of the Swiss Greylanders, and they want their painting back. They don't give a shit about who killed Preston, they just want the artwork. Whoever it is has better security than the corporation, but I think we'll have a name in twenty-four hours.'

'I know Hendrik handed the fake off to Madame Pookie Greylander, but she can't be the one taking action, she's supposed to be a hundred years old.'

'I wouldn't sell her short, Martel. She's probably got all those Swiss doctors shooting her up with drugs and hormones. Maybe her brain is still intact.'

'That is a thought, darling,' I said, standing up and preparing to leave. 'Oh, Dries, before I go, tell me where did you get that fantastic poster of Bobby you've got tacked up on your door?'

'I got it off the Internet. I can send you one if you like.'

'That will be great. I can pay you now.'

Dries laughed: 'That won't be necessary. I'll have it sent to the shop under a phony name like Koffe Trieste. Be on the lookout.'

'Koffe Trieste, that's great!'

Dries stopped laughing and his face went still and solemn: 'Is Bobby really my cousin? He doesn't act at all like Hendrik.'

'He's your cousin alright. They did the DNA test. You guys are brothers in blood. You met him at the hospital the other day. How did you get along?'

'Great! He's really a fantastic dude. Even though he looks like uncle Hendrik, he takes after his gypsy side. He's not at all like the Van der Saars. He's much warmer and more open. I'm meeting him and Venessa at The Bald Hyena tomorrow night. He said I could bring the Viper along if I wanted.'

'Well you guys have fun.' I picked up the packet of papers Dries had prepared for me and stuffed them into my purse. He walked me to the door and opened it. The sweet little kid looked so young, untouched, and defenseless, that I couldn't resist and kissed his cheek. He must have been getting used to me because he didn't pull away. 'Thanks for everything, darling,' I said.

Because of the pressure from the Greylander's Hendrik and I had been having nasty little tiffs and senseless arguments for several days. They were nothing special, just the usual struggle for dominance, plus, he was sore because I had a good relationship with Bobby and Venessa. He was resentful because he'd been fighting against their romantic entanglement for years, and now I was telling him to accept it. The tension between us made life even more difficult and I thought it was time we finally made peace. So, just like a regular housewife, I decided to produce one of his favorite meals and then lure him off to the sack for an evening of hot sex.

Making the food wasn't a problem; Hendrik was a lover of fresh and simple cuisine and I could prepare whatever fish looked best at the market, steam some vegetables, and provide a salad of small leafy greens, with French bread and later a plate of cheese. I hoped to find some pears so I could poach them in red wine for dessert.

On the day of the dinner I got up early and went down to the fish market. I found a nice medium-sized turbot, and the fishmonger trimmed and fileted it for me. By the time he got done, it was super clean and I hurried home and put the lovely flat fish on ice.

I was working pretty much full time down at the shop, filling in wherever I was needed, and after the fish had been carefully stored in the refrigerator, I hurried off to put in my morning hours. I worked a half day and left at lunch to do the rest of the shopping. I'd always enjoyed shopping for food, and the colorful markets of Amsterdam made the task even more pleasurable. They yielded up wonderful produce and food stuffs and I got what I needed to prepare the meal: spinach, mushrooms, fresh butter, jasmine rice, pears, bread, and two kinds of cheese. Although Dutch cheeses are world famous, neither Hendrik nor I really cared for them, so I found a couple of French imports that looked suitably ripe and well kept.

After I returned home with the groceries, I poured dry vermouth on the rocks and added a twist of lemon. Sipping the herbal aperitif made me feel very Julia Child, and I decided to poach the fish using one of her methods, an old-fashioned *court bouillon*. The name sounds daunting, but it's easy to make, you just throw some herbs, lemon, and veg into salted water and boil it up.

After I got the *court bouillon* going, I decided to make the dessert because it had to be cooked on the stove top and left to cool. First I opened a bottle of fruity red and poured it into a big pot adding a stick of cinnamon, a pinch of cardamom a cup of sugar, the juice of one orange, and two cloves. Then I boiled the wine mixture and let it simmer while I peeled the pears, leaving them whole with the stems attached, and placed them in the pot. I adjusted the heat and cooked the whole lot for thirty minutes or so, until the pears had turned a glorious red color and the sauce was thick and spicy. That was the major chore, everything else on the menu was dead easy to prepare.

By this time it was four thirty, and Hendrik wasn't due in until seven, so I poured myself another vermouth and went up to my room. I didn't feel like listening to music or reading, and I certainly wasn't going to let my mind dwell on the Greylander affair so I watched a famous French movie about two lesbians who kept jumping on top of each other and then beating each other up. That really didn't do it for me, so I switched off the TV and took a short nap. After fifteen minutes in a brief and refreshing semi-slumber, I rolled off the bed and went for a shower. Because I was cooking, I didn't bother to present myself in a sexy gown, but rather slipped into jeans, put clogs on my feet, and topped it off with a loose, black linen shirt. The look was appealingly androgynous, but it became female and seductive when I worked it with a jade bracelet and a silver chain with a turquoise pendant. Feeling confident and ready for action, I went downstairs and attacked the vegetables. By the time Hendrik arrived, I had everything organized and prepared except for the fish. He was surprised to see me busy in the kitchen because I seldom cooked. On occasion, I made very nice omelets and once I roasted a chicken with tarragon, butter, and lemon, but we usually ate food from the Dutch equivalent of a deli, or scavenged snacks from the pantry and refrigerator. If we wanted more elaborate food we went for a meal at a restaurant.

'What a nice surprise,' he said, moving towards me and taking me in his arms. He buried his face in my neck: 'You smell of herbs and onion.'

'It's not my usual perfume, but I hope you like it.'

'Not on a daily basis, but at the moment it's quite exciting.' He let go of me and washed his hands in the sink.

'We're having vermouth on the rocks for an aperitif and there are Spanish almonds for the appetizer. Sit down and I'll pour you a glass.'

He sat down and took a handful of almonds from the bowl. I could tell he was pleased that I had gone to the effort of creating a meal just for him, and I thought that maybe I should do it more often. I made a long twist of lemon to put in his glass of vermouth and gave it to him. He took a sip: 'This is much more civilized than a shot of jenever and a chaser of beer.'

'How often do you have that before dinner?'

'Not too often, now that you mention it,' he took another sip. 'This vermouth is good, very herbal, what's it called?'

'It's nothing special, just plain old Noilly Prat, and it is good.'

'I had no idea,' he said, and took another sip.

I turned my back on Hendrik and started pouring the court bouillon into a large, slightly antique fish pan that I'd found in the back of the pantry. Hendrik was watching intently: 'You know, Martel, I haven't seen that pan in use since I was a kid. We had a wonderful cook called Hannah and she used to poach the fish in it.'

'You remember the pan?' That was weird. Why would a child remember a cooking pan?

'Indeed I do. That lady made some great meals for us. She let Willem and me hang around the kitchen and watch her cook. Naturally, she fed us a lot of treats.'

'It sounds like a nice time.'

'It was, until the tabloids started investigating the Van der Saars and calling us war criminals. When Hannah found out about our Nazi connection she went ballistic. Her father was from Berlin and had opposed the Hitler regime. He was thrown into one of the camps and perished there. She was an infant when her father was taken away, but Hannah had not forgotten him. She told Willem and me that she had to leave us. Hannah didn't blame us, or our parents, for her father's death, but she was a woman of principle and she could not work for a family who collaborated with the Nazis. When she left our employ, Willem and I were shattered.'

'I'm so sorry, Hendrik. The whole episode must have been terribly painful.'

'Yes, *schatje*, the pain went deep and the guilt has carried on through the generations.'

I looked at the beat-up old pan and was sorry I'd brought it out. Now the wonderful dinner I'd planned might be spoiled by Hendrik's melancholy feelings, but he seemed to perk up when I showed him the poached pears we were going to have for dessert. He wanted to taste the thick syrup the pears had been cooked in, and I gave him a spoon and let him have a small sample of the sweet, candy-like sauce.

'That's really good, I can't wait for dessert. Will you serve the pears with whipped cream?'

'That's right, darling, but only a daub. The pears don't look right when they're smothered in whipped cream.'

The *court bouillon* was on the boil and I reduced it to a simmer and gently placed the turbot in the pan. It only took three minutes to cook the filets and as I began plating the fish and the vegetables I asked Hendrik to open the bottle of white burgundy that was chilling in the refrigerator. When he picked up the bottle and read the label he said: 'I'm impressed. You're really going all out in the wine department.'

'You'll be even more impressed when you sit down and eat this dinner.'

He sat down and looked at his plate: 'It looks beautiful and smells delicious. What kind of sauce is this?'

'It's just lemon and butter. I like to keep things simple, anything heavier would ruin the turbot.'

Hendrik began to taste his food: 'This is fabulous, Martel. The fish and the vegetables are perfectly cooked. Why didn't you cook for me before?'

'I have. I've made lots of omelets, and once I made a superb roast chicken, but I usually don't have time. It took hours of shopping and prep just to put this simple meal together.'

He nodded blankly, but I could tell he didn't really grasp what I was talking about. He may have hung around in the kitchen when he was a child, but he really didn't know much about food, except how to order it in a restaurant.

I stuck my nose in my glass of burgundy and then took a sip. The wine was exceptional, but it didn't overwhelm the turbot.

Hendrik gave me a sweet look from across the table: 'Thanks, Martel, this is the best it's been in a long time.'

I knew he wasn't just talking about the dinner.

I was drifting to the top when the phone rang. Hendrik was inside me, it felt like he was a bone-fish moving upstream. 'I have to answer,' he said, and reached for his phone.

'Oh, no,' I whispered, flexing my muscles and hanging on.

'Yes, Nikki, what do you want?' There was silence in the room while he listened to the detective. I could feel him go soft and I relaxed and let him slide out. 'I'll be right there.' He moved away from me and stood up.

'What's going on? Where are you going?'

'Out to the Noord. There's a problem at Madame Lillian's.'

'What kind of problem? Is it about the picture?'

'Two burglars tried to get in and Rowley cornered them in the garden. Nikki says the dog defended his territory and left the intruders bleeding. He and Piet are out there now. I have to go.'

'Not without me you won't!' I was out of the bed and into my jeans before he could object.

'Nikki won't like it if you come along. He could get in a lot of trouble if this leaks out. This is not an official investigation. He's doing me a favor.'

'You know damn well I can keep my mouth shut. Explain that to Detective Gripsa.'

'He'll think I'm pussy whipped.' Hendrik laughed, but I could tell he was concerned about what his buddy the cop would say when I showed up at the crime scene.

I kissed Hendrik's cheek, then reached down and tweaked his balls: 'No one would ever call you pussy whipped, darling. You're much too strong and masculine.'

'Yeah, right,' he slapped my hand away and reached for a pair of pants and a black sweater.

'How are we going to get to the Noord? It's eleven o'clock; the ferries have probably stopped running.'

'Jesus, Martel, stop talking like a tourist. There's a fucking tunnel that goes under the river. We can drive right over there.'

'The last I knew we didn't have a car. We'll have to go to the shop and pick up the van.'

'No, we won't, I have Willem's Fiat. He can't drive because of the head injury, so he let me borrow it. It's so small I was able to park it out front.'

'Well aside from the fact that somebody's trying to steal the Rembrandt, and that our love making was seriously interrupted, this is working out perfectly.'

'I would have preferred to stay in bed with you and finish the conversation.'

'Making conversation? That's a nice way to put it.'

Hendrik grabbed my elbow and said: 'We can discuss it in the car. Come on, Martel we have to get out of here.'

The lights were on at Madame Lillian's and she greeted us at the door. 'We've had a little excitement tonight. Two burglars tried to jump over the garden wall, but Rowley cornered them and gave them a couple of bites.'

I looked around, but the dog was nowhere in sight: 'Where's Rowley now?'

'He's out in the kitchen devouring a bone. I thought he needed a treat after all that strenuous work.'

"Where are Nikki and Piet?' Hendrik asked.

'They're in the spare bedroom with the burglars. They had to give them quite a lot of first aid and now they're trying to question them.' She nodded to Hendrik: 'It's down the hall and to your left.'

He took off, but I decided to stay behind with Madame Lillian.

'Come to the kitchen with me, dear,' she said. 'You can congratulate our hero and I'll make you a cup of tea.'

Rowley was lying on a rug in front of the stove chomping on a huge bone that was covered in raw meat. He had blood on his whiskers; whether it was from the bone or the burglars was unclear. Lillian walked around him and put the kettle on to boil.

'I think I'll have a tot of rum. Would you like one too?' she asked.

'No thanks, tea will be fine.' I would have liked a drink, but once again I felt it was necessary to keep my wits about me.

'I need something to settle my nerves after all the excitement. I was terribly concerned about Rowley.'

'He looks like he won the fight. After he gets done with that bone you're going to have to wash his muzzle.'

'Yes, he did get rather mussed up in the fracas,' she said, thus confirming the fact that it was human blood on his whiskers. Lillian poured me a cup of tea and we sat at the kitchen table staring at Rowley who was deep into his bone and paying us no attention.

'Did you get a good look at the burglars?'

'Not really, they had balaclavas over their heads and were wearing dark clothes. Piet has been staying with me, he was sleeping, but he woke up when he heard Rowley barking and growling. He went out and broke up the fight or Rowley would have killed the intruders.'

'It was lucky Piet was staying overnight,' I said, wondering just what the relationship between Madame Lillian and the dog handler actually was.

'Yes, wasn't it,' she simpered, 'I called Nikki immediately and he came rushing over to help.'

'What do you think the burglars were after?'

'I believe it was Nikki's new painting. I'm afraid he was so concerned when he saw what happened that he let slip the painting was a real Rembrandt and not a facsimile.'

'He must have been very upset.'

'My son is devoted to me, and when he realized I might have been harmed because of that painting, he told me the whole story and begged my forgiveness.'

'Did you forgive him?'

'Of course, if it wasn't for the picture I never would have met Piet and Rowley. They have become very dear to me. Those two have brought new life to me and I am grateful. When Piet tires of me, I am keeping the dog.'

'You are very wise, Madame Lillian.'

'For god's sake, Martel, please stop with the Madame and just call me Lillian. I think we're on familiar enough terms. I'm just giving you a preview of how you're going to end up. Hopefully, you'll be lucky enough to have a house and a dog, because your boyfriend is nothing but a low life skirt chaser and a high class criminal. I wouldn't count on him to stick around.'

'He wants to get married.'

Lillian looked shocked: 'This is indeed big news! Hendrik has never considered marriage since the jailhouse coupling that resulted in darling Venessa. You must have very special talents to keep him interested.'

'I'm a good cook,' I smiled. 'But, seriously, how do you know Hendrik so well?'

'Nikki and the Van der Saar boys were schoolmates and great friends. The atmosphere at my house was much less formal than the one at the Van der Saar home, so the boys congregated here. Willem was always the sweet one, but Hendrik was wicked and headstrong, he kept leading Nikki astray. Thankfully, Nikki got out of Hendrik's orbit and went to work with the cops. Unfortunately, he is still susceptible to the Van der Saar influence, as you can see by the mess we're in now.'

Lillian would have continued her vilification of Hendrik, but she was interrupted by a loud scream coming from down the hall. Rowley perked up his ears when he heard that scream.

'My god, are they torturing somebody?' I exclaimed.

'I suppose they are trying to extract information from one of the burglars.'

'Christ, I thought they only did that at Guantanamo and Abu Girab. You Dutch people are civilized. You're not supposed to be pulling this kind of stuff.'

'At one time we had a great empire. How do you think we conquered Indonesia and colonized South Africa?'

Another scream came ratcheting through the air. This time Rowley dropped his bone and stood up. It looked like he was getting ready for action. I stood up too: 'I'm going in there,' I said. I wasn't the kind of person who could sit calmly in the kitchen and do nothing while somebody, no matter how reprehensible, was being tortured down the hall. I was going in there and I was going to break it up.

'I wouldn't do that, Martel. You might see something you won't be able to forget.'

'I'll take my chances,' I said, and ran off down the hall. Rowley did not follow me, he decided to stay in the kitchen with Lillian and his bone.

The door was shut, but it wasn't locked and I walked in. Nikki saw me first and told me to get out. Hendrik turned and stared, his face was blank and he didn't say a word. The two burglars were laid out on a double bed and Piet, stripped to the waist, was working them over with an electronic wand.

I paid no attention to Nikki, but addressed myself to Piet: 'Did you ever live in South Africa?'

Piet lifted the wand from one of the burglar's feet: 'I'm originally from Cape Town. How did you know?'

'By the way you handle the torture instrument; you have a definite South African flair.'

He didn't know if I was putting him on or giving him a compliment: 'Thank you, Madame,' he said.

'I don't think you're getting anywhere with these guys so why don't you let me take over? I'm a CIA operative and I'd like to try out a couple of new techniques. I guarantee I can make them talk.'

Piet glanced over at Nikki who was sitting there with his mouth wide open. The cop was so startled by my aggressive takeover of the torture scene that he seemed unable to make a decision. Fortunately, Hendrik had come back to life and was willing to back me up. He spoke to Piet: 'Let my fiancée give it a try. Go out and have Lillian pour you a drink. Come back when you're rested.'

The dog trainer was still looking at Nikki. His boss finally nodded in the affirmative, and when he got the nod, he laid down his wand and took off for the kitchen. I went over to the double bed to check on the captives. They still had their pants on, so Piet had not yet got to their genitals, which was a relief. The balaclavas had been removed, and I saw the handsome faces of two Italian American bravos of southern Italian descent. They were young men and their eyes were full of tears. I almost felt bad for them.

'Hey, don't worry,' I said, 'I'm not really from the CIA. I'm an art dealer from New York City. Are you the guys that broke into the Van der Saar gallery and roughed up one of the owners?'

The boys looked chagrined, and one of them started to explain: 'That was an accident: we gave the guy a shove to get him moving and he fell and hit his head on a desk and knocked himself out.'

It was an unlikely story, but I let it pass. Hendrik was not so accepting. I could see his hands clenching and unclenching. He was giving off major bad vibes, like he wanted to avenge his brother and smash the shit out of the gangsters.

The second burglar picked up on Hendrik's antagonism and attempted to sound more accommodating: 'We're in Amsterdam on a simple job. We're looking for something that belongs to a friend of a friend. We're here to recover it and return it to the owner.'

'Can you give me a little more detail, like who you're working for?'

'Sure,' the first one said, 'everybody knows we're part of Sally D's crew out of Hoboken. This job is a favor for Sally's dad, the old Capo. Talk about big balls, the old dude is ninety-seven years old and he still wants to keep his girlfriend happy. She's some rich bitch who lives over in Switzerland, and she claims that these dudes,' he pointed to Hendrik and Nikki, 'stole her fucking Rembrandt, and she wants it back.'

'How did you find out it was in the Noord?'

'We put in some bribes down at the cop shop. An officer in the Canine Corps gave us an earful. He was plenty suspicious about the South African dude. There's trouble in the corps because one of their top dogs was taken off duty and the trainer, this scumbag Piet, went with him. Down at the cop shop they think Detective Gripsa ordered it. We came out here to investigate.'

'Do you have pictures of the painting you're looking for?

'Sure,' burglar number one said, 'we got it on our phones, but this crazy fucker took them away.' He glared at the detective.

'The pictures are on the phones,' Nikki confirmed rather grudgingly. I guess he didn't like the fact that I was getting information out of these young Mafiosi without torturing them.

'So, did you happen to get the name of the old man's girlfriend?'

'Yeah, she has a weird name that has something to do with shit. I think it was Poopie or Pookie. The old capo is crazy about her. He said they met at a charity ball in Vienna.'

'I'm afraid she's not getting the picture back,' I said.

'That's OK, this isn't top priority for us. Sally D won't mind; he thinks his old man is senile and he doesn't like him running around with Poopie.'

I turned to Nikki: 'I think we have all the information we need. Why don't you give these guys their phones back and let them go.'

Nikki struggled to save face: 'They can go, but I'm keeping the phones.'

I started to loosen the bonds on the prisoners: 'Do you need to go to the hospital?'

'We never travel without antibiotics and painkillers, so we're good on that end, but if that fucking dog is rabid, we may have to go to the ER.'

'He's a police employee, naturally he has health care and all his shots have been provided for,' Nikki said.

'That means he doesn't have rabies and you're good to go,' I said.

The two boys stood up, and one of them said: 'Lady, we don't know where you came from, but you probably saved our lives. We owe you one. If you ever need help just call Sally Delmonico's restaurant in Hoboken, and ask for Johnny A. or Joey T.'

'I'll keep that in mind.'

The two burglars walked slowly towards the door. You could tell they were hurting because of their tentative movements and dragging steps. They looked to be in their late twenties, but they moved like arthritic old men. When Johnny and Joey finally made it out the door I turned to Hendrik: 'I'm really tired, darling, do you think we could leave now?'

'I don't see why not,' he glanced at Nikki, 'We can go over this tomorrow.'

Nikki glared at him: 'Yes, and tomorrow you can get that fucking painting out of here. You're going to have to settle with that old bag in Switzerland on your own. I put my mother at risk because of you and your picture. Those two bums could have iced her.'

'Get off it, Nikki, they're very sweet boys. They wouldn't have hurt a hair on Lillian's head.' I said.

'I don't need to listen to any more of your lip, Martel. This is between me and Hendrik.'

'Sorry, Nikki,' I said contritely. I had really put my foot in it with the detective, he and Hendrik had been friends since childhood and now he saw me as a meddling bitch.

Hendrik intervened: 'You have my word the picture will be out of here tomorrow. We can discuss the rest of it over cocktails and dinner tomorrow evening. Drop by the Herengracht around eight. Martel will cook for us. She's makes a fantastic roast chicken.'

With that bombshell, Hendrik took my arm and we walked out of the spare bedroom, down the hall, and into the night.

While I was out hunting for the plumpest, most succulent chicken in Amsterdam, Hendrik came home with the Greylander Rembrandt and hung it in the dining room. I was shocked to see the painting. I thought he was putting it in the vault at the shop. There was a sheet of paper taped to the wall under the painting. The message was printed out in large, black letters. It said: 'Please serve dinner in the dining room where we can view this picture.'

"OK, buddy,' I thought, wondering if Hendrik was going to spring some new and elaborate plan regarding the picture and its fate, or if he just wanted us to appreciate the object that had caused all the trouble.

Having Nikki for a guest made for a few changes in my overall menu plan. I had no idea what his tastes were, but because he was a guest I thought the appetizer should be more elaborate than a bowl of nuts, so I settled on a small plate of *fruits de mer* on ice; just a few oysters on the half shell, and a dozen jumbo prawns with lemon slices. The main course would be my famous roast chicken with lemon, butter, and tarragon, served with a delicious array of roasted vegetables. For dessert I'd purchased a fabulous chocolate gateau that I was going to serve with raspberry sauce. If the food didn't convince Nikki of my wifely virtues, nothing would.

This time I was not presenting myself as an androgynous cutie, but dressed like a vamp in a tight, black dress and shoes with three-inch Cuban heels that put me in the six foot range. When eight thirty rolled around, I served the seafood platter and poured a couple of glasses of Muscadet.

While the men chatted in the dining room, I went to the kitchen and got the main course plated and opened a bottle of red. We all sat down and ate with good appetite; everything seemed to be going well. A few witty *bon mots* were tossed back and forth across the table, but I stayed out of it. The meal was being given for Hendrik to regain his status with Nikki and to convince him that I was not a ball cutter. I knew the detective had plenty against me: I was fucking with the old time camaraderie of the boys club by becoming Hendrik's love interest, and not only that, I had interfered in the interrogation of the mobsters and got information from them where the South African torturer had failed.

The Rembrantian burghers stared down at us with supreme indifference, they were cool and smug in the long ago and didn't care a damn about our pathetic relationships and foolish actions. Hendrik had been giving Nikki most of his attention, but now he turned his gaze to the painting and said: 'I've seen better double portraits in provincial museums.'

'You're talking heresy, pal,' Nikki said.

'It never looked right to me,' I said.

'Hendrik took a long, thoughtful sip of his wine: 'Although Willem seldom makes a mistake in his attributions, I think he may have been wrong this time. The signature must have thrown him off.'

Nikki started to laugh: 'You mean I put my mother in jeopardy and risked my career to protect a fucking fake?'

'It's possible,' Hendrik smiled, 'I think I'll return it to Madame Pookie. I believe it's rightfully hers.'

Both Nikki and I looked at Hendrik in disbelief. If this kind of drama kept up, we'd never finish the vegetables. 'Come on, you guys, eat up!' I exhorted. 'You won't get dessert if you don't clean your plates.'

'I don't believe your bullshit, Van der Saar, that painting has got to be real,' Nikki said, picking up his fork and attacking his carrots.

'I can't help it, dude, the more I look at it the more false it becomes. It's contemporary with Rembrandt, but the signature must have been added at a later date.' Hendrik speared a beautifully glazed chunk of potato.

We ate in silence for a minute or so, until Nikki finally said: 'Martel, your cooking is wonderful. I don't think I've ever had a tastier roast chicken.'

'I'm glad you enjoyed it. I used the old Julia Child method. It works every time.'

'It's that faint taste of lemon combined with the herb that makes it so special,' Hendrik said.

While the men were finishing up, I went to the kitchen and began to prepare the dessert. It was a simple assemblage: a swirl of raspberry sauce drizzled on the plate, a thin slice of chocolate gateau decorated by a dollop of whipped cream. I thought about tossing a couple of candied violets on each plate but decided it would be overkill. When I arrived back in the dining room to clear the dinner service Hendrik stood up and said: 'Let me do that for you, *schatje*.'

Nikki looked startled when Hendrik offered to help, and I worried that once again we were violating his sense of gender roles. The guy was totally old school, and I blamed Madame Lillian for that. She doted on her son and must have spoiled

Nikki to death with all her matronly attentions. She had allowed him to think women were mere domestic goddesses designed to comfort and feed the menfolk. Well, that wasn't true in this ménage, and Nikki was just going to have to get used to it. His eyes widened in shock as he watched Hendrik briskly and efficiently clear the table.

Later, when we were all settled back at the table and luxuriating over the taste of the smooth, unctuous, chocolate, Nikki's face opened into a wide smile and he raised his glass to me in a gesture of appreciation and respect. The cop must have decided that I wasn't a ball cutter after all.

Before breaking the bad news about the Rembrandt to the rest of the family, Hendrik and I decided to get married. My reservations about entering into a legal contract with the man I loved seemed to have vanished with his decision to return the Greylander Rembrandt. I was still slightly aghast that Hendrik had been present at a torture session, but rationalized that Nikki and Piet were the perpetrators.

We were married at a hasty ceremony in a judge's chambers with Willem and Nikki as witnesses. I had wanted Venessa to represent me, but she had taken a few days off to go on tour with Bobby and couldn't get back until the night of the wedding, so, rather ironically, Nikki filled in for her.

Afterward we entertained family and friends at the Herengracht with a champagne reception. It was quite a gala celebration, even the socially challenged Dries showed up with his hacker companion, the Viper. They weren't the only unusual guests: Madame Lillian brought Rowley along for the occasion. The dog was the center of attention because he carried a large basket of flowers in his teeth. When Rowley spotted me in the crowd, he trotted right up and smartly presented me with the basket.

Bobby and Venessa got back to Amsterdam in time to make it to the party and they created a sensation when they behaved, unashamedly, like a loving couple. Hendrik turned livid when he saw them making a public display of affection, and I had to poke him in the ribs and tell him to get over it. I also reminded him that it was possible Venessa was not his blood child. That shut him up! We both knew that neither he, nor Venessa, wanted to do a DNA test. They both preferred to live in some kind of half world where the truth was not known or acknowledged.

I thought the Bobby and Venessa kerfuffle added a spicy frisson of scandal to the event and helped ensure the success of the occasion. After my wifely scolding Hendrik must have decided to forgive his errant offspring because I saw him embracing them both and then settling in for what looked to be a jolly conversation.

Madame Lillian joined me for a glass of champagne. I asked about Rowley's whereabouts and she said he was out patrolling the perimeter.

'I noticed you didn't bring Piet along,' I said.

'No, he's back at work these days and we're not seeing as much of each other as we once did.'

'But you're keeping the dog?'

'Oh, yes, Rowley belongs to me now. It's all officially signed, sealed, and delivered,' she smiled. 'Rather like the documents you just signed with Hendrik.'

'That's a novel comparison.' I smiled back at her.

'Yes, isn't it,' she giggled. 'By the way, it's so nice to see Bobby and Venessa together. I do love those children and they make such a beautiful couple.'

'You don't object to their relationship?'

'Not on the basis of them being half siblings. I have it on good authority that Hendrik may not have fathered Venessa. Nikki says that Venessa's mother was a wonderful girl, but like so many others she subscribed to the doctrine of free love.'

'That may be so.'

'Listen, Martel, there are other problems. Are you aware Bobby married a gypsy girl when he was sixteen and that they have two little kiddies?'

'Yes, I am aware. Bobby confided the whole story to me. Face it, Lillian, he's primarily a musician, and everything else is secondary. He's only twenty years old, and who knows how this thing with Venessa will shake out in the years to come. It's possible they may tire of each other.'

'It's more likely he'll tire of his marriage. And then what will happen to his children?'

'Don't borrow trouble, Lillian. The Revata will always take good care of those kids. They are precious to them, and it was Bobby's obligation to the group to father them.'

'I suppose you're right, but what about the poor little girl who gave birth to the babies?'

'Oh, god, I don't know! I'm betting that things will continue as they are. Bobby's not expected to be home much. I think the Revata lead somewhat separate lives based on gender and occupation.'

Lillian did not seem to be registering what I was saying. Her eyes had locked on a far corner of the room and a look of horror was spreading over her face: 'Look over there, Martel! Rowley's got some man pinned up against the wall.'

'Well, go over there and get him off the poor guy!'

Lillian ran towards the corner and I followed. She reached Rowley and called him off before any physical damage was done. Instead of being angry the man looked sheepish: 'I think he just wanted some meat,' he said, and pulled several balls of steak tartare out of his pocket. He put the balls in the palm of his hand and held it out to Rowley who took them eagerly and then wagged his tail.

'There were no serving plates available so I stashed them in my pockets,' he explained.

'That's a likely story,' I thought. Hadn't the guy ever heard of cocktail napkins? I'd never seen the man before and wondered if he was a party crasher who was desperate for food.

Having consumed the meatballs, Rowley tried to take off in search of more victims, but Lillian grabbed his collar and turned him around. When Rowley saw she meant business he sat down and then lowered his whole body to the floor in front of his mistress. While Lillian was disciplining the dog the man slipped away, and the last I saw of him he was slinking out of the grand salon and going for the exit.

Lillian was snapping a red leather leash on Rowley's collar when a woman came up to her and said: 'Miss Collins, it's so wonderful to see you here on this joyous occasion. You were my grandmother's favorite actress and when I visited she always let me stay up and watch *Dynasty*.' The woman held out her hand: 'Please allow me to introduce myself, I'm Samantha Horlech. Perhaps you've seen my column on BloArt.com. Would you mind if I asked you a few questions? Our readers would be fascinated to know what your connection is with the Van der Saar family. Are you an old friend of the groom?'

Lillian looked irritated, and did not extend her hand to meet Horlech's: 'Yes, I'm an old friend of the groom's. I used to wipe his ass when he was a toddler.'

Rowley was still on the ground, but he picked up on Lillian's disdain for the columnist and started growling in her direction. Samantha Horlech was a snotty bitch from an art blog and she had seriously misjudged the situation. Her eyes opened wide when she realized Lillian was not Joan Collins, and she fled without further comment or apology.

'I'm going home,' Lillian said. 'I always leave when they get drunk enough to start mistaking me for Joan. It's a royal pain in the ass.'

'You should be flattered. She's a beautiful woman and quite the actress.'

'I know, I know,' Lillian groused, 'but I developed this style on my own before she ever got that job on *Dynasty*. Now people think I'm copying her.'

'That must hurt,' I said.

'Maybe a little bit,' she smiled wistfully. We kissed good bye while Rowley wagged his tail impatiently. I think he was glad to be leaving. I watched Rowley and Lillian make their way through the guests and when I couldn't see them any longer I went to find my husband.

We went to Venice for our honey moon. It was the middle of winter and most of the tourist spots were closed. We walked around in the fog and the mist like lost travelers who had stumbled upon an ancient, unknown, ruin of a city. It seemed that Venice, whose derelict charms grew ever more enticing with age, was still able to enchant. As we voyaged through her empty streets, we took on the ambiance of the city, we became as transparent as wraiths and as empty as stone. We were still vastly in love.

We returned to Amsterdam, and Hendrik decided it was time to discuss the delicate matter of the authenticity of the Greylander Rembrandt with the rest of the family. There had been a difficult meeting with Willem and Venessa, neither of whom wanted to return the picture to the Greylanders. Willem was still sticking with his original assessment and insisted the painting was genuine. Venessa was backing him up. Because I was now officially a Van der Saar, my opinion was sought by the other three. I had always had my misgivings about the picture and, to the dismay of Willem and Venessa, I stood with Hendrik. We had reached a deadlock, and it was decided that Dries had to be called in to break the tie. Although Dries had no formal training in art history or conservation, he was a Van der Saar and by some right of genetic inheritance he was expected to settle the matter.

Dries came to the meeting with a large file folder and started spreading prints out on his father's desk. They were all double portraits by Dutch artists of the Golden Age. We crowded around the desk to see what he had brought to the meeting, but there was nothing on that desk that looked like the Greylander Rembrandt.

Dries stood back, nonchalantly puffing on an electronic cigarette while we examined his display.

'How many times have I told you not to smoke those things?' Willem snapped. He was irritated, but it wasn't about the E-cigarette.

'Sorry, Dad,' Dries kept on puffing. He pointed at one of the prints: 'That one is a fully authenticated Rembrandt.'

'We know that, Dries!' Willem was infuriated by his son's comment, and it looked like he was getting ready to go off the deep end. I hoped his head injury had fully healed. It would be horrible if he had a stroke or a heart attack.

'I don't think this is really your area of expertise, Dries,' Venessa's voice was sweet as honey, 'Your father is a world famous expert and his attribution is correct.'

'I have my doubts,' Dries said stubbornly. 'The Greylander portrait is old, but it's just not right. It must be by another artist whose work hasn't come down to us. I think the artist actually had those initials and it's a coincidence that they match with Rembrandt's.'

'Wow, that is some original thinking,' I said. I had to hand it to the kid, none of the pros had even entertained such an idea.

Willem looked at Venessa: 'I think we're fucked, darling.'

'It seems that way,' she said.

'If we're all agreed, I'll take the picture back to Madame Pookie,' Hendrik said.

'We're not exactly agreed, Daddy,' Venessa said, 'but Dries has cast the deciding vote, and it's now three against two. You guys win, but I still think you're wrong.'

'We could debate the authenticity of the painting forever, but we'd never reach a conclusion that satisfied everyone. As you say, Venessa, it's three against two, so why don't we all have a drink and forget the hard feelings,' Hendrik said.

Venessa looked sulky and didn't answer, but Willem managed a weak smile and said: 'We might as well bring out the celebration brandy.' He went to a drawer in a cupboard and pulled out a bottle of XO.

Dries sidled up to his father and watched him pour the prized elixir into paper cups: 'Dad, can you pay me the money you owe for the research on the Greylanders? We really need it. The Viper and I want to go to Moscow to learn how to climb and crawl.'

'Climb and crawl? What the hell are you talking about?' Willem's hand shook and he almost spilled the brandy.

'It's sort of like Parkour, only you do it barefoot on tall buildings and bridges and dangerous towers. The Viper and I decided we've been sitting in the dark too long and now we want to get some fresh air and exercise.'

'Can't you take up jogging or tennis?'

'No, it wouldn't be the same. We're thrill seekers; we need the excitement and the challenge. We have no fear of death.'

'You're too young to fear death.'

'You owe us the money, Dad,' Dries whined.

'I'll pay you tonight, but don't come crying to me when those Ruskies throw you in jail for mucking about on their buildings and bridges. Before you leave for Moscow you better make out a will and advise me if you want cremation or burial.'

'Don't be so negative, Uncle Willem,' Venessa said. 'I follow free climbing on YouTube and, believe me, those kids are fantastic. They even have girls doing it. The death rate isn't that bad; they've only lost three boys and one girl this year.'

'I'm sure their parents were amused,' Willem said, handing out the paper cups.

Dries took his cup and gingerly lifted it to his lips. He put it down fast: 'Can I put some Red Bull in this?' he asked.

I thought Willem was going to smack him one, but Hendrik quickly intervened: 'No, Dries, you'll have to drink it straight. Just remember in Russia even the young ones drink their Vodka without mixers. You'll look like a wimp if you keep adding Red Bull to spirits.'

'OK, I'll give it a try,' Dries grimaced and took another sip.

Willem lifted his paper cup in Hendrik's direction: 'Make sure you get Madame Pookie to hand over my copy and bring it back to me. I'd like to keep it as a souvenir of this unfortunate episode.'

'I've already talked to her personal assistant. It's going to be a simple exchange of paintings. I'll bring the copy back to you, but I wouldn't count on hanging on to it. We may be able to sell it to one of our clients.'

'Martel can make up the provenance,' Willem said. 'I've noticed she's good at that.'

'Thanks, Willem,' I said, basking in his approval and happy that his mind was getting back on business. Although Dries was still struggling with his drink, the rest of us were enjoying the XO and behaving once again like a happy and united family.

I went to Geneva with Hendrik to make sure he stayed out of Pookie's clutches. According to what my husband said, the Greylander heiress had shot up one hormone too many, and was constantly on the alert for new sex partners. He had spoken with her on the phone and she had been quite angry, going so far as to threaten a law suit, or a prosecution. Hendrik feared she was in a blackmail mode and might try to lure him into the sack to make him pay for the theft of her picture. As unlikely as this scenario sounded, I could see that Hendrik was uneasy about the meeting, so I said I would go along as back-up. I didn't think she would try anything if I was in the room.

Pookie sent her personal airplane for us; she was in a hurry to get her hands on the Greylander Rembrandt and wasn't trusting of public transportation. Her aide said that after our meeting with Madame Greylander we would be expected to find our own way home.

We were the only passengers, but the plane was set up to carry at least ten people. It was decorated in a very feminine style; the seats were upholstered in luxurious beige leather and the walls were painted pale pink. As we waited for takeoff, a pretty boy in a beige uniform served us glasses of pink champagne accompanied by strawberries dipped in chocolate. I was waiting for him to hand me an orchid, but apparently that wasn't part of the service.

It was a short hop, slightly more than an hour, from Amsterdam to Geneva. We were meeting Pookie at the Grand Hotel Kaminski where she maintained a suite. The Kaminski was a posh five-star on the edge of the lake, and we had booked ourselves a room for the night, hoping to relax and enjoy the deluxe amenities after our most likely traumatic meeting with the aged heiress.

After landing I expected a visit from customs officials as Switzerland is not part of the EU, but none appeared. Instead, a Cadillac Escalade drove up on the tarmac next to the plane. A chauffeur, smartly dressed in a dark suit and cap, came on board and assisted Hendrik in removing the crate that contained the Greylander Rembrandt. Together they loaded it into the Escalade.

As we sped through the quiet streets of the clean and well maintained city, I gawked out the window at the rather nondescript architecture and the beautiful natural setting that was highlighted by an intensely blue river that flowed into an intensely blue lake. The fabled Alps were not much in evidence; the city seemed to be surrounded by foothills, although you could see a couple of snow-capped peaks off in the distance. The sights were new to me because I have a tendency to avoid the enclaves of the super-rich and I'd never been to Switzerland before.

The hotel was located smack on the shores of Lake Geneva, right in front of a soaring water sculpture known as the *Jet d'Eau*. This great plume of water has become an identifying symbol of the ridiculously prosperous city, and it was considered incredibly chic to stay at a hotel with a view of the giant fountain. When we arrived at the Kaminski, a uniformed lackey opened the door and ushered us out of the Escalade. Hendrik and the driver went round to the back, removed the crate and put it on a luggage cart. Another lackey led us into the lobby where a slick looking guy with suave manners took us to a private elevator and pushed the button to take us up to the royal suite. After a short silent trip the door opened and deposited us in the middle of an elaborately decorated salon.

The place was overloaded with crystal chandeliers, Persian rugs, and gilded furniture. There were a couple of soft looking couches upholstered in rose brocade that looked vaguely suitable. Offsetting the ostentatious decor were huge floor to ceiling glass windows that opened onto a large balcony. The windows offered a fine view of the lake and were right in front of the *Jet d'Eau*.

The elevator door closed, and Hendrik and I and the crate were left alone on the periphery of the room. Madame Pookie did not keep us waiting; she soon appeared leaning on the arm of a male attendant who was dressed in white scrubs. He could have been a doctor, but because he was quite muscular I pegged him for a masseur. The attendant deposited Pookie on one of the couches and left the room. She gestured toward a chair and told me to sit down. She glared at Hendrik: 'Alright, Van der Saar, get that picture unpacked and let me see it.' Her voice sounded like sandpaper had been applied to her vocal chords and then been left to clog in her throat.

'Yes, Madame Pookie, right away,' Hendrik spoke with the subdued voice of a servant. I suppose he had no choice but to be subservient, considering the shit he'd pulled on her.

While Hendrik was taking the crate apart, Pookie watched him with the sharp eye of a raptor. Her focus on Hendrik's actions allowed me to take a good look at the ancient billionairess. I had to admit she looked a lot better than expected, mainly because she had resisted the extremes of facial mutilation that have become so popular in recent years. Her face and neck had been tucked and tightened, but there were no signs of Botox, collagen, fat injections, or other fillers that had a tendency to make the victim look like a contemporary version of Bozo the Clown.

Her face, framed by a wig of pale, straight hair that stopped at her shoulders, was reasonably pleasant. The face could have passed for a well preserved eighty, but it was the gnarled and desiccated body, that gave her away. It was a fact that not even the greatest youth doctors were able to correct the ravages of extreme old age, and even the wealth of the Greylander's could not stave off the inevitable decay. Pookie was striving desperately to correct these tell-tale imperfections and had dressed herself in a flowing, peach colored confection of a dress that had a high neck, long sleeves, and a flowing skirt that reached to mid-calf. It was a brave effort and might have worked in a dim restaurant, but in the bright light from the windows she reminded me of a skeleton dressed up for a Day of the Dead celebration.

By this time Hendrik had got the picture out of the box and was displaying it to his client. My husband was behaving so obsequiously that I half expected him to kneel down in front of the old hag and beg for forgiveness. Pookie had pulled out a pair of diamond studded cat's-eye glasses and began avidly surveying the piece. 'Oh, yes, this is it,' she slavered. I could see a line of drool forming on the edge of her thin, heavily glossed and pinkish lips. 'I'd like my painting,' Hendrik said, finally showing some spunk.

'I'll have the boy bring it out,' Pookie lifted a tiny, pink phone to her ear and shouted some instructions into the receiver. Soon the masseur in the white scrubs appeared pushing a cart with Willem's copy tossed carelessly on top.

'I'd rather expected to see your brother here instead of this creature.' Pookie pointed at me.

'Fuck off, Pookie, that's no creature, that's my wife. Surely your spies must have notified you about the wedding.'

'Oh, yes, I did hear about that transaction. She must be totally misinformed if she married you for your money,' she paused. 'You Van der Saar boys will be coming up paupers after I get done with you. Presently you owe me a million Euros, and that's before I take you into court and ruin you.'

'If you live that long' Hendrik said.

'Are you threatening me?' Pookie laughed and stuffed a cigarette into a gold holder. 'Light me, baby,' she said to the masseur.

The masseur let go of the cart, reached into his pocket and retrieved a Viet Nam era Zippo, which he soon sparked up and used to light her cigarette.

Pookie puffed and exhaled. Apparently, she had forgotten about Hendrik's implied threat because she started mooning about Willem: 'I do so adore that boy, even though he sent me this forgery. It is such a disappointment not to see him. There's no one like darling Willem, so talented, and with that beautiful, natural blonde hair. I adore those golden braids.'

'He doesn't have the beautiful hair anymore,' I said, finally interjecting myself into the fray, 'Those fucking thugs you sent over from New Jersey gave him a head injury and damn near killed him. They shaved his head at the hospital.'

'Is he alright?' For the first time in our encounter I saw real emotion creep over Pookie's face. Unfortunately, I couldn't identify the emotion. She turned to Hendrik: 'I blame you for all this, Van der Saar! You were the one who convinced Willem to make a copy and keep the original. You're a rotten punk, and I'm going to have your ass in jail.'

To my great surprise Hendrik walked over to Pookie and said: 'Your time is just about up, babe.' She took a hit from her cigarette, laughed, and fell over on the sofa. Hendrik's words must have had a huge effect because she started choking and turning blue.

I looked at the masseur who was standing dumbfounded with the Zippo in his hand: 'Can you help her?' I asked.

'I'm her toy boy, not her doctor. I don't know any first aid.'

'Call the house doctor,' Hendrik said.

Pookie was calming down, she'd stopped choking and her breathing had become shallow and weak. The boyfriend found her phone and called the desk. The staff of the elite hotel wasted no time in getting up to the Royal suite. There were four of them, one of whom billed himself as a medic. The guy jumped on Pookie and started banging on her chest. We all stood around and watched as he beat the hell out of the poor old gal. Unfortunately, the hundred year old had finally given it up and nothing the hotel doc did could bring her back.

'What happened to her?' the man in charge asked.

'We don't know,' Hendrik volunteered. 'I'm her art dealer. We were having a meeting and she had a seizure. Her attendant called the house doctor for help, but she must have expired before you people got here.'

'I'll have to get a police officer up here to take your statements.'

'That will be fine,' Hendrik said.

When it came time to leave, Hendrik packed up the Greylander Rembrandt and left Willem's copy in the suite.

Hendrik and I were living it up in an executive room at the Kaminski. It was late night and we were out on the balcony viewing the *Jet d'Eau* and indulging ourselves in a platter of spectacular looking hors d'oeuvres and a bottle of champagne.

'You must have scared her to death, darling,' I said.

'I certainly hope so. The fucking bitch deserved it.'

'Do you think the Greylanders will make any trouble?'

'I doubt it. I'm sure they'll be happy that she's finally gone. She was a troublesome wench, what with her interest in maintaining an active sex life in old age. They couldn't have been too happy when she started running around with that Mafia don from New Jersey.'

'It sounds like he was way too old for her. If I recall correctly, one of the thugs said he was ninety-seven.'

'If I know Pookie, she hooked up with him for cheap thrills. She probably loved being associated with a real gangster.'

'And he was able to provide her with muscle when she was looking for the Greylander Rembrandt.'

Hendrik looked thoughtful: 'She died before I could ask her who tipped her off to the fact that her painting was a copy.'

'It could have been Bowden Bork,' I said. Bork who was known in the trade as BB, was a well known bottom feeder who published sensationalist biographies of long-dead artists. The bios were short on facts and long on sex, violence, and addiction.

'Did you notice Pookie had BB's book on Caravaggio prominently displayed on the coffee table? I heard she and BB were great pals, and that she often entertained him at her chalet in Gstaad.'

'You may be right, Martel. The last time I saw BB he was lurking around the shop trying to take a meeting with Willem. BB claimed he was writing a biography of Rembrandt and needed to consult with Willem about the master's technique. He made such a pest of himself that Willem finally let him in the studio. Maybe he saw the copy and later sold the information to Pookie.'

'That sounds about right,' I said. 'Do you think we should have a chat with BB?'

'It will be up to Willem whether he wants to pursue the issue. It was his deal from the beginning. He was the one who convinced Venessa and me that the Greylander picture was a true Rembrandt.'

'I guess he'll be overjoyed when we come back with the original.'

'Yes, it will help take his mind off the problems with Dries. He's terrified the kid will lose his life climbing on a rackety old TV tower in a Moscow suburb.'

'You Van der Saars worry too much about your kids. From what I've seen, Dries is quite well coordinated for someone who has spent the last five years locked up in a dark room. I doubt that either he or the Viper will make a misstep. They are very smart boys.'

'That's another thing. Willem thinks Dries and the Viper are lovers. It worries him that his son won't talk about his sexual preferences.'

'I doubt they're lovers. They both look asexual to me.'

'Is that supposed to be reassuring? I don't understand your blasé attitude toward our kids. How can you make such statements when you've never bothered to have any children.'

'It's easy,' I smiled and poured myself another glass of champagne. 'It doesn't take any kind of genius to pop out a bunch of kids. I'm more interested in studying human behavior than producing children. I study the little brats the way I do adults. We're all a bunch of animals and you know it.'

'I know it, but I prefer not to talk about it.'

'But that knowledge should direct your behavior.'

'It does, but not where the kids are concerned.'

'Wake up, darling, the way you view your children is totally atavistic and animalistic.'

'You're such a fucking smart ass,' Hendrik said, standing up and pulling me out of my chair: 'How's this for animalistic?' he asked, dragging me towards the bedroom.

Willem was amazed when we walked into his studio with the Greylander Rembrandt. A smile spread over his face as he watched Hendrik unpack it.

'For you, brother,' Hendrik said, beaming back at Willem.

'How did this happen? I thought we had lost it forever.'

'You're not going to believe this, but Pookie dropped dead at the moment of exchange.'

'Did you two help her along?'

'No, not at all,' I said. 'Her assistant was in the room with us when it happened. He told the cops exactly how it went down. His story matched perfectly with ours.'

'How much did you pay him?'

'Not one Swiss Franc. We didn't have to. The woman was so old she was due to go at any time. The excitement must have sent her over the edge.'

By this time Willem and Hendrik had hoisted the unframed painting and put it on a large easel in the back of the studio.

'What happened to the copy?' Willem asked.

'We left it with Pookie. It's part of her estate.' I said.

'Did you find out who identified it as a forgery?'

'No, she died before we could ask, but Hendrik and I think Bowden Bork may have been involved.'

Willem looked uncomfortable: 'You're right, it must have been BB. He barged in one day while I was making the copy. The Greylander Rembrandt was out in full view.

'Can't we forget the whole sorry mess?' Willem didn't seem to have much appetite for pursuing the investigation. In fact, after the first flush of joy and surprise on seeing the painting his enthusiasm seemed to have faded.

'It's your call, brother,' Hendrik said.

'Then I say let it be. At the moment I feel like putting the picture in the vault and letting Venessa worry about it after we're dead. Sorry, but I'm in no condition to discuss business. Dries and the Viper took off for Moscow to learn free climbing, and I'm worried sick about them. I had a huge fight with Dries before they left. Nothing I said could convince him to give up this psychotic fixation. I'm afraid he's gone off on a suicide mission.'

'Those fucking idiots!' Hendrik exclaimed. He rushed to his brother's side and embraced him. For a moment I thought Willem was going to cry, but instead he said: 'I need to get out of here and straighten up. Let's go over to the coffee shop and smoke some ganja.'

'I'll stay here and make sure the Greylander goes in the vault,' I said. I thought it best if Willem and Hendrik were left alone to confront this new piece of family misery.

PART FOUR

A few weeks later, I went down to Hendrik's office around closing time, thinking I might be able to coax him out for a drink. He wasn't there, but his secretary said she was expecting him back at any minute, and offered me a cup of tea.

As I sipped my tea and waited for my husband, I wondered what was troubling him. We were not connecting emotionally, and he had become remote and subdued since we came back from Geneva. In fact, the atmosphere in the shop had grown increasingly glum, what with Willem moping over Dries absence, and Hendrik slinking around like he had something to hide. We should have been celebrating because we'd retrieved the Greylander Rembrandt and banked the million euro restoration fee, but the aged cognac remained in the drawer while the two brothers sank deeper into sadness and desolation.

By the time I finished my tea, Hendrik arrived and told me to sit tight because he had to speak with Willem. He was gone for about fifteen minutes and when he came back there was a stricken look on his face. I stood up and he put his hand between my shoulder blades in the familiar gesture he always used when he wanted to move me from one area to another.

We went to the Brown Café and had our usual: jenever and beer. We chatted a bit about the melt in the Arctic and whether the genius of Dutch engineering would be able to save Amsterdam from the coming deluge. It was hard talk, but Hendrik was not giving it his full attention. Finally he said: 'I've been seeing a MD and having tests all week.'

'It must be serious,' I said. To my knowledge Hendrik had little faith in medical doctors and never consulted one.

'I'm afraid it is, darling,' he said, grasping my hand and explaining that he was in the throes of a fast developing lymphoma. It was a bad strain which had spread to the bone marrow and there wasn't much hope for survival. Still, the doctor had scheduled aggressive chemotherapy for next week. When telling me the sad facts Hendrik had become cool and matter of fact. He related the prognosis like he was discussing a business deal. He may have been fine with the news of his impending doom, but I was so startled I knocked over my jenever. 'I'll get you another drink,' he said.

While Hendrik was up at the bar I tried to collect my thoughts and regain some composure, but it was impossible. I started to cry. Hendrik returned with more jenever, and I hastily wiped my eyes, but that didn't stop the flow, and soon I was sobbing and starting to go totally out of control.

'Get a grip, Martel!' Hendrik put the glass of gin down in front of me and said: 'Drink up. It will help.'

When I couldn't manipulate the glass to my mouth, he held it to my lips and practically forced the drink down my throat. 'Do you want a pill?' he asked.

'What have you got?' I was choking and sobbing but I managed to get the question out.

'I have Xanax and Clonazepam and OxyContin. Bobby gave me a herbal remedy. It's the best of the lot for calming anxiety. Bobby's been using it when he gets cravings for heroin.'

'A couple of Xanax will be fine.' He handed me the pills, and I swallowed them with a swig of beer. I was in no mood to experiment with some unknown herbal potion. I knew how the Xanax would affect me, but only god knew what the herbs would do.

'Does Bobby know about the lymphoma?' I asked.

'No, presently it's just you and Willem. I thought I would tell Venessa and Bobby when I made up my mind about the chemo. I'm not really keen on having this kind of radical treatment. The patient gets very ill and may die from the side effects. I don't understand the point of it, seeing as I'm terminal anyway.'

'In the States people do it to please their families. A lot of the terminally ill would rather die in peace, but they are expected to take radical treatment to prove they have the fighting spirit. People are brainwashed by big pharma and the medical establishment into thinking that prolonged suffering is the way to go.'

'You sound bitter, Martel.'

'I am. I've seen too many people die that way. It's very undignified and dehumanizing and I don't want that for you.' The minute the words came out of my mouth I regretted them. Even though what I said was true I had no right to influence Hendrik's decision.

'It sounds like you won't stand in my way if I decide to skip the chemo.'

'No, I won't, it's up to you.' I was having a hard time accepting that Hendrik would soon be gone, and I felt like giving in to grief and despair, but fortunately the Xanax started to kick in. 'How does Willem feel about it?' I asked.

'He's with me whatever I decide.'

'So what do you want to do, darling?'

'I think I'll pass on the chemo. I can have a couple of good months, and when the disease takes over I'll call a suicide doctor.'

'It sounds like you've got it all planned out.'

'Actually, I do. I guess extreme chemo was never an option.'

'Are you in pain, darling?''

'No. But sometimes I feel listless and anxious and my bones ache.'

'Do you remember the time we had the blood ceremony?'

Hendrik laughed: 'I'll never forget.'

'When I cut you with the knife the blood flowed out in a black stream. I wonder if the color was a symptom of your lymphoma.'

'Most likely,' Hendrik said, 'although at the time I didn't think much of it.'

'I thought the black blood meant you were either an alien from outer space, or a vampire.'

'I hate to disappoint you, but I'm just a mortal man,' Hendrik said, taking my hand and kissing it. 'Would you like to go back to the Herengracht and have sex?' He smiled wickedly: 'The knowledge of impending loss should add an element of desperation to our lovemaking. Just imagine how poignant each touch will be. The whole act will be drenched with sorrow. It could be one of our best fucks, Martel.'

'You are such a bullshitter,' I said.

Hendrik may have been playing at sophistry, but he was correct, that's exactly what our lovemaking turned out to be.

As the weeks passed, the Van der Saar family displayed solid Dutch practically and arranged for the succession. No one objected to Hendrik's decision to forgo chemotherapy and he continued to spend his days at the shop maintaining his workload. He looked fit and healthy, the disease was not yet draining him of life, and it was easy to fall into denial and think that the lymphoma had magically left his body and that he was in remission. Still, we prepared for his departure, and it was decided that Willem would take Hendrik's place as chief executive officer. Surprisingly, I was expected to assume

Hendrik's position in the marketing area, and I spent most of my work days with him learning the nuances and style of his presentations and sales approach. I was being schooled in the Van der Saar tradition, and our relationship was that of master and apprentice. During business hours we were no longer husband and wife. I was to carry on until Venessa was seasoned enough to take over. Presently she was preoccupied with schoolwork and had yet to finish her dissertation. In her spare time she was expected to be in the shop assisting me. As for Dries, it was hoped he would survive the free climbing experience and join the firm at a later date.

One afternoon during this period Venessa came into my office with a piece of paper in her hand. 'Look, Martel, I printed this off the Net.' She tossed the paper onto my desk: 'Dries and the Viper posted this on Instagram.'

I took a good look at the picture and started to giggle. Dries and the Viper were seated at what looked like a night-club table. They were colorfully attired in matching red T-shirts that featured a portrait of Josef Stalin under a lively hammer and sickle motif. The boys looked shit faced drunk and were surrounded by a bevy of gorgeous young Russian women. Dries held a bottle of vodka proudly aloft while the Viper cuddled one of the girls.

'How times have changed,' I said, almost collapsing in laughter. 'Has his father seen this?'

'No, let's go show it to him,' Venessa said, a sly grin on her face.

Willem was in a meeting when we got to the studio, and we decided to wait until he got out. We went in his office and Venessa sat down at his computer: 'I found a video of the boys on YouTube, but I don't know if we should show it to Willem. He's not too steady on his feet since the head injury, the shock might give him a stroke,' she brought up a video: 'Take a look, Martel, what do you think?'

The video showed Dries and the Viper sneaking into a building site and climbing the skeleton of an unfinished skyscraper. The building was tall, and when they got to the top they had a superb view that stretched all the way to Siberia. The boys worked in bare feet and without ropes or tools. The climb had been jaw-dropingly difficult, but when they reached the summit they did not rest on their laurels, instead they began to crawl out on the exposed beams. Acting in unison they lowered themselves off the beams and into the air. At first they hung from the beams by both hands like trapeze artists, but then they took one hand off the beam and hung by one arm as their bodies dangled out into empty space. It was a frightening performance, and one that I did not think Willem would be able to tolerate.

'Let's just show him the picture,' I said.

'Pretty scary, isn't it?' Venessa smiled. She seemed intensely proud of her cousin and his friend.

'Yes, but it's also frighteningly beautiful,' I said.

'This is real performance art!' Venessa was enthusiastic. 'I wish I could write my dissertation on this mode of expression, but those old frumps at school wouldn't stand for it.'

Just then Willem walked in followed by his secretary, Irene. He was giving dictation and she was trailing behind taking notes on an old fashioned steno pad. Willem stopped dictating and noticed us: 'Oh, hello you two, what brings you to my lair?'

'We've got a big surprise for you. Wait till you see it!' Venessa gushed.

'I hope it's not another Rembrandt.' Willem smiled at Venessa and then turned to Irene: 'Get that typed up and I'll sign it this afternoon.'

After Irene left Venessa jumped up from the computer and ran to Willem with the print in her hand: 'Look at this Uncle Willem. Dries and the Viper have surfaced. They're living it up at a nightclub in Moscow.'

Willem took the print and studied it. 'I wonder who made those T-shirts?' he mused. 'They show a great sense of design and the portrait of Stalin is authentic 1930s propaganda art. It's a nice piece of work, but I'm surprised the boys are running around with a picture of that tyrant on their chests. '

'They're just kids, Willem. It probably wasn't a political choice,' I said.

'I don't care a damn about their fucking T-shirts,' Venessa wailed, 'look at them, Uncle Willem, they're with girls, and they're smiling. Dries never used to smile. He always kept a tight lip, and now it looks like he's happy.'

'I can see that, Venessa, and I am deeply touched.'

I looked at Venessa: 'Maybe we should leave, darling. I'm sure Willem is terribly busy.'

'Yes, of course,' she said. We started for the door.

'No, stick around. I want to talk to you about Dries,' Willem said. He sat down at the computer. The screen was black and he hit a key: 'I'll be with you in a minute; I just have to get some dates for Irene.'

Venessa's face got very pale and she ran towards Willem's desk, but it was too late. In her haste to show Willem the picture of Dries and the Viper she had forgotten to sign out of YouTube, and now Willem was sitting in front of a video that was labeled *Dutch Daredevils Go Wild in Moscow*.'

'You weren't supposed to see that,' I said.

'Then why is it on my screen?' He clicked on the video.

'It's up there because you didn't turn off your computer when you went to the meeting.' I was trying to deflect the blame from Venessa, but I knew what I said was pretty lame.

'I'm sorry, Uncle Willem, I just wanted to show the video to Martel,' Venessa chimed in. She looked scared and sounded contrite.

Willem paid no attention to our excuses because he was caught up in the action on the screen. When the boys finally climbed back down to safety and were greeted by a gaggle of cops he relaxed: 'Is Hendrik around? I want him to see this.'

'I'll call his office,' I said. I got Hendrik on the first ring and told him to meet us in the studio. He said he'd be right down. After I hung up my focus was back on Willem. 'What did you think of the climb?' I asked.

'I think they're thrill seeking morons, but aside from that it was an exciting piece of work. I didn't think those two little bastards had it in them.' He paused for a moment and then said: 'The cops took them away. Do you think they're in jail?'

'I doubt it,' Venessa said, 'the photo was posted after the climb. They seem to be celebrating their success.'

'I hope you're right because I don't feel like engaging with a bunch of Moscow cops. The bribes would be outrageous. '

The door opened and Hendrik walked in. When he saw his family members gathered around the computer he gave us a wary look: 'I hope you haven't called me here to have a conference about my illness.'

Willem smiled, 'No, Hendrik, it's much more serious. Take a look at this video and tell me what you think.'

The video played through again. It was the third time I'd seen it, but it remained eminently fascinating and I couldn't help but hold my breath when the boys started dangling in space.

'It's fucking brilliant,' Hendrik exclaimed. 'I don't understand how those two puny little shits developed the skills to perform this kind of stunt.'

'They probably trained day and night,' Venessa said. 'Also, it helps to be in an environment where your hopes and dreams are encouraged by a peer group of like-minded people.'

'What's that supposed to mean?' Willem asked. He was taking her comment as a slight on his parenting.

Venessa backtracked, 'I just meant he was with people who could give him the skills and support to meet his goals.'

'That's enough,' Hendrik commanded, 'let's not get off track here. Willem, what are you going to do about this? Frankly, I don't like the idea of Dries and the Viper continuing in this suicidal activity. They are going to fall to their deaths if they continue.'

'You don't know that, Daddy.' Venessa was really hot on free climbing. If she liked it so much, maybe she should take a trip to Moscow and get trained in the art.

'You're right, *shatje,* I don't know, but you have to admit it does seem possible. Think about it, we don't want to lose Dries or the Viper. We have to stop them.'

'I'm going to Moscow and bring them back,' Willem said. He looked at Hendrik: 'Will you come with me brother?'

'Of course, Willem, you know I've got your back. Although I do wonder if that's the right approach. These kids are flushed with triumph after their great ascent, and I doubt if they'd welcome two middle-aged relatives busting in and trying to bust their balloon.'

'You may be right,' Willem said.

'Maybe Bobby could help,' I said. 'I know he has a lot of influence on Dries. The kid adores him.'

Venessa had been sitting quietly at the corner of Willem's desk. She seemed to have taken her father's words to heart. I understood her enthusiasm for the art; you had to be a fool not to see the brilliance. These kids were the ultimate in nihilism, and you could write a whole paper on their existential activities. Venessa was a scholar and she was taking free climbing from a philosophical point of view, but now that Hendrik had forced her to see that two young lives might be dashed to pieces after a long, hard, fall, she was giving it a different take:

'I'll call Bobby,' she said.

We all trooped over to the Herengracht that afternoon to meet with Bobby. For some reason he had been disinclined to meet at the shop, saying he had something to show us and he wanted to do it in private. We went to the kitchen and I made a pot of Italian roast. Willem lit up a joint, and passed it to Hendrik. Venessa was sitting close to the door and when she heard the bell she ran out of the room to greet Bobby. When they entered the kitchen, Venessa was in the lead, she was carrying a large piece of bright colored hand luggage that was decorated with teddy bears. Bobby came behind her. He had a little girl under his arm and a fat baby strapped to his chest. The whole room fell out in shock, but I noticed Hendrik had a huge grin on his face. Bobby went directly to Hendrik and dropped the little girl on his lap: 'Lucia, this is Grandpa Hendrik,' he said.

The girl looked at Hendrik and smiled. She seemed perfectly at ease with this strange man. 'Hi, Grandpa Hendrik,' she said.

Hendrik was speechless. He looked all teary eyed and bent down and kissed Lucia on the top of her head.

Bobby turned to Venessa and said: 'Help me get this kid off my chest. He weighs a ton.'

Venessa was another one who seemed perfectly at ease. She loosened the straps on the carrier and took the baby into her arms. I got the idea that she knew these children quite well and that Bobby must have been bringing them to visit at her apartment.

'Hi, little fatty,' Venessa said to the baby. He was a cute little guy in a blue romper suit decorated with the ever popular teddy bear motif. She wiped a spot of drool off his chin and handed him to Hendrik. Now grandpa was covered with children. The baby looked at him with wide eyes and reached up and grabbed a hunk of his hair and pulled. Lucia laughed and took a hunk of hair for herself.

'Cut it out, you two,' Bobby said, sitting down by Willem and taking a hit off the joint. 'So what did you want to discuss?' he asked.

'It's Dries,' Willem said.

'Oh, yeah, I saw that video of him and the Viper on YouTube. Those guys are into some dangerous shit.'

'I want juice,' Lucia said. 'Grandpa I want juice.'

'Yes, sweetheart,' Hendrik said, and looked helplessly at Venessa.

'There's orange juice in the refrigerator,' I said.

'I think there's some special kiddie juice in the bag. She'd probably rather have that.' Venessa opened the carryall and pulled out a cup of juice and handed it to Lucia. It wasn't a spill-proof cup and the child dribbled juice on her pretty, pale rose smock and down onto Hendrik's trousers. He didn't seem to care that she'd stained his expensive tailoring, but just sat staring at her with that same blissed out smile on his face.

I didn't blame him for staring, the child was close to being beautiful; already she had masses of dark hair, and her sweet face was decorated with large, long lashed, hazel eyes and the beginnings of a prominent nose. She looked to be about three and a half years old.

I could hear Willem and Bobby down the table talking about Dries and the Viper: 'Do you know where they're staying?' Bobby asked.

'No, but we've got a lead, they were celebrating at a club called 'The Fugitive.'

'Never heard of it,' Bobby said. 'We've got some contacts with the Ruska Roma. I'll get them on the case. Those little Dutch boys shouldn't be too hard to find.'

Just then the baby started to bawl. Venessa reached into the bag and pulled out a bottle filled with a creamy yellow liquid which I took to be expressed breast milk.

'Lucia, get off grandpa's lap, he has to feed the baby,' Venessa said. She had a wicked glint in her eye like she was pulling a huge joke on Hendrik, but he didn't seem to notice.

'No, I won't get off,' Lucia said, 'I like this grandpa.' She leaned back into Hendrik and put her head on his chest. The baby continued to bawl, in fact, he was going into frighteningly loud paroxysms. Venessa went over and stuck the bottle in his mouth, after that she took Lucia off Hendrik and put her on the floor.

'He's going to shit his pants when he gets done eating,' she informed her father.

Hendrik had regained his cool: 'I do believe I remember that from your infancy.'

"OK, just so you know.'

Lucia, no longer the center of attention, started to cry. 'Why don't you dance for us, Luz?' Venessa asked. 'Look, you can get up on the table and it will be like a big stage.'

'OK,' Lucia stopped crying and climbed up on the table. Already at three years old she was a performer. Willem and Bobby were locked in conversation down at the other end of the table. Lucia walked over to them and said: 'Daddy, play guitar, I want to dance.'

'I didn't bring a guitar, honey, but I can clap for you.' He started to beat out a flamenco rhythm with his hands, and the little girl did a few childish spins and stomps. Her body hadn't yet got the coordination to actually dance, but she did seem to be moving to the rhythm her father was pounding out. Lucia got a little carried away on one of her spins and dumped on her ass. Bobby stopped clapping and they both started to laugh. Willem, who looked to be stoned out of his mind, was laughing too.

I walked over to Hendrik. The baby had finished his bottle and Hendrik was burping him.

'Let me hold him,' I said. Hendrik handed me the baby and I held him close. The child was a dead weight and smelled like a barn. The odors of sour milk and half-digested baby shit surrounded him. He looked at me and smiled and we gazed into each other's eyes in what seemed like a sublime moment of perfect communion. I embraced the moment, but all the while I was thanking god that I would never have the experience of being the mother of such an adorable, but rancid, little brat.

Venessa came and took the child away and carried him to the loo to change his diapers. Lucia came trailing after them saying she had to go pee-pee. I was surprised to see Venessa performing these traditional female duties with such skill. She acted like she actually enjoyed caring for the children, and I hoped this wasn't leading to more heartbreak further down the line. I went to Hendrik and sat next to him and held his hand: 'You must be over the moon, darling,' I said.

'Yes, I never thought I would see those kids. They are Revata, and I understand that, but they carry some of my genes, and it is very kind of Bobby to bring them to me.'

'Bobby's a fucking mensch,' I said. 'I think he's setting things up with Willem to get Dries and the Viper back.'

Hendrik looked pensive and ignored the Dries and Viper problem: 'I hope Venessa is not too attached to the children. She seems very comfortable with them.'

'I think Venessa is naturally competent around children. She's acting like an efficient nanny or a professional nursery school minder. Those kids belong to the Revata, and she knows it.' I only half believed what I was saying, but I wanted to reassure Hendrik – he didn't need any more problems.

'It's wonderful to meet them, but I'm getting tired now. Do you think we could go upstairs and rest for a while?'

'Yes, of course, Bobby won't mind.'

Hendrik got up and went down the table to Bobby and they embraced. He said something to both Bobby and Willem and then he turned and came back to me and we went upstairs. Venessa and the kids were still in the loo.

The Ruska Roma located the boys in a suburb of Moscow. The town was called Krylatskoe, and sections of it were fairly rural. In fact, the Roma reported that wild boar sometimes roamed the streets and sent a picture to prove it. The area was also a haven for disaffected youth, and the less affluent areas of the suburb were packed with encampments of dedicated free climbers, Parkour artists, snowboarders, and skateboarders.

Dries and the Viper had been accepted into a commune whose members were top climbers with big reps worldwide. The Ruska Roma had infiltrated the commune and learned the boys were training with Boris 'Space Needle' Ulanov, a nineteen-year-old veteran who was famous for his ascent of the Chung King Tower in Hong Kong. Ulanov's tutelage did not come cheap, but Willem had paid out plenty of cash for the Greylander project, and the boys were spending it on training. The Ruska Roma advised Bobby to come quick if he wanted to retrieve the boys, because the 'Space Needle' was prepping them for a big climb on an undisclosed target in two weeks' time.

I met up with Bobby and Venessa at the apartment in the De Pijp. Bobby was taking off for Moscow that afternoon, and they had asked me over to discuss Hendrik's health. Unlike the last time I was at Venessa's place, she served tea and cookies without the consoling benefits of drugs or alcohol.

'How much longer has Hendrik got?' she asked.

'I don't think he knows. If he does, he hasn't confided in me.'

Venessa frowned: 'That's so typical of my father.'

Bobby was nibbling on a cookie: 'Did you put pot in these?'

'It was supposed to be a surprise. Can you taste it?'

'A little bit.' He finished off a cookie and started eating another one.

I glared at Venessa: 'Why in the hell did you do that? I have to go back to work this afternoon.'

'Don't worry, Martel, it probably won't have much effect. It was just a bit of leftover weed.'

'I already ate two of the damn things.'

'You didn't get much of a dose,' Bobby consoled, 'the cookies are small and the dope is weak.'

'You better be right.' I hated the body high you got from eating cannabis. Others could handle it, but I always got logy and semi-paralyzed. I was worried about the effects of the cookies, but Venessa was yapping on about her father:

'So what does the oncologist say about Daddy's condition?' Venessa asked.

'As far as I know, he's stopped going to the oncologist,' I said.

'From what I've seen, he looks to be doing fine,' Bobby said, taking another cookie off the serving plate. 'If Hendrik was being treated by a cancer doctor, his hair would be falling out and he'd have lost forty pounds.'

'He's such a stubborn old fool; he's going to die without making any effort to stay alive.' Venessa was starting to get emotional.

'I don't know what you're getting upset about,' I said, 'You agreed to his plan when he told you he was terminal.'

'I changed my mind,' she said. 'I can't stand to lose my father. I don't know what I'll do without him.'

'Well, darling, I'm afraid you don't have anything to say about Hendrik's treatment, or lack thereof.'

'I could get a court order and force him to have chemotherapy.'

'Oh, no, you couldn't,' I was getting pissed. 'Don't you even dare think about bringing lawyers into this!'

'Calm down, Vennie,' Bobby said. 'Hendrik has made his decision, and there is nothing you can do to change it.'

Thank god Bobby was on the side of reason. Maybe she would listen to him.

'You are all so cruel and unfeeling.' Venessa started to cry.

'No, we're not,' Bobby said. 'We're just abiding by Hendrik's wishes. I hate to tell you, baby, but he's the important one, not you. It doesn't matter what you think or want.'

'Venessa, you have to understand that Hendrik will not survive, even with extreme cancer treatment,' I said, trying to explain.

'There's always hope,' she sobbed. 'We have to hope.'

'I'm sorry, but there is no hope.'

Bobby put his arm around Venessa in an effort to comfort her and to stop her sobs, but she jerked away from him: 'I'm going to force him to have treatment.' Her voice was high and out of control and I knew she was going hysterical.

Bobby looked helplessly at me: 'I have to leave in about five minutes to go to the airport. The plane for Moscow takes off at two thirty. I can't miss it, the Ruska Roma think Dries and the Viper are headed to Dubai in the next few days.'

'Go ahead and leave. I'll take care of her,' I said.

Bobby let go of Venessa and stood up. He scooped the rest of the cookies off the serving plate and wrapped them in a napkin. Venessa didn't seem to notice he was leaving; she was too wrapped up in her own hysteria.

'Good luck, darling,' I said as Bobby hurried out the door. He was on a mission, and I was stuck with a caterwauling idiot. What to do? I had to get back to the shop for a meeting, and Venessa showed no signs of calming down. If she didn't stop soon, I was going to have to call emergency and have them come and take her away. Still, I thought I might be able to stop her hysteria without resorting to such desperate measures. I grabbed her shoulders and forced her to look me in the eye, then I slapped her hard in the face. It felt good when I slapped her. I was sick of the way she was carrying on. Hendrik had enough fucking problems without Venessa going psycho and causing trouble.

'Go wash your face and take a tranquilizer.' I ordered. 'We're going to work.'

I followed her into the bathroom and watched as she applied cold water to her face and eyes. While she was fixing her face, I went through the medicine cabinet and found a bottle of Klonopin. I shook one out and put the bottle in my pocket. She took the pill and swallowed it.

'You don't need any more because you ate all those pot cookies,' I said, 'They should start sedating you any minute now.'

Venessa was not making any objections or mouthing off about her father's plight, and I thought that maybe things were going to be OK.

'Hendrik is dying, and you are going to let him die in his own way. Get it?'

'Yes,' she said. At the moment she sounded meek and was acting passive. I only hoped it would last. Fortunately, I had borrowed Willem's tiny car and we didn't have to cope with public transport. Venessa got in willingly and I took over at the wheel. Just as I started to pull out of the parking space I felt those two pot cookies starting to kick in, but luck was with me and I was able to get us safely to the shop.

Bobby came back from Moscow with Dries and the Viper. I don't know what he said to persuade them to return to Amsterdam. Maybe they were getting cold feet about the climbing and finally realized they could be dropping to their death at any minute. Willem was so happy to get them back that he threw a party over at the 'No Exit' coffee shop. The boys were treated as heroes, and even the Viper's mom and dad showed up for the occasion. The parents were a pair of solid citizens from Utrecht and were totally perplexed by their son's outrageous endeavors. Unlike the Van der Saars, they were pretty straight and did not partake of the pot and hash that was circulating freely.

Madame Lillian arrived with Rowley, and somebody must have slipped him a hash brownie because he got loaded and fell out on the floor and started turning somersaults. Bobby brought the kids and they both seemed to have caught a contact high; Lucia was dancing and singing like a trooper, and the baby was rolling on the floor with Rowley.

It was a jolly time, and the only one who put a damper on the party was Venessa, who clung to her father in a tearful pose. Hendrik was gentle with her; I had told him about her threats to force him to have chemo, and he didn't want to get her riled up. Still, she was cramping his style, he wanted her to go away so he could enjoy the festivities and play with his grandchildren. Finally, Venessa got the message and went to join Bobby and Dries who seemed to be deep in discussion with Willem.

The rest of us were watching videos of the boys climbing exploits and having a jolly time when the outer door opened and who should walk in but my old buddies from New Jersey, Johnny A. and Joey T. They were escorting a suavely dressed elderly man who hobbled along on a walker. I assumed the old dude was Pookie's boyfriend, the ancient Capo. Johnny and Joey were both looking uncomfortable and gazed at me with beseeching eyes: 'Hello, Ms. Martel' one of them said.

'We're sorry to intrude, but Don Gulio wants a word with your husband,' the other one said.

Rowley, who had been playing with the baby, stood up and started advancing toward the New Jersey contingent. It seemed he had not forgotten his previous encounter with Johnny and Joey because his hair was bristling and his fangs were showing.

'Tell him to climb down, will you, Lillian,' I said.

Lillian, dressed in five inch heels and a silver lamé gown walked over to Rowley and gave him some hand signals. The dog looked miffed, but turned around and went back to the baby and sniffed his diapers.

Don Gulio in the meantime was dragging his walker towards Hendrik. 'You fucking asshole, you killed the love of my life!'

'I did nothing of the sort,' Hendrik was indignant, 'Pookie dropped dead on her own. Nobody helped her.'

The old Don pulled out a Glock and started waving it around. All eyes were now on the New Jersey mobsters, but no one in our crowd moved a muscle except Willem, who was slowly advancing up behind Don Gulio. Johnny and Joey just stood there looking confused and helpless.

'I loved her,' Don Gulio said. He pointed his gun directly at Hendrik, but didn't pull the trigger. After a long moment, he dropped it on the floor.

'Pick up that gun! There are kids around here,' I shouted at Johnny and Joey. They both scrambled for the gun almost knocking heads in their enthusiasm to grab it. Finally, one of them picked it up and stashed it in his pocket.

The old Don let go of his walker and slumped into a chair at Hendrik's table. 'What were her last words?' he asked. I was sitting next to him and could see the tears running down the crevasses of his wrinkled cheeks.

Hendrik replied: 'I think she said, *You're a rotten punk and I'm going to have your ass in jail.*'

'Yes,' I agreed, 'those were her last words. I was there and I heard them. After that she fell on the couch and died.'

The Don laughed through his tears: 'That does sound like Pookie,' he said. 'Her bark was always worse than her bite.'

Lucia had been dancing on a table when the Don walked in and spoiled her act. She came over and climbed up on Hendrik's lap: 'Who's that, Grandpa?' she asked.

'That's our friend Don Gulio. He traveled a long way to come to the party.'

Lucia looked at the old Mafioso suspiciously: 'He was going to shoot you with a gun,' she said.

'It was a toy gun, honey. He was just playing.'

'I want that gun. I want to shoot him in the head.'

'You can't have it. His friends threw it away.'

Lucia started to cry. Maybe her contact high was wearing off, or maybe she had been exposed to too much excitement for the day. When the baby heard his sister crying, he started bawling too. Suddenly, it felt like the party was over.

The Viper's family grabbed their son, thanked Willem for his hospitality, and fled. Madame Lillian snapped the leash on Rowley and went outside. Bobby took his kids and left with Venessa and Willem and Dries. Johnny A and Joey T helped Don Gulio to his feet and attached him to his walker. The old man was still crying, but at least he no longer wanted to fill Hendrik full of lead. The boys from New Jersey were deeply contrite and assured us they would all be on the first flight out of Schiphol in the morning.

Hendrik and I were left alone in the coffee shop. He picked up a joint and lit it: 'We might as well get high,' he said. 'I hear weed is good for cancer patients.'

The little soirée at the coffee house was not the last party Willem threw that month. He gathered the staff and a few business friends for a goodbye dinner in honor of Hendrik's departure from the firm. This bitter-sweet event was held at a charming venue in the Frankendael Park.

The restaurant De Kas was housed in a remodeled greenhouse and surrounded by vegetable and herb gardens. The whole set-up was steeped in Dutch tradition and seemed marvellously fitting and right for a Van der Saar event.

Hendrik had been in his element that night and accepted the toasts and plaudits of his associates with modest good humor. I was unsure if the guests knew of Hendrik's cancer, or if they just thought he was taking early retirement. A lot of wine was poured, and, towards the end of the party the mood became sentimental. I got pretty wasted on the wine, so I can't remember much of what was said, but I do have an image of Hendrik making a farewell speech that was greeted with wild applause. When the speech was finished Willem came to his side and they stood arm in arm at the head of the table with their wine glasses held high. It was a fine end to a glorious evening.

Hendrik was starting to lose his appetite and began slowly dropping weight. The food he liked best was hazelnut gelato which he ate morning, noon, and night. I tried to tempt him with soups and pastas, but he didn't have much interest, although one night he single-handedly devoured a platter of roast beef with horse radish sauce. I guess he needed the B vitamins in the meat.

I was eating the gelato along with him, we ordered cartons of the hazelnut ice cream from Fior di Gelato. Although Hendrik was beginning to look like an Auschwitz survivor, I was gaining weight around the middle. It probably didn't help that I was drinking iced vodka with the gelato. It was a good combination and helped keep the anxiety down.

As Hendrik's disease progressed, he started taking OxyContin and drifted into a drugged oblivion that must have been similar to that experienced by junkies. He started to play a lot of Chet Baker music and seemed to find peace and strength from listening to Chet's deeply evolved meditations on love and death. I listened along with him, and I do believe that Chet, who is often unfairly portrayed as an evil junked-out demon, went about as deep as you can go into interpreting areas of pure emotion.

In the last days of Hendrik's life I took to sleeping with him. He was a sweet bundle of bones that I loved to hold next to me. He was usually zoned out of his mind, and I often joined him in oblivion by taking an OxyContin or licking on one of his Fentanyl lollipops. It was if we were both dead together, but still breathing, and still sharing our love.

One night he woke me at around three am and said: 'Martel, I just had a dream and I want to replicate it before I die. I dreamt of a dinner party with all our nearest and dearest. It was here in the dining room of the Herengracht and the Greylander Rembrandt was on the wall. In my dream the dinner was a joyous occasion and Bobby was playing the Concierto de Aranjuez on the guitar. He finished playing and the party broke up. You and I went to my bedroom to wait for the suicide doctor. When the moment came you held me in your arms while I left this world.'

'That's a great script, darling,' I said, 'and I think it can be managed. I'll get on it tomorrow.' My words were calm and businesslike, but in my mind I was thinking: 'Jesus Christ, what next?'

I had a vision of the suicide doctor, dressed in a black coat and black fedora, carrying a little black medical bag, climbing the back stairs to Hendrik's room. As I watched the doctor climb the steep, narrow stairs I heard Bobby's rendition of the exquisitely melodic Concierto de Aranjuez playing softly in the background.

I came back from my reverie and reached out for my husband and we embraced. Our bodies moved in unison, and damned if we didn't start to make love. We were poised on the edge between life and death and each movement was fraught with meaning. It was a strange and overwhelming event that was weirdly timeless. It felt like we were swimming in a sea of bliss.

After making the necessary mental adjustments and forcing myself to accept that the day of the party was going to be the day of Hendrik's death, I got down on the plans for the dinner. He was going out in a great burst of conviviality, unafraid of sharing the ecstasy and the pain of his last day on earth with family and friends. The Van der Saars and the Viper were easy invites, even though I dared not tell anyone but Willem that this was to be Hendrik's last supper.

I made sure I spoke directly with Detective Nikki Gripsa, stressing the importance of the occasion so he could take time off from his police duties and attend the party. After that I made a call to Nikki's mother, Lillian, requesting that she leave Rowley at home. We all adored the big rascal, but since Piet's departure the dog had become rather headstrong and attention seeking, and I didn't want his antics to disrupt the dinner.

Next, I talked to Bobby, and he said it would be an honor to perform the Concierto for his father. He loved the Joaquin Rodrigo piece and had been playing the adagio for years. I asked if he was bringing the children, but he said that was a no-go because the Revata women had gone off on a shopping trip to Paris and taken the kids with them.

Even though I was putting a good face on Hendrik's imminent demise, it didn't mean that I wasn't feeling sadness and despair. One had to participate in daily life, and I did not allow myself to appear needy and introspective. Instead of falling into a funk, I decided to prepare the entire party menu. It would be a labor of love, a festive offering to the guests and to my husband. The cooking would also keep me so occupied I wouldn't be able to think about Hendrik's suicide trip.

I decided on the Julia Child chicken with lemon, butter, garlic, and taragon, only this time I would roast five or six plump birds. The menu was essentially the same one I served to Nikki and Hendrik months ago, but instead of meager little plates of seafood there would be giant platters of *fruits de mer.* I would not be holding back for this final feast, and there would be lobster, crab, mussels, scallops, and langoustines along with the shrimp and oysters. It was a pity that Hendrik's stomach had turned so weak, I doubted he would be able to partake of the seafood.

I labored for days on the purchase of food stuffs, and, just like a rich dope dealer, ordered a case of Cristal champagne. The champagne was good for starters, but I also raided the Van der Saar cellars for choice vintages to serve with the meal. Madame Lillian offered to bring over a dozen individual lemon tarts, and I happily accepted because her pastry making was on a professional level. According to Hendrik, she had learned the art many years ago when she worked in a Paris patisserie. I thought the lemon tarts would be a lovely ending to the meal and go well with a glass of Cristal, but I also knew there were people, myself included, who liked to finish a nice dinner with a taste of chocolate, so I ordered up the best chocolate gateau in town, knowing full well that Bobby, Dries, the Viper, and perhaps others, would consume portions of both desserts.

On the day of the party, Dries and the Viper arrived at around eight in the morning carrying boxes of tulips. Hendrik wasn't really up to the task of assembling huge bouquets, so the boys filled several large vases with water and then put the flowers together under his direction. The flowers were red and white striped tulips, the only variation being that one group had straight edges and the other had ruffled edges. By placing them together the effect was harmonious, but with a subtle difference that caught the eye and for a moment challenged the brain. Hendrik was pleased with the effect and congratulated his helpers; he said he couldn't have done better himself.

The boys took off, and Willem arrived with the Greylander Rembrandt. Hendrik wanted it hung in the dining room where his guests could view it while eating. I assisted Willem in hanging the picture, and after we'd got it on the wall I cracked a bottle of Cristal. Hendrik's stomach had not yet reached the point where it would reject a glass of the bubbly and he drank the wine with pleasure.

'The picture looks great with the flowers,' Willem said. 'It's taking me straight back to the Golden Days of the Dutch renaissance.'

'Yes, it seems to belong in this room,' I said.

'I still think it's a Rembrandt,' Willem said stubbornly.

'You may be right, brother.' At this late date Hendrik seemed willing to change his opinion.

'I knew you'd finally come round,' Willem smiled.

I decided to get my two cents in: 'It must be the contrast with the tulips, because it sure didn't look this good the last time we had it in here.' A nasty thought crossed my mind: 'Have you been working on it, Willem?'

'Of course not, Martel. You don't see any wet paint, do you?'

I had to admit the painting was dry and didn't look like it had been tampered with. Still, Willem had his ways. Who knew what he was up to when he was locked in the confines of his studio? In spite of his denial, I was still puzzled about the painting and thought something had been altered, but I couldn't figure out what.

Hendrik was sitting at the dining table grinning like a Cheshire cat. If he knew that Willem had been doing some retouching, he wasn't sharing his knowledge with me. The two brothers seemed to be having one last moment of mischief before they parted for good. I poured them each another flute of champagne and left for the kitchen to start preparing the chickens.

I had a few qualms about the party and was concerned that I might break down when Bobby started playing the Aranjuez Concierto. The piece was tinged with deep sadness and grief, which was only slightly alleviated by the beauty of the melody. I was skating on emotional thin ice and I knew it, but I was even more troubled by the thought of what Venessa might get up to.

She had been controlling her emotions since the outburst at her apartment. There had been no more hysteria and no more crazy talk of getting a court order to force her father to have chemo. She seemed to have resigned herself to the fact that he was dying in his own way and there was nothing she could do to stop him. Nobody except Willem and me knew that this was to be Hendrik's last day on earth, but I was sure that most of the guests would pick up on the vibe, and I hoped Venessa would not take it upon herself to try and save her father from the ministrations of the suicide doctor. I didn't want the dinner party to end in a knockdown, drag-out fight between myself and Venessa, two females who, each in her own way, loved Hendrik with a pure and passionate intensity.

I put such thoughts out of my mind and started to work. I had five chickens and kilos of vegetables to prepare. By the time the helpers arrived, my work was done and I trusted them to roast the fowl and the veggies while I went to my rooms and got myself together for the party. I hadn't seen Hendrik in hours and I stopped by his suite to see how he was doing, but he was laid out on the bed fast asleep.

When eight o'clock rolled around both Hendrik and I were dressed and groomed and ready to greet the guests. He looked a prince in one of his bespoke suits which had been taken in and restructured for his shrinking body. The tailors had done a masterful job, he appeared as suave and commanding as he had before the cancer struck.

I left Hendrik sipping Cristal and schmoozing with the first arrivals while I went to the kitchen to supervise the plating and serving.

Lillian swept into the kitchen carrying a large pastry box. She was wearing a sea green taffeta gown that fell from her shoulders like waves in a Turner seascape. She dropped the box on the kitchen table, and gave me a quick kiss. She said: 'Martel, I've just been in the dining room, and it looks fabulous. The tulips and the Rembrandt are a perfect match, in fact, I don't think I've ever seen a more spectacular décor.'

'Hendrik and Willem are responsible for the dining room. Tell them about it, I'm sure they'd love to know your reaction.'

Lillian gave me an inquisitive look: 'The painting is real, isn't it?'

'Truthfully, Lillian, I have no idea.'

She grabbed a flute of Cristal off a tray and drained it in one gulp. 'Darling, correct me if I'm wrong, but I'm getting the idea that this may be Hendrik's last night.' She was starting to tear up and I worried that she might spoil her elaborate eye make-up.

'Don't cry, Lillian,' I said, 'I can't stand to see all that black soot run down your cheeks. Stay pretty for Hendrik, you know he always had a crush on you. Don't spoil his memories by looking like a make-up disaster.'

I took a piece of paper towel and blotted her eyes. Lillian picked up another flute of Cristal, lifted her chin, and tossed her head of bouffant hair; she was going into *femme fatale* mode.

'You look gorgeous now,' I said. 'This is the way Hendrik wants to see you. Don't let him down by going hysterical.'

'Thanks for putting me on the right track, Martel. Don't worry I won't start crying,' she paused. 'Why don't you check out the tarts before I go back to the party?'

I opened the lid of the box and looked down at thirteen fine examples of the pastry chef's art. 'They are wonderful, Lillian, not only do they look beautiful but the lemon smells so good I can barely stop myself from tasting one.'

'I made a baker's dozen,' she said, 'let's split one. They're light; a few bites won't spoil our appetites.' She picked up a table knife and cut one of the tarts in half.

I took my half and bit into it, the sensation was one of pure lemon with a slight hint of sweetness that tickled the taste buds and made you long for another mouthful. I followed the lemon tart with a sip of Cristal: 'I think we've got a winner here,' I said.

'Yes,' Lillian smiled, 'I do believe the combination of *tarte citron* and champagne is close to perfection.'

Hendrik sat at the head of the table with Bobby and Venessa on either side. I was doing my duty down at the foot of the table with Willem and Dries beside me. Nikki was seated next to Venessa and they were chatting it up. Lillian was across the table next to the Viper and he was autographing a photo of the Moscow climb for her. Since Dries and the Viper returned from Russia, they had become quite the local celebrities and never went anywhere without stacks of PR prints in case one of their fans wanted an autograph. Willem was slumped in his chair looking wasted on weed; he was so stoned he wasn't partaking of the delectable seafood that had just arrived at table. He kept staring at the Greylander Rembrandt with a dreamy smile on his face.

Dries was busy demolishing one of the sea food platters, but he wasn't so overcome by gluttony that he didn't have time to glance at his father: 'Come on, Dad, eat up. This could be your last chance for *fruits de mer* because all the seafood is dying out.' He put a large scallop, two belon oysters, and a langoustine on his father's plate.

Willem smiled beatifically and speared the scallop. 'Thank you, Dries, for putting the food on my plate, and thank you, Martel for arranging such a beautiful presentation of so many endangered species. The seaweed draped on the platter is a nice effect.'

'Don't start on the ecology,' I warned. 'I was just trying to make something nice for Hendrik and our guests.'

'Sorry, Auntie Martel, I didn't mean to make you feel guilty.' Dries began scarfing up a couple of large, pink shrimp.

Willem was eating seafood, but his eye was still on the double portrait of the affluent Dutch couple. Dries followed his father's gaze, stopped, and took a good look: 'Dad, is this the same painting we had in the shop? It looks different. It looks like a real Rembrandt.'

'That's just an illusion, son. The painting is being displayed in an historic room that has period details, so the picture looks like it belongs here. And, those splendid bouquets of tulips that you and the Viper helped arrange set it off to perfection. It is looking very much of the period.'

Dries gave his father an odd look, but went back to his seafood and let the authenticity of the Greylander Rembrandt pass without any more comment.

I was eating the seafood too, it was fresh and tasty, and I only hoped that the genius of Dutch aquaculture would be able to keep these species alive in the years to come. Down the table Hendrik was relishing the party and acting like a true *bon vivant*. I was surprised to see his plate was full of oysters, lobster, and crab. This was indeed a surprise, I didn't think he'd be able to get them down.

The seafood platters were taken away and the roasted chickens and root vegetables were served along with Grüner Veltliner and Clos Vougeot from the Van der Saar cellars. The chickens looked like they belonged on the cover of a gastronomy magazine with their crisp, caramel-colored skins and a garniture of large, browned, mushrooms. When the detective saw the roast chickens he smiled down the table toward me and said: 'Martel, those chickens look so succulent and juicy I think they will drive me to desire.'

'You make eating a chicken sound like an erotic experience,' I said.

Nikki laughed: 'It could be. I hope your cooking doesn't send me to the red light district later tonight.'

Lillian gave her son a dirty look; he was a hard-nosed cop, but he was still her baby, and she didn't like him running around the red light district and consorting with prostitutes.

I stood up and started carving the chickens because I didn't think Hendrik was up to the task, but he surprised me by coming to my side and taking the knife out of my hand. He carved the chickens with swift, sure, strokes of the blade and his hand never wavered. When he finished, the last chicken he looked at me and winked. He seemed to be in a playful mood, it must have been the oysters he'd just eaten.

Lillian took a nice piece of white meat and a smaller piece of the dark. After sampling both she said: 'Excellent, Martel. The true test of a cook is how she prepares a roast chicken.'

Venessa piped up from down the table: 'Martel, you have to teach me how to make this chicken and veggies. Please, Martel, they're the best.'

'Any time you're ready, darling. Just let me know.' I was happy my main dish was a success, particularly with Venessa, who, like so many young women, was a notoriously finicky eater.

I could hear Dries and the Viper making juvenile sex jokes about breast and leg as they shared a chicken. The Moscow maniacs were having a ball, but Bobby had suddenly turned morose and was just toying with his food. He must have figured out that something was up with Hendrik and that this festive meal was actually his father's last supper.

I hadn't spoken to Bobby since the evening began and now I observed him sitting next to Hendrik like a reflective shadow of the older man. Since Bobby had stopped shooting smack, his golden glow and Bodhisattva tendencies had diminished. I wondered if there was a correlation between his drug taking and his semi-divine qualities. That was possible, but I decided it was more likely that his saintly aura had diminished because he had entered the adult world and been faced with the realities of fatherhood, the difficulties of placating the women in his life, and the problems of making a living out of an art form that was relegated to an obscure area on the margins of world music. There was also the angst of living between two cultures. Shit, that would be enough to make anybody lose their psychic connection and stop glowing. Still, Bobby was a genius musician, and no one could ever take that from him.

Venessa was not aware of the sadness emanating from Bobby's corner because she was still laughing it up with Nikki. I turned to Lillian: 'Venessa and Nikki seem to be really hitting it off tonight.'

'It's always like this when they get together. They're like two peas out of the same pod,' she paused and took a sip of red burgundy, 'I don't think it will do any harm to tell you, darling, but I think Nikki is Venessa's father. He was always crazy in love with her mother and had a complete breakdown when she took off with Dieter. That's when he joined the cops. He wanted to put the past behind him, but he still couldn't break the tie with Hendrik. As Venessa grew older, he became convinced she was his daughter.'

'If what you say is true, then you're Venessa's grandmother.'

'I believe I am,' she said proudly.

'I hope you're going to be there for her when Hendrik dies. I won't be able to help her because I'll be totally out of my mind with grief and despair.'

'Don't worry, Martel, Rowley and I will take good care of her. She can stay at my house until she recovers.'

'Just don't keep her too long. We're going to need her down at the shop.'

I barely had time to process Lillian's revelation when there was a moment of confusion that interrupted my thought. The kitchen helpers came in and removed the chicken carcasses and the dirty plates. While this was going on, there was some action at the head of the table. Hendrik stood up and shoved his chair aside. He had a dinner napkin over his mouth and his face had turned a nasty shade of green. Bobby grabbed his arm and hurried him along to the lavatory in the hall. I was hoping and praying that Hendrik would not vomit until he got to the toilet. Lord Shiva answered my prayers and Hendrik held it down.

Venessa had been so busy gabbing with Nikki that she hadn't caught the full effect of Hendrik's absence from the table. She looked bewildered and seemed uncertain as to what was going on. The Viper, seeing her confusion, said: 'Your Dad just went to the lav. He'll be right back.'

The helpers were uncorking the Cristal and serving the lemon tarts and the chocolate gateau. By the time Hendrik and Bobby got back, people were indulging themselves in the luscious desserts. I noticed that Hendrik's face had turned from the vomity green to a whiter shade of pale, and that he flashed a sweet smile in my direction. Thank god I had placed a bottle of mouthwash in the downstairs loo this morning, so he was able to cleanse his mouth of the noxious residue.

I watched carefully as Hendrik took a glass of Cristal and picked delicately at a lemon tart. Bobby had buried himself in a double serving of the chocolate gateau and was simultaneously drinking a glass of red and a glass of champagne. The poor kid, I really felt for him. It had been a rough night and it wasn't over yet. Thank god we had the good food and drink to get us through.

Dessert was almost over and Bobby, who was supposed to play the Aranjuez Concierto after dinner, seemed disinclined to bring out his guitar. He said something to Hendrik, then stood up and walked down the table toward me: 'Sorry, Martel, I can't play tonight. Hendrik told me what's going on when we were in the toilet. I know I'm not being professional, but I'm afraid I might break down while I'm playing.' Bobby leaned over and gave me a kiss before he walked back to sit by his father.

Things were starting to get painful, but the scenario had to be played out and I was the director. I tried to get Willem's attention, but he was still staring at the fucking painting. He was so out of it I figured he was on more than hash or weed. Maybe he had got into the barbiturates. I knew that he was unable to face the loss of his brother and that this was his way of dealing with the grim reality. I turned to Dries: 'Why don't you and the Viper take your Dad home and let him rest. He's really out of it.'

Poor little Dries, I hated to ask him, but he just smiled and said: 'OK. Can we take the rest of the cake with us?'

'Sure, go right ahead.'

'How about a bottle of that red wine?'

'When did you start drinking wine?'

'The Space Needle taught us to drink when we were in Moscow, but he never gave us any wine that tasted this good.'

"OK, darling, enjoy it. But right now do me a favor and get your Dad out of here. I want everybody to leave and you can start the exodus.'

The Viper saw what was going on and came over and gave me a hug and a kiss. Since his stay in Moscow he had become quite the ladies' man: 'Thanks, Martel, it was really beautiful. I'll never forget it.'

'You're welcome, darling.' I kissed him back.

It took both Dries and the Viper to get Willem on his feet and out the door, but they managed quite well, even with the added baggage of a bottle of wine and a box of cake.

Nikki and Lillian exchanged glances. They both knew it was time to go and I asked them to take Venessa with them. She was drunk and had eaten a lot of food that probably wasn't going to agree with her body chemistry. She didn't seem to have any idea of what was going on with Bobby and Hendrik, because she just kissed them goodbye and went off with her putative father and alleged grandmother.

I looked at my watch. It was eleven o'clock and the suicide doctor was due in at midnight. Bobby was still hanging around and I gave Hendrik an inquisitive look. He put his arm around Bobby's shoulders and asked: 'Do you want to stick around for the main event?'

'I guess I can take it if you can,' he smiled wanly. 'I might need to be a little high when…' he struggled for words, 'the doctor comes. Have you got any drugs?'

'I don't have any injectables, but there are bottles of OxyContin and a package of Fentanyl lollipops. The lollipops are supposed to be eighty times stronger than morphine.'

'That sounds like big pharma bullshit,' Bobby said. 'A couple of Oxys will do it for me.'

'I think I'll have one too,' I said. 'I don't want to be sucking on a lollipop when the doctor arrives.'

Hendrik and Bobby both snickered; even at this desperate moment they still had dirty minds.

We all got loaded and laid out on Hendrik's big bed and listened to Chet Baker and Paul Desmond and a bitching rhythm section play the adagio from the Aranjuez concierto. When the doorbell rang, Bobby jumped to his feet and went downstairs to let the doctor in. They came up in the little elevator, and when I saw the doctor he was not as I imagined. He was a plump, rosy chap who looked like he might have been a dairy farmer or a cheese maker.

Dr. De Jong had never met Hendrik and didn't have a clue as to who his patient was, but he must have been a jazz fan because he was well aware of the fact that the handsome young man who answered the door was the world renowned guitarist, Bobby Janacek. While the doctor made his preparations, Hendrik asked Bobby to play the Aranjuez again. As the music began to flow out of the speakers, Dr. De Jong said: 'A wise choice, Herr Van der Saar. Many of my patients go out to this music, although they usually play the Miles Davis version. Like you, I prefer Chet and Paul.'

Bobby moved a chair close to the bed and took Hendrik's hand. I stayed beside my husband. I was cuddled into his side and rested my head on his chest. Both Bobby and I were in the way of a clean shot, but somehow the doctor managed.

Hendrik said: 'Be kind to Venessa,' and then he was gone.

After Hendrik's death most of his ashes were disposed of in the Herengracht canal and the back garden of the house. A small portion was taken by Willem, and tossed, in the dark of night, around the perimeter of the shop.

The mourning period lasted for ten days, and the windows and main entrance of Van der Saar Fine Arts were draped in black bunting. Hendrik's PR portrait, the one where he looked like a Spanish aristocrat of the old school, was blown up and edged in black and put in one of the windows. In the other window a large, candid photo of Hendrik walking through a field of tulips with a three year old Venessa perched on his shoulder was displayed to fine effect.

Bobby was given Hendrik's suits and haberdashery, and he very kindly offered Dries a choice of the suits. The Viper was also remembered, and given a fine cashmere sweater and a Hermès foulard. Before the boys finished decimating Hendrik's wardrobe, I went down and raided his sock drawer.

As I ran my fingers through the rich excesses of natural fibers, I reflected that Hendrik had decorated his body with the finest clothes and fabrics, but he was no arriviste tycoon, rap star zillionaire, or broken down shadow of hereditary monarchy, none of whom could hang clothes on their bodies with such finesse. He was merely playing the role of art hustler to the wealthy, and dressed himself in a manner that was devised to awe and impress. It was a role that had been bequeathed to him by generations of Van der Saar merchants and conmen.

I filled a shopping bag with his precious socks and carried them off to my bedroom. They would be mine to keep and I would wear a pair of them to bed every night for the rest of my life.

We kept the shop closed for ten days. It was a time for deep mourning, a time for introspection and memory, a time to process death and learn to live with the absence of the beloved. Of course, mourning lasts longer than ten days, sometimes it lasts forever, but in this formal period the Van der Saar family had time to express or repress their feelings of loss. After that, it would be business as usual.

I stayed at the house in the Herengracht, the only occupant, alone with a paralysing grief. Although I had watched Hendrik sicken and die and cared for him in his last days, I was ill-prepared for his loss. He had been such a great and brilliant spirit, a man who brought so much beauty and joy into my life that it seemed impossible to accept his death.

Even though it was the height of summer the rooms were cold and my body was chilled. I wrapped myself in Hendrik's favorite sweater and spent most of my time huddled under the duvet, reliving every moment of our time together. His scent was still on the sweater, and that brought him close and there were times when I thought I could feel him in the bed next to me.

As I lay in bed, I wondered if it was time to end the tawdry spectacle of my life. It would be easy: a bottle of Hendrik's best cognac and a handful of sleeping pills. It was the traditional route for heartbroken females, and I asked myself why not join all those silken damsels who had perished for need of a vanished lover. Why not? I was sick of this fucking charade we call life. Death would be a new adventure, and who knows, I might even meet up with Hendrik somewhere out there in a parallel universe.

I reached out and grasped the bottle of pills on the bedside table. When I opened the cap, the bottle was empty and

I realized that I had been medicating myself into oblivion. No wonder I hardly ever got out of bed and my brain had turned to mush. The bottle of XO on the table was only half full, and may have contributed to the damage. I must have had a subconscious wish for suicide, but now the wish had risen to full consciousness and I needed more pills.

I got out of bed, my legs felt weak and shaky from lack of use, and I wrapped Hendrik's sweater tightly around me. I was going to have to go into his room and search for his stash of narcotics. The room had not been entered for days and I dreaded the thought of looking at Hendrik's bed and perhaps seeing a replay of his entire death drama. However, need conquered fear, and I walked down the hall and opened the door.

The room was dark, empty, and cold, and there was an odd, rotted, vegetal stink in the air. The odor certainly wasn't left over from Hendrik, even in his last days he exuded his familiar personal scent of pine needles and warm honey. After my eyes adjusted to the dim light, I saw a decaying bouquet that had been left to rot on a table close to the window. The floral display, a typical Dutch mélange of blown out roses, drooping carnations, livid fruits, and frowzy tulips, had become a true *nature morte*, oozing rot and decay. When I pulled the drapes and opened the windows to let some sunlight and air into the darkened room, a huge and spectacular cerulean blue butterfly flew in and circled the bouquet.

The unexpected arrival of the butterfly caused my heart to flutter and then break into a rapid, agitated beat that banged away in my chest like a hammer. I had seen the blue butterfly before, in this very room, on the day that Hendrik and I had agreed to marry. At that time, the insect had appeared as a magical symbol of the life to come. Now, as it hovered over the rotted flowers, I felt it as a malign influence. Maybe it was the spirit of Pookie Greylander coming back to gloat over Hendrik's death and to take her revenge.

The butterfly settled on the remains of a red and white tulip and closed its wings. Apparently there was no food to be had in the shrivelled flower, because, after a few moments, the butterfly opened its mighty wings and swept out the window like an insect version of Dracula. The evil bug was gone as suddenly as it had appeared.

I took a quick look out the window, the butterfly had vanished into the sky, and the street and the canal path were deserted. It was a perfect opportunity to get rid of the stinking, rotting flowers, so I picked up the vase and dumped the contents out the window onto the cobbles below. After that the room began to smell better, and I was able to concentrate on my search for the drugs.

There were no pills or lollipops on Hendrik's bed table so I headed for the bathroom where he usually kept a stash in the medicine cabinet. I opened the cabinet. The drugs were gone. I took a further look around but there was nothing to be found, and I figured that Bobby must have relapsed and secretly taken the lot.

Now I was totally fucked; without sleeping pills or dope there was no way I was going to kill myself. Jumping, strangling, or cutting my wrists did not appeal, so I'd probably have to stay alive and learn to live with the horrible, empty pit in my stomach, the melancholy pain in my heart, and the full-on sexual feelings that popped up in my genitals when I thought back on Hendrik's physical appeal and masterful lovemaking.

Opting to live for the time being, I put my suicidal impulses on hold and headed downstairs. I hadn't eaten in days and I interpreted the gnawing emptiness in my gut as a need for food. When I got to the kitchen, I was surprised to see Dries standing in the middle of the floor with a broom in his hand.

'Hi, Auntie Martel, there was a big mess out front and I just cleaned it up. I think somebody left a floral tribute to Hendrik on the stoop and some jerk came by and destroyed it.'

'Thanks, Dries, that was really sweet of you,' I said weakly. No way was I going to tell him the truth about the flowers. I went to the refrigerator and opened the door: 'I was just going to make some lunch, would you care to join me?'

'Sure,' he smiled, propping the broom up in a corner and sitting down at the table.

All I could find in the refrigerator was a tub of reasonably fresh chicken salad, a wheel of Camembert, and an avocado. I hurriedly put the Camembert in the microwave on low heat and let it nuke for ten seconds. After that I arranged some slightly wilted lettuce on two plates and put a scoop of chicken salad and a few slices of avocado on each plate, spritzing both with lemon and hot sauce. The Camembert, which, after its stint in the microwave looked fairly ripe, was placed on a platter and surrounded by crackers. For drinks I found a couple of bottles of Belgian brew hidden in the back of the refrigerator.

'Willem sent me over to see how you're doing,' Dries said between bites of chicken salad. 'He's sorry he neglected you, but he's just too fucked-up to come by.'

'I hope he's not in serious trouble.'

'It's serious enough – he keeps himself locked up in his studio and I can hear him crying and cursing and pounding on the wall. I guess he really misses his brother.'

'That's understandable, they were very close.'

'Like Vincent and Theo?' Dries asked, referring to the Van Gogh brothers. The kid was a typical Van der Saar, always getting off with an art history reference.

'Similar, but not quite,' I said. As I recalled Theo went stark raving mad and died only six months after Vincent's death. We were getting into dangerous waters, and I thought it best to change the subject: 'I've been out of the loop for a while, how's Venessa doing?'

'She's out in the Noord with Nikki's mom. The dog is taking care of her. He sleeps in her bed at night and lets her cuddle him like a big teddy bear. During the day he makes her work in the garden.'

'They say that work is the answer to grief.'

'Willem says that's true, it's in the Dutch tradition. He's going to be back on the job on Monday and wants to know if you'll be there too.'

'Of course, darling, you couldn't keep me away.'

'Thank god you're coming back,' Dries was relieved and his face showed it. 'I doubt that Willem can go it alone.'

'We're all in this together,' I said. 'I'll help where I can.'

'I know you will, Martel. You're the best.'

'Speaking of the best how's the best guitar player in the world these days?'

'Bobby's OK, he's with the Revata. I saw him the other day and he gave me something to give to you.' Dries reached for his rucksack and pulled out a plastic bag and handed it to me. 'Bobby wanted to give it to you himself, but he knew he'd done wrong and was afraid you'd nail him to the wall. He couldn't face you, Martel.'

I took the bag and opened it. Inside were the drugs that Hendrik had left behind. Apparently, Bobby's theft had saved my life. An hour earlier I would have used the drugs to kill myself, but now that I had resolved to live I didn't need them.

'Bobby doesn't need to worry, I'm not mad at him. Tell him to call me, we can talk it out.'

'Sure,' Dries said, popping a piece of Camembert into his mouth.

'And how about you, Dries, are you alright? It must be a big job looking after your father.'

Dries lower lip started to tremble and I thought he was going to cry: 'The Viper's been staying with us, and if Willem gets too crazy, he helps me restrain him.'

'Has he been smashing up his paintings?'

'Only a couple, and they aren't completely destroyed. He's patching them up today. I think he's beginning to learn to live with his loss.'

'I'm glad somebody is.'

'Don't talk that way, Martel, we need you to be strong for the family's sake.' Dries lower lip started to quiver again: 'Willem's worried you might go back to the States.'

I laughed: 'He *really* must be out of his mind. I've got nothing left over there and I never want to go back. I'm afraid you guys are stuck with me.'

Dries smiled: 'That's great, Auntie Martel. You know we love you and want you around forever.'

'And I love you too, darling.' Now I was the one who was starting to tear up.

'I bet you haven't been out of the house in days,' he said. 'Let's go for a walk down by the canal. The fresh air will do you good. Maybe we can stop some place for coffee.'

'I'd like that, Dries. Just let me comb my hair and freshen up.'

The pain and the emptiness were still with me, but I was going to suck them in and soldier on. I knew that was the way Hendrik would want it.

As head of the family, Willem was expected to live in the Herengracht house, and not long after the period of mourning ended he and Dries moved in. They brought the Viper with them, and he found a space on the third floor. There was plenty of room for everyone, and we hoped that Venessa would soon return. Willem made very few changes, the Greylander Rembrandt remained in the dining room, and the main rooms were always full of flowers.

Venessa was living with Lillian and Rowley, but I was too fatigued by my own grief to check and find out what was going on over in the Noord. I knew Venessa was in good hands, and when she bothered to show up at work, she seemed in reasonably good spirits. The plan was that she would eventually take over the sales and marketing area, but at this point she wasn't ready, and we just let it ride. I could have used her, she actually knew a lot about the business, but she seemed disinclined to spend any more than twelve hours a week at the shop.

I was busy putting a presentation together when Dries walked into my office, wearing one of Hendrik's suits. The suit had been tailored to fit his slender frame and, by wearing this piece of silk and wool, he had become an entirely different person, someone similar to my late husband.

'Jesus, Dries, what happened to you?' I gasped.

'I got a haircut and put on some of Hendrik's clothes.'

He turned like a model and asked: 'What do you think, Martel? Dad says I look pretty cool.'

'Honey, you look like a billion bucks.'

'I want to work with you, Auntie Martel. I want to learn the business and take over Hendrik's place.'

'I'm sorry, Dries, but Venessa is in line to do that.'

'You better talk to her. I think she wants to do something else with her life.'

'Like what?' I thought for a moment. 'She's always been interested in free climbing, I hope you haven't hooked her up with the Space Needle.'

Dries smiled: 'No, no, it's nothing like that. She's coming in to work this afternoon. She'll tell you then.'

'I can hardly wait,' I said, wondering if Lillian had convinced her to follow in her footsteps and go to Paris to learn to be a pastry chef.

'Can I start working with you today?' Dries asked.

'Sure, why not,' I said. 'Did you learn any Russian while you were in Moscow?'

'I can speak in the vernacular,' he said proudly. 'The Space Needle and the rest of the group didn't know any Dutch and their English wasn't that great either, but we managed to communicate.'

'That's good,' I said, 'because we can start you right now. Two Russian clients are coming in, a gentleman and a lady; you can show them the pictures we have in the showroom. If you sell anything, call me and we can do the finishing details together.'

'Wow, that's great! I can hardly wait to get started.'

Dries sold the Russians a pair of nineteenth century Dutch flower paintings by a prolific but unknown Dutch master named Dirk de Vries. I was amazed that he did so well on his first try, and his father was in seventh heaven. We broke out the celebration cognac and were having a shot when Venessa walked in. We offered her a drink, but she said no. She was all smiles, but she didn't want to party – she wanted to talk to me.

I took her up to my office and made us both a cup of tea. 'What's up, Venessa?' I asked.

'I don't know where to begin,' she said. 'Did you know my mother is dead?'

'No. I thought she went to South America with Dieter.'

'She was in Bolivia, but she got killed in a shoot-out with a CIA death squad.'

'Did Hendrik know? He never told me.'

'Sure he knew, but he didn't tell me either. He was a devious old bastard and kept a lot of information to himself. I just found out about Greta's death from Nikki.'

Venessa glared defiantly over her tea cup at me: 'Nikki's my real father. We did the DNA test right after Hendrik died.'

I couldn't think of anything to say, so I said something stupid: 'How does it feel to have a cop for a father?'

'It's not that bad. Nikki's an unusual kind of cop.'

'That, he is,' I said. I could feel a terrible rush of blood going to my brain and I wondered if I was going to have a stroke. Both Hendrik and Lillian had their doubts about Venessa's parentage, but now it was official, she was not Hendrik's blood child. Poor Venessa, she didn't deserve the shit that her elders had dumped on her.

'Don't look so sad, Martel, I have good news.'

'You do?'

'This means that Bobby and I aren't related, so it's OK for me to have his child, and guess what, I'm pregnant!'

I could see that Venessa was happy, perhaps even ecstatic. I tried to be happy for her too: 'What does Bobby think about the baby?'

'Right now he's a little confused. It came so fast after Hendrik's death that he couldn't process it. He was upset when I told him I was pregnant and right after that he took off for a tour of Scandinavia,' she sighed. 'At least, he's not insisting I get an abortion.'

'Don't worry, he'll come around.'

'He'll never marry me.'

'I don't suppose he will.'

'It's OK. We'll always be together, one way or the other.'

'I think you're right about that.'

'If it's a boy, I'm going to call him Hendrik. Just think, Martel, we will have another Hendrik Van der Saar in the family.' Venessa giggled. 'Even though Nikki's my blood father, it's just an accident of birth. I'm a real Van der Saar no matter what.'

'That you are, darling. Nothing can ever change that.'

Venessa's baby turned out to be a boy and was named Hendrik just as she promised. We were all thrilled about the birth and wanted Venessa to come home to the Herengracht, but she stuck it out with Lillian in the Noord. She said she felt safe there because Rowley was protecting the baby. The dog had really taken to the child and slept on a rug in front of his crib. Venessa said Rowley was a good nanny, but when he wanted to change Hendrik's diapers she wouldn't allow it.

One day, when baby Hendrik was about three months old, Venessa decided to bring him over to the Herengracht so he could start to get acquainted with his Van der Saar heritage. Bobby came in from the camp and brought Lucia along so she could meet the new baby. He left Sebastien at home. The little guy was in the rambunctious toddler stage, and Bobby said he wasn't fit for social interactions.

Bobby and Lucia arrived before Venessa, so we hung out in the kitchen. I took a good look at Luz and noticed that she had changed her style. She was usually dressed in cute, pastel-colored smocks with matching tights, and her dark hair always hung down her back in loose curls. Not today. Today she wore slim black pants that looked like they belonged on a flamenco dancer and a loose white shirt. She stomped around in little black boots with tiny Cuban heels and her hair was pulled severely back from her face and plaited into a single braid.

I asked Bobby: 'What's going on with Luz? She looks like a *flamenca.*'

'I took her to see the Ortiz brothers flamenco show when they came to town last week. The youngest brother, Desi, is eight years old and he's already doing solos. They call him The Gadget because he's mastered so many steps in such a short time. Lucia saw him and fell in love. She wants to learn flamenco and work with The Gadget.

'She just turned four years old, surely you're not going to indulge her?'

Bobby smiled, 'Of course I am. If she practices hard, she'll be as good as The Gadget in a few years.'

Lucia had been listening to our conversation: 'I'm going to Spain to learn to dance,' she said proudly.

'That's nice, sweetie,' I said, placating the child.

'She's really going, Martel. My mother and my wife are taking her down to Seville next week. They'll stick around for a month and make sure she gets settled in.'

'My god, Bobby, that sounds so extreme!'

'Hey, man, we're gypsies, that's how we roll. We believe that dance, music, and voice, require training from early childhood. You never amount to shit if you start when you're a teenager.'

'I guess you're right,' I admitted reluctantly.

'Luz told me she wants to dance the male parts. She doesn't like those polka dot dresses the women wear.'

'Don't tell me she's a gender bender.' I was shocked. Little Luz was only four years old and already she wanted to be a guy.

'No, I think she's pretty straight. She's got a big crush on The Gadget, but she's a smart kid and figured out the men have better choreography and wear better clothes. Fortunately, there's a tradition of women dancing the male parts so I think she'll get along OK.'

'I seem to remember that,' I said, searching my brain for an ancient black and white video of the great flamenco queen, Carmen Amaya, dancing in a trouser suit and acting like a big macho. I think she ended the act by smoking a cigar.

Luz stomped on the floor and ran to the kitchen door: 'Here comes Venessa and the new baby!' She held the door open, and Venessa entered carrying a baby tote. She took one look at Luz and said: 'Hey, sweetie, you're looking cool. I hear you're going to Seville to study dance with the Ortiz family.'

'The Gadget's going to teach me!'

Venessa set the baby carrier down on the table and picked the little girl off the floor and gave her a big hug and a kiss.

'The Gadget's a little young to be teaching,' Venessa said.

'You'd be surprised,' Bobby said. 'When the Ortiz were in New York last year, they gave some master classes, and the old Grandpa had the Gadget putting the girls through their paces. I was told the Gadget was a good teacher, but the New York chicks couldn't dance for shit.'

While Bobby was talking he was peering into the baby tote to get a look at little Hendrik, and I wondered if this was his first glimpse of his son.

Venessa put Lucia on the ground and threw herself into Bobby's arms. They went into a big clinch and then kissed passionately.

Luz giggled: 'Venessa is Bobby's girlfriend.'

'When did you start calling your father Bobby? I thought you called him Daddy.'

'Bobby's his real name,' Luz said.

She was acting like a true sophisticate and didn't seem to care if her father was double-timing her mother. I thought Luz was being just too precocious for words, and that maybe she could use a little discipline. It seemed to me that the Revata's child rearing practices were overly permissive.

She went over to the table and pulled the blankets back on the baby. 'He looks just like Bobby and Grandpa Hendrik,' she observed, then she poked her finger in the baby's chest. 'Do you think Grandpa Hendrik is in here?'

'I suppose he could be,' I said.

Luz was up on the table trying to get Hendrik out of the carrier. Bobby and Venessa were still making out and couldn't even see what she was up to. I pushed Luz aside and took Hendrik in my arms.

'Grandpa Hendrik is in this baby!' Luz squealed excitedly.

'How do you know?'

'Because he's talking to me.'

'Yes, and what's he saying?'

'He's saying, *Have Martel take me in to look at the Rembrandt.*'

'Did he say anything else?'

'He told me I looked cute in my new outfit.'

I inspected the child in my arms; he was gurgling and cooing and spitting and acting like a normal baby. I wondered if Luz was channeling a demon.

Bobby and Venessa had uncoupled and I could hear Venessa speaking to me: 'Martel, will you watch the kids while Bobby and I go up to my old room?'

'Sure, why not?' Just make sure you don't make a baby while you're up there.'

'I'm not having any more kids,' Bobby said.

'You're not the one I'm worried about,' I said. I pointed at Venessa: 'I don't trust her. She probably wants to have another kid so she can be even with your wife.'

'Don't be ridiculous, Martel,' Venessa said, 'I'm not in competition with Mouchi. She has her place and I have mine. Aside from that, Hendrik is a one-shot deal. Even with Rowley and Lillian helping care for him, I can barely manage. He's cutting into my study time, and I still haven't finished my dissertation.'

It sounded like Venessa was telling the truth; hopefully she was on birth control and there would be no more mishaps. She and Bobby were anxious to go upstairs, and I understood that need, but first I had to let them know what was going on with the baby: 'Luz says Grandpa Hendrik is inside the baby and that he's talking to her.'

'That fucking Hendrik, he has to barge in everywhere,' Venessa said.

'Have you had any recent communication with him?'

'I'm not sure, sometimes when I'm with the baby I feel Hendrik's vibe, but he never talks to me in words.'

Bobby looked at his daughter and said: 'He speaks to Luz because she hasn't had time to build up adult defenses and barriers to occult phenomena.'

That sounded good to me and I was willing to accept his explanation, but before I could reply, Luz started up again:

'The baby wants to see the Rembrandt!' she shouted.

'Do you know what a Rembrandt is?' I asked.

'No,' Lucia admitted.

'Rembrandt was a man who painted pictures a long time ago. We have one of his pictures in the dining room. I think that's what Hendrik wants to see.'

'Let's take him to the dining room,' Luz said. 'He wants to see that picture real bad.'

Bobby and Venessa were so caught up in their love affair that they didn't pay zip to what Luz was saying. I watched in dismay as they walked out of the kitchen and headed for the lift. When baby Hendrik saw his mother leaving he started to bawl. I took hold of Luz' hand, and we all went to the dining room and sat down at the table and looked at the Rembrandt. Hendrik stopped screaming and started jumping up and down in my arms like an infant lunatic.

'It's not a pretty picture,' Luz said. 'I don't know why he likes it.'

'Why don't you ask him?'

'OK, I will.'

There was silence while Luz communicated with the baby. Finally she said: 'Grandpa Hendrik says it's a long story and you know all about it.'

'I guess I do, darling. What else does he say?'

'He's going away now. He won't come back anytime soon. He loves you and says you'll meet again.'

The baby stopped jumping and relaxed in my arms. He went to sleep, and I thought I could see a wisp of energy move out of his body. It was all so fucking strange that I suddenly felt weak, as though the energy was moving out of my body too.

'Do you feel like taking a nap, Luz? We can go to my room and sleep on my bed for a while.'

She held out her hand: 'Yes,' she said, 'talking to Grandpa Hendrik makes me tired.'

We went up to my room and had a good sleep. When I woke, the children were clustered around me and there was nothing left of Hendrik's presence. That wisp of energy I had seen leaving the baby's body had been Hendrik's spirit, and now he was gone, leaving us alone in the material world.

ABOUT THE AUTHOR

Patricia Ketola was born in North Dakota and brought up in Minneapolis, Minnesota. She studied cultural anthropology and art history. An adventurous sort, she traveled the world and experienced many different cultures and personalities.

Landing in New York City, Patricia became a middle manager in a financial services operation. On the side, she moonlighted in an art gallery and became involved in the fine arts and antiquities trade. Later, she moved to the mountains of Colorado and worked on a mushroom farm.

Dirty Pictures is Patricia Ketola's first novel. Her insight into Roma culture comes from informants who shared anecdotal knowledge relating to this misunderstood and persecuted group.

She currently lives in Minneapolis and works on her second novel, *Surfers*.

To learn more about Patricia Ketola please visit *www.betimesbooks.com*

Printed in Poland
by Amazon Fulfillment
Poland Sp. z o.o., Wrocław

50708542R00139